To Bob—
In Love & Friendship,

4-1-96

Cast a Single
SHADOW

Cast a Single
SHADOW

John Charles Cooper

Northwest Publishing, Inc.
Salt Lake City, Utah

Cast a Single Shadow

For information address: Northwest Publishing, Inc.
6906 South 300 West, Salt Lake City, Utah 84047
JC 5.12.95 / AC

PRINTING HISTORY
First Printing 1996

ISBN: 0-7610-0309-6

NPI books are published by Northwest Publishing, Incorporated,
6906 South 300 West, Salt Lake City, Utah 84047.
The name "NPI" and the "NPI" logo are trademarks belonging to
Northwest Publishing, Incorporated.

PRINTED IN THE UNITED STATES OF AMERICA.
10 9 8 7 6 5 4 3 2 1

Preface

The mountains of western North Carolina come as a shock to the traveler who first drives down from Michigan or Ohio to the Carolina Coast, or to the Tar Heels and Sand Lappers of the tidewater south who drive north. Americans think of mountains as far out west and of Indians as living in Wyoming or Arizona. To travel east from Knoxville, Tennessee, is to climb higher, ever higher into the Smoky Mountains, spiraling up the side of one Tennessee valley to another and then flat out upward into the massive granite backbone of the continent. The highest peak east of the Rocky Mountains stands in western North Carolina, Mount Mitchel, named for a university professor who measured its height—and now lies buried on it. In the extreme western area of the state, lies also a large Indian reservation, home of the eastern band of the Cherokee nation.

The Native Americans are the descendants of those few hundred "Indians" who escaped the forced deportation of their tribe from Georgia, where they had legally settled and founded a culture on a par with that of the whites. One of the so-called "civilized tribes," the Cherokee had an alphabet invented by a chief named Sequoyah, a printing press, and a newspaper, when they were forced to move on foot along the Trail of Tears to Oklahoma, in 1838-1839, by order of President Andrew Jackson and his successor in the White House.

In the eighteenth century, the Cherokee had fought the settlers in the Carolinas, and during the Revolution, sided with the British, hoping to regain their hunting and farming lands in the Piedmont and Appalachian foothills. With the founding of the United States, the Cherokee saw the futility of further armed resistance and adopted a constitution based on that of the U.S., and soon, thanks to Sequoyah's alphabet, were literate, living in homes like the Scotch-Irish settlers around them. But gold was discovered where the Cherokee lived, and white schemes resulted in their expulsion to the west. Not all submitted to the exodus. Some clans fled deep into the rugged Smoky Mountains. Others fled deep into Florida.

Those who sought freedom in the mountains are still there, and, as was the case with Sequoyah—also called George Guess— who was half white, among these three-thousand-plus free people, men and women of mingled blood are not rare.

"If your eye is single, your whole body is full of light."

Luke 11:34

I

Is It Real, This Life I Live?

1

The gang of boys ran happily over the slippery, wet grass, their brown, bare feet securing firm purchase, though the meadow sloped upward. Each boy wore a blue shirt and dungarees, faded and torn, and long, straight hair. Though most of them were thin, their arms and legs were firmly muscled and already their chests, heaving as they raced, looked broad and deep like those of the elders who followed them at a slower pace.

"Stop at the top, boys," a gray-haired man in plaid shirt and Oshkosh overalls called. "Just stand easy there. It will be sunset soon, so we'd better get started."

3

The boys obediently slowed down and wandered around the top of the ridge that overlooked a deep, wooded valley. The higher mountains beyond the valley were only partially visible through the drifting, heavy white mist that gave this range its name: The Smoky Mountains. Wisps of "smoke" trailed over the ridge and gave the boys a damp, almost wet sensation on their lower legs. None of them seemed to mind. They were born and bred to these misty heights, and only blowing snow could make them cold.

"Let's gather some dry wood, now," the overalled elder ordered. "You, Buddy, Roger, Dan, get some rocks for a fire pit."

In a few minutes a space was cleared and a shallow hole scooped out with tough hickory branches. Rough stones were laid in a circle around this pit, and the driest branches the boys could find were arranged inside. Longleaf, the elder, squatted by the circle and knocked the thick back of his hunting knife blade against a flint rock, angled so the sparks dropped on to the dried milkweed tinder he had taken from a pocket and laid on a rock. When the tinder smoked, he put the knife and flint aside and fed tiny branches to the budding flame, then moved the fire under the wood in the pit. Soon a campfire was roaring, and the boys were warming their hands, talking excitedly.

"This is like the old days, eh?" boy excitedly asked boy.

"Be seated, all," Longleaf said. "To pray. To think. To look without on the stars and to look within on the shadows that reveal our life.

"It is time, now, to be serious. This is no game. We are not playing at being 'Indian.' We have come to set these boys on the right path, to commune with The Spirit that fills the Universe.

"It is time to be silent."

Everyone sat quietly, though not rigidly. From time to

time someone shifted position slightly. The sun's rays disappeared in the graying evening. Slowly the deep gray turned to black. A light wind sprang up, moving the mist away and, like the opening of a window, allowed the stars to appear.

The stars, seen from that altitude, five thousand feet above sea level, and from that attitude, one of meditative reverence, were blindingly glorious. Stars could be seen distinctly, as individuals placed at lonely intervals from each other, and not as mere clusters of indistinct, cloudy white. The planets hanging low on the horizon were easily separable from the true stars that hung higher in the velvet sky.

Buddy Nighthawk felt a lump in his throat and warm tears in the corners of his eyes. Every clear, black night sky made him think of Wakan, of the Great Spirit, of God.

The group continued silently gazing at the stars. If time passed, no one noticed. Nothing was said. Each person was left to his own thoughts. These tribal people listened for no external voice, but for the voice that speaks within.

After a time, the wind shifted and the smoky haze drifted over the seated group again. The stars were masked and a dozen heads tilted downward almost in unison. The time had come to look within in earnest.

Longleaf's eyes closed. In a moment the blackness behind his eyelids turned to light. Colors played there and shifted dreamily from shape to shape. Longleaf saw a file of shuffling forms, carrying a burden. He witnessed his own funeral. He would not walk this way with the growing boys again.

Dan looked into himself and saw the figure of a racing dog. Massive shadows milled about, and the leaping dog jumped at them. Dan knew he would help herd his father's cattle this next year and he would get a new dog to help him.

Buddy closed his eyes and saw only darkness. He closed them tighter and produced only bursts of red and yellow behind his eyes. Then he remembered not to rush things. To gaze within just as he had gazed at the stars. He relaxed.

Soon the place of vision lightened. Buddy's breath caught in his chest. He didn't exhale for many seconds. Buddy saw, as in a newsreel in a Saturday afternoon movie, cities and towns, highways and railways, airplanes and ships, islands and oceans, mountains and deserts, tall buildings and masses of people. This tour of the globe ended and was replaced by an empty screen. Buddy saw himself, grown tall and broad, dressed in strange clothing. Yet, stranger still, Buddy saw his adult self cast two shadows, one to either side. Both shadows stretched out to an equal distance, and the image of himself hesitated, moved a step in one direction, stopped, then moved in the other. The vision faded. Buddy opened his eyes, exhilarated yet vaguely disturbed. He was surprised to find himself exhausted.

Longleaf, seated across from Buddy, stirred. "Time to rest. Time to sleep," he called out softly.

Men and boys stood up slowly and stiffly. They stretched, then silently found level spaces, lay down, curled up under winter jackets they had brought, and fell asleep.

In the morning the group walked home, thoughtfully looking at the trees, their own feet, the ground. Even the youngest boys were quiet until they neared home; then, as at some hidden signal, they began to chatter and race in circles until they reached the village. They had been to the mountain, had their vision, and life must go on.

A small cabin, covered with black tarpaper and a few bare boards, stood at the edge of the Cherokee town of Okonolufte. Tarpaper shacks have leaky walls. Moonlight and noises penetrate them easily. Moldy streaks of gray white moon rays lighted the iron cot on which Buddy Nighthawk lay, feigning sleep. He could hear his parents talking softly together in their creaky four-poster, on the other side of the rough-studded wall. The newspapers tacked on the studding for warmth had dried and torn and did little to muffle either childish cries, trips to the slop jar, or parental conversations in the depths of night.

The father's voice, rich and full—even in it's half-whisper, observed, "This is an opportunity for the boy, Margo. There's nothing here for him. Nothing on this reservation. Not even a decent school."

"But he's our eldest son. The oldest of the three we have left. We've lost two already," the mother's soft voice hissed belligerently. "Just six years ago we lost our last child. Don't you want to keep any of them?"

Big John replied, "But that was permanent. This isn't. What if his grandparents carry him away? We can see this boy every summer. The city isn't the grave. He can even come home at Christmas."

Well," Margo responded, "it's set then. Buddy gets the bus for Ashville in the morning. God help him among the whites."

"That's pretty bitter for a white to say."

"Only a white can realize the distance he will have to go."

"Buddy's only half-Indian and light-skinned at that. He looks white, which is more than you can say for Chester and Janet," John said quietly. "All the whiteness flowed into him and not so much into his brother and sister.

"Really, you know," Big John spoke half-aloud and raised up on one elbow to look down on Margo's shadowed face, "Buddy is more than half white in his soul. He has...oh, I don't know...a ruthlessness, a drive that I've never seen in a full-blooded Cherokee. He's relentless in everything he does, from school to hunting rabbits, even to this move to his grandparents'. Buddy' ll get somewhere. He ain't gonna cry. He's gonna do. That's white, the Scotch-Irish, I'd guess."

Buddy, wide awake, choked back a sob. He smiled grimly and willed himself to sleep. Visions of gaily colored buses and

trains moved through the air before his eyes. He rubbed his
eyes, yawned, relaxed. He slept.

The next day was the first full day of summer vacation.
Chester and Janet, who slept crammed up to Buddy's cot on
iron beds of their own, grumbled when Buddy got up early to
wash and pack. They pulled the tattered cotton blankets and
torn quilts, which mountain nights demanded, high over
their heads, though the rising heat would soon drive them out
of bed also.

Washing was no problem. Buddy pulled on trousers and
high top shoes and strode through the narrow alleyway
between beds to the wooden door that issued out on to the
dilapidated back porch. He went out to the well, drew a
bucket of water, poured some in a cracked gray-blue pan and
splashed his head, face, neck, hands and arms. Buddy dried
on a damp strip of towel hanging on the clothesline. Turning
to a mirror fastened to one porch support, he dug out a
broken-toothed comb and carefully ran it through his long
brown hair. Even neatly parted and combed, it looked crude
and disheveled as it curled in long strings around his neck and
ears. Buddy squinted in the mirror and was pleased to see how
fine, how light in color his hair really was. Out of his high
cheekbones, even with their slightly almond-shaped appearance, gray-blue eyes looked back at him. "Indians don't have
blue eyes," Buddy thought.

He went back into the cabin through a second door and
found his mother frying mush. His father was already eating.
He could hear his younger brother and sister dressing and
whispering in their bedroom.

"Sit down and eat," Big John said heartily. "No rabbit this
morning, but it's your own fault. You didn't work the traps
last night."

"Mush is okay. Can I have coffee?" Buddy responded.

"Sure. Use this cup. It's not cracked much," his father

replied.

Buddy ate and drank in silence. His father broke it. Big John seriously, yet all in a rush, wanting to get his farewell over.

"Son, you're goin' off today. I know it's for the best. Lots of kids go off to school. You're lucky you got white grandparents who think enough of you to give you this chance. Don't mess up. Study hard. Obey them and work. And, if our paths ever cross again, I hope we'll still be friends."

Buddy felt a tremendous rush of emotion. He sensed tears behind his eyes. He'd never really liked his father, but never really disliked him either. Big John wasn't a drunk like so many of the others. He hadn't been in jail. He was just unlucky in getting and keeping jobs. Buddy resisted his impulse to gush out a reply. He restrained from reaching out, turned away from the table silently, in confusion, and caught the tears glistening in his mother's eyes.

"Now, the boy ain't going off forever. He'll be back from time to time. Ain't that so, Son?" she scolded, unwilling to see the finality in Buddy's leaving that Big John recognized. Buddy froze inside at this unusual display of feeling. He tried to stuff back the panic that rose in his chest.

"Sure, it's so," Buddy answered dully and, rising uncertainly, left the cluttered kitchen. He did a good job of damming up the hot liquid that burned his eyes and seemed to fill his upper nostrils. Buddy packed his belongings in silence, ignoring the good-tempered jabbering of his brother and sister.

The bus had to be boarded at a crossroads near the Blue Ridge Parkway. The old Trailways Coach, coming down from Virginia, left the parkway and drove to a spot where a ramshackle motor court with six bed-sized cottages, a combination gas station/bus station/general store and a Primitive

Baptist Church announced the presence of civilization. Buddy walked to this crossroads alone, carrying his belongings in a scuffed and battered suitcase. It wasn't heavy. He had five dollars in his pocket, sent to him by his grandmother in last week's mail. The road was hot and dusty, and his feet hurt in last season's field shoes.

As the sun moved higher in the sky, it seemed that his shadow fell first this way, then that. Sweat on his eyebrows fell over his long lashes, and looking through this strange prism, it seemed he made two shadows on the road, not one. Buddy bit off the tiny shoot of regret that started to sprout in his mind. He pushed away a nagging sense of something lost and preached to himself. "The past is the past. The past is dead. I am like the spirit that goes on its long journey after the body is buried," he thought. "I cannot think of those who say good-bye to me, but only of what lies ahead. I must not look back." Buddy knew from the depth of his twelve-year-old soul that to turn back at this point was to miss the promise of the future.

Buddy had no fear of the future. Whatever came would be better than the past, he thought. He had no clear vision of what would come, either. "Whatever comes, I'll make the best of it," he dared to think. "I'm not an Indian. I'm not white, either. I'm me," he told himself so many times while waiting for the bus that he almost believed it when he stepped aboard.

"Goin' somewhere, Chief?" the red-faced bus driver asked when Buddy paid his fare.

"Yeah," Buddy answered, his face flushing red, too.

Buddy's grandparents met him at the Ashville bus station. He knew them from their many summer visits and the several times he and his mother and the other children had visited them at Christmas. He even liked them in spite of their obvious hatred for his father. With this knowledge their first question came as no shock.

"Did that no-good try to stop you coming?" Mrs. Gordon asked.

"No, ma'am," Buddy replied, knowing exactly what she meant.

The bus trip to Charleston was uneventful. Buddy watched the neat farms of the Piedmont flow by the half-opened bus windows. He stared at the red brick, three-story buildings in the market towns and the ugly, massive courthouses in the county seats. He read the Burma Shave signs and billboards to pass the time. The bus was hot, and made drowsy by the heat, old Mr. Gordon slept and snored in a pleasant, low tone. Mrs. Gordon bought Buddy ice cream and pop at rest stops and talked quite kindly to him. He was sleepy, but could not sleep.

Night was drawn up deeply around the many lighted buildings clustered together on the thumb of land that stretched between the Cooper and Ashley Rivers out toward the open ocean. Buddy felt his pulse race as the bus drove over the high railroad viaduct, and once more he could see the old, eccentric city of Charleston brightly marking the dividing line of land and sea. This was exciting. This, this city, was where Buddy wanted to be.

By midnight he was settled and in bed in the Gordon's tiny bungalow.

"Good night, Buddy. Say your prayers," his grandmother called from across the narrow hall.

"Good night," he called from the double bed he was given in the room that was to be his own. Buddy snuggled into the clean, white sheet, under the thin bedspread, warm in the semi-tropical night of the Low country. He fell asleep without prayer. In this country of white and black people, he didn't know which god to pray to, or for that matter, how to pray. His mother would know and, in that moment, in the depths of his sleeping mind he missed her and wished her there.

2

His family, in the mountains, had not been able to afford milk, and now Buddy found he loved it. At once, he took to eggs, bacon, and the white grits his grandmother fastidiously prepared. Trying a little of everything, Buddy had even sprinkled Parmesan cheese from a green, porcelain container on his sunny-side-up eggs that first morning in Charleston. Later, as he sat in the dazzling June sunlight on his grandmother's back stoop, playing with her dozen cats, his stomach grumbled and churned with a fullness he had never known.

Tiger, the gray striped mother cat, who in one moment

was fiercely hunting food for her half-grown kitten, and was in the next on his lap rubbing her velvety head against his chin, soon became his favorite. She quickly learned to wait on the stoop for this boy to emerge from the dark interior of the house. From the back stoop, as he played with his newfound pet, he could watch his grandfather quietly and expertly work in the miniature garden. Steadily and with good humor the old man pulled weeds, pruned tomatoes, and dusted green beans. Eventually, Buddy began to work with this quiet, oversized man, raking and hoeing for him along the lush growth of carrots and cabbages. Though few words were exchanged between the two, he grew to believe that the old man liked his company, and, for the first time, Buddy began to relax and feel accepted.

The entire garden was not large, perhaps twenty feet by twenty feet. But it was the finest, neatest garden Buddy had ever seen. It lay at the back of the Gordon's small, fenced-in backyard, to the left of a white one-car garage. Between the old wooden building and the rows of vegetables was a small fenced area. At its center was a chicken coop. A half-dozen mixed-breed hens and one goose-stepping white rooster moved in a steady circular flow, crowded in the small yard, and cussed at nothing in particular in their low, angry clucking monotone.

"See, 'Squire,'" Buddy's grandfather would say with his usual good humor, "get the tiny sprouts of grass out of the rows, like this," and he would pull the sharpened hoe edge-wise down the short, straight rows with practiced ease. The ground was black and rich, a gumbo of the swampy soil the city rested on and the acrid chicken droppings the old man mixed with the earth, along with potato peelings and coffee grounds every spring.

"I see how you do it," the boy replied, dragging a hoe so old that it was but a crescent of rusted steel on the edge of a much-taped handle down an adjoining row, "but it's hard for me to do."

"You'll learn. Just be careful there. You're doing fine," the red-cheeked giant replied. "You'll soon learn."

As the months of June and July sped by, the reason for Buddy's move to Charleston and the Gordons' leapt to the foreground. Mutterings of "Too thin!" "Too dirty!" "Too raggedy!" and "Too stringy!" were constantly being thrown at him by his grandmother. Her sole purpose in life seemed to center around scrubbing him clean, fattening him up and "bringing out the white boy"; and, in a sense, she was right. He was skinny to the point of scrawniness, regardless of the endless amount of food he seemed to be able to put away. His hair had never known a barber's touch, only the annual clipping under a bowl by his father. Fingernails were broken, scabs prominent on arms and legs. Even a summer's worth of baths and tooth brushing didn't seem to remove the red clay ground into his pores or remove the yellow stain from his teeth. In desperation, Mrs. Gordon fell on the boy in a flurry of cleaning. Nails were scrubbed and pared. The barber was visited. Dr. Jacoby, the dentist, tried, unsuccessfully, to clean Buddy's teeth. Dr. Gruder, the Gordon's family physician, announced the boy had worms, was slightly anemic, and was twenty pounds underweight for his height. With this news, Buddy had fresh cakes of yeast and vitamin pills added to the cheese he sprinkled on his morning eggs.

Surprisingly, he rarely thought of his family; though, due to the regular prompting of his grandmother, he learned to keep his mother in mind by writing to her every week. Each Saturday his grandmother gave him a sheet of white paper, an envelope and a blue, three-cent stamp. He would then proceed to write. After asking how everyone was, he wrote exclusively of the new things he was doing. By noon, the letter was ready for the mailbox at the end of Simmons Street. Just as regularly, the postman brought him a letter from her. He would read them once and then put them away bound in neat stacks with rubber bands.

During these early months, Buddy began to fill notebooks with drawings and badly composed poetry, and pages and pages of cheerful self-reporting to his mother which seldom found its way into the real letters.

> *Dear Mother,*
>
> *How are you? Fine, I hope. We're all fine here. I helped Granddaddy cut grass and pull weeds this morning. This afternoon we'll take the bus to Magnolia Cemetery and clean the family plot there.*
>
> *Yesterday, Grandmother took me shopping for school clothes. I got a nice red, button-up-the-front sweater. Grandmother called it a name but I can't remember what. I got brown shoes with thick, "waffle" soles, some long-sleeve shirts, white ones and blue ones, tan slacks, black slacks and dark blue slacks, socks and underwear. I got a new haircut. It cost 50¢! And I bought some Wildroot Cream Oil. Now, I've got a really tall pompadour!*
>
> *Wednesday night I took the bus to Aunt May's and had supper. We had poached eggs with milk on toast, and her great cream cheese ice cream for dessert.*
>
> *How is Daddy? And how are Brother and Sister? Give all my love.*
>
> *I miss you.*
>
> > *Love, your Son,*
> > *Love, Buddy*
> > *XXXXXXXXXXXXXXXXXXXXXXXXXX*

And, having done that, Buddy felt better, even when his

grandmother spoke sharply to him, and his grandfather was silent.

After a month and a half of trips up and down King Street for "shopping and doctoring," as Buddy commenced to refer to the experience, his grandmother sighed in resignation and sent him out the door with the exasperated command, "Mind the teachers!" and "Come home immediately after school." When she didn't hear him answer, she stuck her head out the front door and yelled, "Did you hear me?"

As Buddy turned out on to the sidewalk he raised his hand and yelled back, "Yessum!"

The two months of Grandmother's scrubbing made Buddy look pretty much like all the other boys in the class. Nonetheless, the thought of going to a big city school made Buddy nervous. He was used to being around adults. He'd never really had to deal with people his own age. Frankly, he was scared. In his first eleven years on the reservation and in the surrounding national park land, Buddy and his brother and sister found few playmates. Their lifestyle marked them as Indians, so they were off limits to most whites. Buddy's light skin and gray-blue eyes made his acceptance by the Cherokees an on-again, off-again thing. Sometimes the Indians' traditional acceptance of the down and-out embraced Buddy and his family; at other times, hostility against the whites overflowed on to Big John, Margo, Buddy, his brother and sister.

It was this background that determined Buddy's response to his new classmates, who greeted him with the rude and near cruel stares and under-the-breath comments common to children when faced with newcomers. His response was silence. He simply turned, or tried to turn, away. If the others seemed to reject him with words, he rejected them with indifference.

No stranger to rejection, or even childlike persecution, he remembered the war years, 1942-45, when half-blood children like himself, with the slightly almond-shaped eyes, were taunted and even beaten by the white children in the mountain towns, who called them "Japs." Not realizing at the time his own eyes were slightly tilted and possessed a "squint," Buddy sometimes wondered if the other half-breeds really weren't Japanese—as only the Japanese, who were regularly derided and vilified on radio and in the small-town Saturday matinees, had "slanty" eyes, as far as he knew. One of the boys Buddy ran trap lines with in the winter still had the name "Chink," given him in 1942, even in mid-1945. Somehow the eye shape of Indians seemed normal to Buddy, and only the sight of other half-bloods brought on these thoughts.

Stoicism only looks peaceful on the surface. Underneath that facade of indifference Buddy felt pain, loneliness, and outrage. Not only were his feelings hurt, he was often beaten, if only lightly, punched, kicked and harassed by boys his own age and older. Without realizing it, Buddy replayed the whole history of the weak in showing his indifference, in not fighting back, or even showing fear where these incidents occurred: the bus stop, the lavatory, the gym and in the darker recesses of the playground. Yet the time came when he could no longer turn his back.

Buddy walked down the wooden corridor to the south end of Mitchell Grade School. Lost in thought, he sauntered down the steps and over to the shade of the old-fashioned steel bell tower that, though detached, seemed to anchor the end of the long brick building. Leaning against a leg of this tower, Buddy occupied his time telling himself stories, fabulous adventures in which he starred. All these stories were based on his reading of Admiral Perry's polar explorations and the adventures of other heroes in the jungles of New Guinea, portrayed in *The National Geographic*. These magazines, read in the school library, were his sole diversion, beyond the fifty-year-old religious books in his grandmother's small bookcase and the pop music that came over her tabletop radio. Buddy's interest was aroused only by his history textbook.

He was thinking, at that moment, of Admiral Byrd's flights over the pole when a hulking, fat boy, two grades ahead of him, suddenly punched him on the arm. "Move, creep!" the kid barked.

Without thinking, Buddy drove straight from his daydreams of courage into the reality of action. He lashed out with his right fist and struck the kid's nose so hard it jarred his arm up to the shoulder. The bigger boy sat down with a bump. Grabbing his bleeding nose with both hands, he screamed, "You hit me when I wasn't looking!" and started to cry.

A crowd, both boys and girls, gathered, staring stupidly at the former playground pushover, standing red-faced over the now wounded bully. The bully cried in shame, pain and shock, while Buddy, coming to a realization of what he had done, began to shake all over.

The children parted as two white-haired teachers scurried forward. Quickly these elderly women marched Buddy and his persecutor off to the principal's office. Once there, Mr. Studemeyer, a white-haired old gentleman, forced the boys to tell what happened, truthfully, solely by the tone of his voice and the frown on his face.

"Both of you, bend over," he ordered. "Grab hold of your knees. You're going to get a taste of the 'Board of Education.'" He reached for a worn fraternity paddle on top of the nearby filing cabinet. Moving swiftly, he gave the larger boy a stinging blow on the backside, which was just as suddenly repeated. The boy broke out in loud sobs and began bleeding at the nose again.

"Go down to the school nurse and get that nose packed, mister. Right now!" the principal commanded. "Your friend here is going to get the same medicine you just got. Don't let me hear of you two fighting again."

The broken bully half-ran from the office, slamming the glass-paneled door behind him. Buddy still held his awkward stance and looked indifferently at the principal and his paddle. His heart was pounding and his thoughts were racing but he was determined to keep a straight face.

The old man stepped behind Buddy and said, "Boy, don't fight around school, you hear?"

"Yes, sir," Buddy answered.

"Then, take this," Mr. Studemeyer said and tapped him lightly on the buttocks with his paddle. Buddy looked around in surprise. The old man winked and roughly whispered, "Get out of here."

Buddy didn't mentioned the fight to his grandparents. He never spoke of his classmates' hurtful treatment of him, either. But, then, they never asked about school and the other kids. He guessed that because they and their neighbors were older, they never seemed to think it odd that he had no playmates, no friends who visited. Buddy listened to the radio that night, drew pictures of airplanes on his notebook paper, briefly skimmed his textbooks and then went to bed. As he had no alternative plans, and despite his appearance of cowardice among his peers, no fear either, he prayed neither for courage or luck. He mechanically recited the Lord's Prayer that his grandmother had taught him and went to sleep, expecting no reply.

The next day, the walk to school and the school day itself passed without incident. The seventh grade bully was not to be seen. The other boys were silent in the halls. It seemed that, as Buddy ignored them, they would now ignore him. However, Buddy was indifferent, not stupid. He knew they couldn't leave it alone. An ambush was coming.

He left the main entrance of the school at two-thirty and walked north, toward home. As he crossed a side street a block from school, he was suddenly confronted by a gang of over twenty boys, among them Jeffrey, the bandage-nosed bully. Before he could move to fight or run, Buddy was overwhelmed. Physically picked up by a dozen hands, he was thrust up on top of a low brick wall. Sun-browned hands pressed hard on his mouth, and bodies leaned against his legs. His arms were pinned to his sides, his head held rigidly, facing front. He tried to will his heart to slow down but could not completely stifle his fear.

"Well, you skinny nigger Indian, you're in for it now," the injured Jeffrey gloated. "What's a nigger Indian need to walk around this town with?" he asked the crowd.

"An Injun haircut!" a thin-faced boy shouted.

"Right," someone called back. A chorus of cheers rose from the pack of twenty.

"So, let's give 'im one," a voice from behind Buddy, on the other side of the wall, spoke hatefully in his ear.

And they did.

The boy behind the wall was standing in a flower bed belonging to the Chilton Arms Apartments, something he would never have dared to do under other circumstances. But this day he had a pair of hair clippers borrowed from his mother's pantry—a small crime which now earned him great stature with his friends. Paul, that was his name, was otherwise an unexceptional boy, but today he was a star. As the others held Buddy, he began to clip off Buddy's hair; first one side, then the other. He did a thorough job, although a barber would need to correct some of his mistakes later that afternoon, and soon Buddy had a wide strip of hair running front to back. All the other hair was clipped away. Once done, the

gang stepped back, more out of awe at what they had dared
to do than to inspect their handiwork.

"Now, that looks right nice," a number of them shouted
out. A few others giggled. Then the lot of them rapidly
considered the possible repercussions of their act and ran
away.

Buddy sat for a few moments on the wall and then
tentatively touched the strip of hair. He jumped down and
began the walk home. He dreaded what his grandparents
would say and do. He had nowhere else to go. He remembered
the old man, Longleaf, from the reservation. Once on a trip up
to the mountain he had stopped and looked at the steep,
rocky path that led up its rocky side. It had seemed to be
impassable. Longleaf had come up behind him, stopped,
looked up the treacherous incline and shook his head saying,
"When there is only one path before you, you take it," and
then proceeded with agility up the trail. Now Buddy followed
the sidewalk that led to his grandparents' house, pretending
not to notice the stares of the people he passed on the long
walk back.

In Mr. Gordon's words, "Mrs. Gordon durn near had a
heart attack." Buddy had turned up at about his normal time,
but looking like a savage.

"What happened? Who did this? Why?" was all she could
say.

"Nobody" and "Nothing" was all Buddy would say. He
refused to show his anger or grief.

Finally, Mr. Gordon gave Buddy a dollar to go to the
barber. "I guess he'll have to shave your head, Son," he
observed.

"Uh-huh," Buddy grunted and left the house. Mrs. Gordon was still crying.

She was calm when Buddy returned but grew upset again

when she called him out to her on the back stoop. The boy still had a Mohawk haircut. He told the barber to make the strip of hair shorter, so it would stand up, to make it straight, and to shave the rest of his head. If he was an Indian, he thought, then he'd look like one, or at least like the comic book picture of an Indian held by his classmates. Buddy had never seen an Indian with a Mohawk, and only a few old men with long hair. Most that he knew had short haircuts, "white walls," or even crew cuts if they were marine corps and army veterans. Buddy would not be made a clown, would not be dishonored.

"I'm going to wear this haircut to school all year," he said. "No matter what. If the hair grows out, I'll shave it again."

And he did, for two more weeks, until Mrs. Gordon, who had no idea of what had happened to Buddy that day, had as much playing Indian as she could stand and, for the next six months, escorted Buddy to the barber shop and personally supervised the trimming and evening of his hair.

Mr. Studemeyer heard about the incident, saw the hair and would not take action when the teachers complained. Buddy had one friend at school, although he did not know it, since no teacher told him of their failure to have him expelled. His classmates also said nothing, although they turned away now out of shame, not rejection. It was all the same to Buddy. His life was almost empty, filled only with food, radio, the backyard cats and, increasingly, books.

Buddy's Aunt Lydia had recently married a returning army veteran, a heavy man, red-faced from too much drink but genial and accepting. Buster's job was full-time employment with the local National Guard unit, and he regularly drove an army jeep around town. Besides the Armory and the Idle-Wild Club, a kind of drinking establishment disguised as a restaurant and run by Buster's brother-in-law, Buster liked to go fishing and crabbing. He was kind enough to take the boy along.

Though Buddy found going out to sea with several drunken men frightening at first, it was decidedly better than doing nothing. And nothing is what a person did on the coast of the ocean if he didn't fish, swim or sail. It was on these trips to the ocean that Buddy learned how to swim, a skill not easily acquired by Indian boys who live in the mountains. He also had the chance to fish, dig clams, go after oysters in their beds with tongs, and to catch the quick gliding sand and hammerhead sharks that filled the broad harbor, tidal inlets, saltwater bays, and brackish river mouths surrounding Charleston. Having no other enjoyment, Buddy spent hours in summer swimming in salt water and fresh. At first he was frightened by the water that covered his mouth, nose and eyes; yet, after a time, he dared to jump in and push his head under, finding that he could always break water and find another breath. To submerge, even in rough water, did not mean he would drown. If he relaxed, just went with the flow, not fighting it, he would float or, at least, pop up again. Once the fear was gone, it was only a question of playing about, of learning to pull with his arms and kick with his legs.

One Saturday Buster pulled up to the curb in his battered truck just as Buddy finished mowing the Gordons' tiny front lawn. "Come on, get your stuff. We're going fishing," Buster called out to him.

"Okay, where are we goin'?" Buddy delightedly called back.

"Out to sea, boy, off the Isle of Palms," his uncle crossly replied. "Come on!"

Buddy ran inside, asked permission of his grandmother, grabbed a hat and bathing trunks and ran outside. Buster, just a shade under the influence, roared down the streets of Charleston toward a friend's house. Steve, the fishing partner, was sober and mercifully drove the old truck that carried their tackle over the long, scary Cooper River bridge. On Sullivan's Island, they picked up a boat at another friend's dock on the inland waterway. Powering out through Wapoo Cut, they entered the open sea. About a mile off shore, the men rigged the heaviest tackle they possessed on strong, saltwater rods. Buddy looked at the huge hooks and asked, "What are we fishing for?"

"Sharks," relied Uncle Buster.

"Sharks?" repeated Buddy.

"Sharks?" he said again.

"Sharks," Buster said flatly, "and don't ask why. You'll see later."

Buddy looked over to Steve for some clue, but he only scratched at his three-day beard growth, took a swig of Wild Turkey and shrugged his shoulders.

All afternoon the three of them fished for sharks, sand sharks, and hammerhead sharks, some fairly small, two feet or so long, but some much larger, four and five feet long. At first Buster tried to tie the captured animals to the side of the boat and leave them in the water but other sharks rushed in and gouged huge chunks out of their unfortunate relatives, so he began to bang them on the head with a hammer and throw them in the bow of the boat. Sharks are too dumb to know they're dead, so the bluish bodies continued to writhe and slip and slide around the bow of the boat. As Buddy watched the seething mass of shark flesh pile up, he felt his anxiety mount.

As supper time approached the boy finally asked Buster why they were catching sharks. His uncle, who had taken in considerably more Wild Turkey than sharks, just looked disgusted and said, "You'll see."

Before darkness came, Steve sat at the helm of the boat, though somewhat less ably than earlier since he, too, was now tipping freely from the Wild Turkey to ward off the chill of the ocean air, and steered the low-riding boat toward shore.

Moving into the cut with an incoming tide, Steve maneuvered them back behind the island to the waterway and their anchorage. Bringing the boat close alongside the small pier, he called for Buddy to make fast. The boy leaped to the pier and tied off the lines fore and aft. Buster, who had been sitting with eyes half-closed then came to life and barked out, "You, boy! You get some gloves out the truck and bring me a pair, too. The heavy ones, you know."

"Okay, Uncle Buster," Buddy called back over his shoulder as he ran toward the truck.

Returning with the two pairs of heavy leather gloves, Buddy asked, "What now?"

"Well, hell, we're gonna unload those sharks," Buster answered.

And with much hesitation and difficulty, Buster and Buddy unloaded the now dead but nonetheless uncooperative sharks. Coarse as sandpaper, their lifeless bodies flopped every which way, as the two heaved the defunct marauders of the sea on to the dock.

"Steve, bring the truck closer," Buster commanded.

Slowly, he backed the battered Ford pickup to the land end of the pier. Buster looked at Buddy. "So," he said.

"So, what?" Buddy asked.

'So, put them damn things up in that truck," Buster answered in a soft, reasonable voice.

Still wondering what in the world was going on, the boy helped his uncle load a dozen assorted dead sharks in the pickup bed. Once done, Buster stripped off the messy gloves and threw them on the floorboard of the truck and said, "I'll drive this time. Let's go."

Buddy crawled in the middle, astride the gear shift, and Steve took the door. The sharks smelled awful, something like a cross between burning tires and a burned-down outhouse. Buster, with life-long experience of driving drunk, drove precisely, if not slowly, across the high, open bridges. At the foot of the bridge, on Meeting Street, he turned right and drove toward his home near the western boundary of the city, near the Shootzenplatz, the old shooting range turned picnic grounds that marked the edge of civilization and the beginning of the phosphate and fertilizer factories that dominated the "north area" on the Ashley River side. In fifteen minutes, Buster pulled up before his own small house, jumped out and called, "Buddy, bring the gloves!"

"Huh?" Buddy thought but knew it was not a good time to be asking any more questions. He scooped up the gloves and followed Steve from the cab.

Steve stood watching with a silly smile while Buddy and Buster pulled the grim-looking creatures over the lowered tailgate and dragged them to the middle of Buddy's aunt's front yard. Soon there was a pile of dead sharks three feet high, but smelling higher, situated right where his aunt could see them when she opened the front door.

"Don't worry, Son, I won't tell her you helped me," the now quite drunk Buster offered. "But, you see, she just made me so damn mad this morning." He turned and stumbled across the pile and fell flat out.

Steve gave the boy a ride home but no explanation. When he entered his grandmother's living room, she sniffed the air, looked up and cried, "Go take a bath."

Lying on the beach that summer, one year after leaving the Blue Ridge, he was surprised that he no longer missed the rugged mountains and tall trees of his boyhood home. He loved the sea and its ever changing shore. The salt water that got into his mouth was no longer bitter and strange. It was sweet. He was happy by this ocean and when in town truly missed the dual shadows he seemed to throw on the wet, dark sand as he looked down for shells through eyelashes wet and salt rimed from constant immersion. The V-shaped waves that came rushing at the eroding beach baptized and cleansed him with their endlessly cresting thick gray froth and airy white foam. Buddy no longer needed to be washed clean of the grime and neglect of his first twelve years.

He learned no special style of swimming, though he knew a backstroke from a butterfly, but he could swim fast and far and under water for long periods of time. The good food and medical care was transforming him from a skinny kid into a broad-shouldered, deep-chested young man. No further sacrament of washing, but a ritual of inner cleansing, an exorcism of his sense of meaninglessness, the casting out of that mute and dumb spirit which kept him from feeling anything beyond the sun's warmth and the water's inexorable power, was needed now. Somewhere within himself Buddy sensed this, though not in clear thought. He was not yet capable of applying the words of the Holy Book, read to him by his grandparents and spoken of by the pastor at Sunday services, to himself. He had heard that this kind of spirit can be cast out only by prayer, by fasting, by suffering, but he did not know what it meant. In the immediacy of the moment, which was all he knew, he made do with the ocean's leavening and its sacred water that daily poured abundantly over his body.

Although the ocean was sacrament enough for Buddy, it was not for the Gordons, or at least for Mrs. Gordon. While Grandfather Gordon was through-and-though Scotch-Irish and reared a Methodist, Grandmother Gordon was Scotch-Irish on only one side. Like Buddy, in her flowed the genes of two fierce races, the dour Scots, on one side, in her case, and the grim but worldly oriented Germans on the other. This German strand held on tenaciously to its religious heritage with the same fervent belligerence that the German armies showed in defending the sacred soil of the Fatherland. Mrs.

Gordon's mother was of the Wurtz family, German, German Lutheran, and she, Mrs. Gordon, strove to retain a sort of immortality by preserving the strict Lutheranism of her ancestors. Actually, it was because of Mrs. Gordon's desire to see at least one of her grandchildren baptized and reared in the old faith, as much as her high regard for education, that caused her to skillfully disengage Buddy from his family over several years of visits. When Buddy reached thirteen, having already attended church for months, Mrs. Gordon called Pastor Schmidt and set the machinery of Buddy's salvation into motion. Not really understanding all that was involved in this affair, as he had rarely attended church in the mountains and knew what a church was like only from Christmas visits with his grandparents, Buddy made no protest when Pastor Schmidt appeared one day and plans for his baptism were made.

The pastor was a medium-tall man with graying, curly hair and a scar on one cheek that reminded him daily of his foolish enlistment in World War I. Buddy was drawn to the scar, since so many men he had known had similar marks on their temples or cheekbones, the talisman of youthful knife fights or military service. And, although Schmidt was orthodox and rigid in matters of doctrine, the easygoing manner of the pastor, who sipped several glasses of wine during his visit, put Buddy at ease.

'Ordinarily, son," Schmidt began, "I'd wait and baptize and confirm you at the same time. But your grandmother and I have concluded that such an event wouldn't be wise. It would make you different from the other young people who were baptized long ago, as infants, you see?"

"I think so," Buddy answered.

"So, fine. It's decided. You will be baptized Sunday. Is that all right with you? I have a gentleman in his thirties and his baby son to baptize also, so you won't be in the chancel alone, okay?"

"Yes, sir. But what do I have to do?" the boy asked with a catch in his voice.

"Well, I'll baptize you as I would an adult. Just like Mr. Bowers. You'll both kneel down at the Communion rail. Mr. Bowers, the man I mentioned, will hold his baby. You'll just kneel there. I'll start, right after the announcements and before the sermon, by baptizing the little one in the regular way. Then, I'll ask Mr. Bowers—and you—if you believe in Jesus Christ as your Savior and you'll both answer 'Yes,' and I'll sprinkle a few drops of water on your heads, one at a time. All right?" Pastor Schmidt leaned back into the Gordons' overstuffed couch smiling to himself, then once again leaned forward, staring Buddy intensely in the eyes. "You do believe in Jesus, don't you, son?"

Buddy hesitated slightly. What he had heard this man say on Sundays about Jesus sounded all right to him. He had even read some words of Jesus, printed in big red letters, in a worn and fading Bible his grandmother kept on the telephone stand in the hall. Buddy looked at the pastor and said, "Yes."

"Fine. Sunday it is, then," Schmidt said, smiling and slapped his hands on his knees. "See you in church."

Soon after, he left, shaking Buddy's hand as he went out the screen door. Buddy blankly watched him go down the steps and turn out of the yard and head up Simmons Street.

Sunday morning came, bright and warm. Dressed in the suit his grandparents had given him, his neck constricted by a starched collar and tightly tied blue tie, Buddy sat three pews back, near the end, on the pulpit side of the Emmanuel Lutheran Church. Buddy pleased his grandparents by singing lustily, something he was glad to do, as he had enjoyed learning the old hymns with German, Welsh and Latin titles that the congregation sang over and over. All he knew of

Christianity he had learned from these hymns. The names of John and Charles Wesley, Martin Luther, and Zinzendorf were familiar because they so often appeared at the top or the bottom of the pages of music that made up the bulk of the service book he leafed through Sunday by Sunday. He knew baptism was a name-giving ceremony; beyond that, he knew nothing.

When the time came, Pastor Schmidt ponderously turned from the altar to make his announcements, then he called Mr. Bowers, his little son and Buddy forward. They knelt closely together, just outside the Communion rail. The hand-carved wooden baptismal font had been moved near the altar and opened. Schmidt read through a part of the service. Then he asked who would sponsor these new Christians. At once, Mrs. Bowers and her parents and Buddy's grandparents came forward and stood behind them. Mr. Bower's baby was baptized first, then the man himself. The pastor stopped to dry their foreheads with a linen cloth, then turned to Buddy.

"By what name shall this child be called?" he asked in a booming voice.

Buddy froze inside when his grandmother answered in a voice to match the pastor's, "Martin Charles Gordon."

"Martin Charles Gordon," Pastor Schmidt said, "I baptize thee in the name of the Father, the Son and the Holy Ghost."

Buddy didn't know what to say. The water ran in little rivulets down his high forehead, into his left eye, and over his prominent cheekbones. There really was nothing he was required to say. The pastor intoned, "Amen," and Buddy silently took his seat.

There flashed through his mind, as he smoothed wrinkles from his coat and trousers, the idea that now the Indian in him was dead. A glance at the half-tolerant expressions on people's faces in the pew across the aisle convinced him quickly that such was a groundless fear or a useless hope. Blinking back tears, he looked steadily at the rose window above the rear of the chancel, staring so intently that the flickering candle flames and the tall, plain brass cross on the altar seemed to cast double, even triple shadows on the snowy white linen draped across that holy spot. In his trance, it seemed as though, in a regular cycle, the altar disappeared and reappeared before his eyes. Somehow, the Jesus he had read about seemed missing here in the perfumed candles of this dark, yet, oh, so white spot.

3

Buddy did well in his first years of school in Charleston. Possessing a quick mind, and with no social life to distract him from constant reading, he was a good student. While his teachers found the childish scrawl, the overly large letters in which he wrote hard to read and soon realized that his previous education had not taught him to spell, they were amazed, nonetheless, to discover the wide extent to which his vocabulary had developed. "He reads mountains of material," one teacher wrote in a year-end report, "and he understands what he reads." Though Buddy was slowly overcoming the deficiency of his early schooling, he had not yet begun to understand the society in which he now lived.

Buddy particularly liked English literature and history. In literature, the poets, early and modern, and in history, the sagas of classical Greece and Rome were his particular favorites. Mathematics was of little interest to him, as were sciences, except for biology. Buddy seemed to enjoy dissecting worms, frogs, dogfish and even fetal pigs, as he moved into high school—remembering, perhaps, the rabbits, squirrels, and 'possums he'd trapped and skinned as a youngster. Social sciences were boring, yet he read widely in the area, and on the recommendation of a social studies teacher, was passed from sixth grade to eighth. What might have been a social disaster for another child caused Buddy no problems. He had no close friends in either grade.

After the move upward, the school counselor tested Buddy's IQ and was mildly surprised to find his intelligence quotient seemed to be in the highest upper percentile measured by the test. The only result of this testing was a short note to Buddy's grandparents, mentioning his high potential, and a low-key suggestion to Buddy himself to enroll in college preparatory courses. With absolutely no concept of just what options were open to him in high school, Buddy—in a stroke of highly intelligent ignorance—agreed.

As ninth grade wore on and dropped behind, and the tenth grade opened up, Buddy found the college prep courses a mixed blessing. He was required to take geometry and trigonometry, which he greatly detested, and ancient history, Shakespeare, advanced biology and American government, which he found delightful. The special seminar in Shakespeare met in a little room around a small wooden table, and was led by Mr. Sherman, a small, round, balding man, who was thrilled to read the majestic lines of *Macbeth* and *Julius Caesar* with his few, chosen pupils. Buddy fell in love with the life of study one week into the course. If the enormity of the idea had not overwhelmed him, he would have decided he wanted to be a teacher, but nothing in either home he had known prepared him to dare such a thought.

Buddy's experiences from age thirteen to seventeen ranged from the profound to the absurd. The days seemed to rush by although the hours often felt like the glacial movement of Greenland's icecap. In order to get in physical shape and stay that way he began to walk to and from school, two miles each way along the hot sidewalks of fall and spring and the cold, wet streets of January and February. In doing so, he began to make friends.

A block west of the high school of Charleston, on the corner of Rutledge Avenue, stood an old grocery converted to a pinball parlor. Stopping there brought Buddy into contact with other outsiders. He met Mike, who rode a motorcycle, which was odd for that day and school. Suddenly, Buddy found himself at Simmon's Street faster than the city bus could manage. Mike, a good-natured sort, began to introduce the boy to others on the fringe of Charleston's life—and through them to employment.

Buddy's grandmother had arranged for his weekend employment after he turned thirteen. Mrs. Gordon—for Buddy and Mr. Gordon and everyone else always thought of her as "Mrs. Gordon"—did all her grocery shopping at Cohen's grocery a few blocks across town on King Street. One Saturday, as Buddy picked up her bags of goods at the checkout counter—it was Buddy's job to carry the heavy bags home since the Gordons had no car—she spoke to old Mr. Cohen, the owner. "Sam, don't you need another bag boy here? This boy," pointing toward Buddy, "is a hard worker."

The old gentleman, polite but direct himself, replied, "I don't know. Maybe. Let him come in next Saturday for a tryout."

As Buddy and the old lady walked out, she whispered

hoarsely, "You got the job. Don't mess up!"

He did, in fact, get the job. The next Saturday Buddy was there at 7:00 A.M. waiting on the sidewalk with several older boys from more modest parts of town. He got the job—at a gratifying three dollars a day, plus a dollar for Friday night and tips—despite a heavy-handed approach to grocery bagging that he had to fight to overcome.

Mr. Cohen worked one cash register and his son, Abe, the other. Buddy found himself working with the old man in mid-afternoon. It was hot and all were tired. The old man was peevish but nothing like Grandmother. Buddy, in an attempt to work faster and ingratiate himself with this man, dropped a carton of eggs. It struck Mr. Cohen's thick wrist and large gold wristwatch. Egg white ran down his fingers and a large golden yolk burst on the watchband. Mr. Cohen's face flushed and an apt Yiddish curse began to form on his lips when he glanced down at the boy's face. The intense look of fear stopped him in mid-syllable. "Just go get a rag," he muttered with disgust as he watched the egg white and yolk mix in mid-air and stream down on his new shiny black wingtips.

That night, when the little brown envelopes with salary were distributed by Abe, the younger Cohen handed Buddy his pay and said, "Dad said you did all right today. Come back Friday at 4:30." The force of this simple sentence struck the boy so powerfully that he could not speak. He nodded and ran for the door and home.

At school, Buddy did well in everything but math. Reading was part of his life, taught him at an early age and modeled by his mother, who read continuously for escape when permitted by time and money. She had unwittingly given him the base needed to glide through most courses without much preparation. In the mountains Buddy read what was available in the school library, and read old copies of the classics that his mother bought at the used furniture, clothing and book store in a nearby town. He found that most of the books required in English were ones he had read, for pleasure and escape, years before. Two classes, however, were new and utterly fascinating to him: the section on Shakespeare in English and Mr. Brehart's ancient history. Buddy found *Macbeth* and *Julius Caesar* endlessly enjoyable—and even more exciting, the small groups that Mr. Sherman formed in class to discuss the plays in depth. What most other boys professed to hate, Buddy knew he loved.

"What is the problem in *Macbeth*?" the rosy-pated instructor asked. And Buddy, as yet knowing nothing of tragic flaws or original sin, tripped over his tongue to answer, "Macbeth is strong and brave but proud. His spirit points two ways, to good and to selfishness. His problem is that he follows the wrong path. His weakness is his strength."

In the Scottish Laird Buddy saw that everyone's spirit cast a double shadow, that every human being faced two ways and that to choose the wrong path was to invite destruction. He saw this, mentally, as an intellectual proposition, and sensed it deep within although he did not, in any useful way, yet apply it to himself.

Mr. Brehart was, without doubt, the most interesting person Buddy had yet heard speak. The "Professor," as the young men called him, lectured about Socrates—a wise man who knew he had a spirit within him who spoke to him of right and wrong—and who listened to that little voice with religious devotion. The teacher spoke of Socrates at his trial, of his bravery and good humor and of his obstinate refusal to disobey the spirit, who signaled to him his approval of Socrates' rejection of surrender by simply keeping silent when the death penalty was read out. Socrates seemed to the boy to embody all the dignity and respect for justice that was best in the characters of the Native Americans and white mountaineers he had known in growing up. The grandeur of the Athenians and the power of the Romans impressed him but it was the unity of purpose, the hard rock of human dignity that Buddy saw in Socrates and the later Stoic philosophers that won his heart. West's and West's *The Story of Man's Early Progress* became his Old Testament, the plays of Shakespeare, his New Covenant.

Shakespeare and ancient history changed school from dreaded chore to a looked-for opportunity. Unfortunately, balance and common sense are not the major gifts of teenage boys, and Buddy let his other classes slide. As much as he enjoyed drawing in notebooks and the margins of his textbooks, he did poorly in drawing class and was worse in geometry. The high school of Charleston in the 1940s was a magnificent institution, solely for boys, offering a college preparatory course that was arguably better than most college liberal arts offerings, although Buddy, with these two exceptions, did not appreciate the opportunity. Literature and history allowed his imagination to run free; mathematics, and a responsible approach to drawing, demanded discipline, attention to the rules and respect for details. More than most teenagers, Buddy lacked tolerance for such boundaries, gradually sloughing off the discipline that grew out of politeness as well. With hormonal determinism, he shifted toward MacBeth's weaker side.

The interior of the pinball shop was dim, the brightly colored panels of the high-legged machines clear as Roman candles bursting over the baseball stadium on the Fourth of July. Buddy walked in, blinked, and saw Mike gently tapping the side of a Las Vegas machine that suddenly registered TILT.

"Sonofabitch!" Mike exclaimed as Buddy walked up behind him. Mike looked around as the tall, lanky boy looked down over his shoulder.

"What's shakin'?" Buddy asked.

"Nothin'," the older but shorter boy replied. "I ain't got

the bike today, so I'll walk uptown with ya."

"Okay," Buddy agreed.

Once on the street headed west, the heat began to wilt both boys. As they crossed a small alley, a milk truck slowed and a cheerful voice called out, "Wanna ride?"

"Yeah!" they answered together.

The driver, named Max, offered them small cartons of chocolate milk as they drove slowly along, drinking one himself. "Yeah, I graduated Charleston High five years ago," he announced. "Didn't go to college. Just been hanging around town. Worked for the *News & Courier* at nights for a while, then landed this really easy job last year."

"Neat," Mike said. "We're looking for work, too. You know, so we can have some dough while we're still in school."

"Maybe I can help," Max opined. "My stepdad is foreman of the *Courier*'s press room nights. I'll introduce you. Ya never know."

"Great!" Buddy exclaimed, thinking that the heavy hand-edness he'd displayed once too often at Mr. Cohen's would not prove to be the same liability.

Max let Mike off at Hampton Park and took Buddy to the corner of Simmons Street, turning into a driveway so as to return to his route. "I'll look for you two tomorrow along the street," he promised.

"Okay!" Buddy called back over his shoulder as he began the short sprint home.

Buddy and Mike needed money, as all teenagers do, but with an extra hitch. Several nights later, while racing through the darkened streets, Mike piled the Harley into the picket fence that surrounded the "Hanging Tree" on Ashly Avenue, just east of Hampton Park. This huge old oak caused the narrow street to fork and go to either side of its massive trunk. A four-foot-high white fence encircled its raised base; the tree's long, heavy limbs stretched like a giant cartwheel, just above the street. It was as easy to hit as the ground itself, of course. The question was why Mike did hit it, for it was equally easy to avoid. This question was never answered but the headlight, front fender and the front fork of his bike were considerably decommissioned when he rammed it head on, throwing both boys inside the narrow perimeter of the tree. Buddy ended up with a scraped knee and sore side, Mike with an ache in his neck and shoulders. Neither was seriously hurt but the Harley demanded intensive care for which neither Mike nor Buddy was able to pay. Max's promise of a chance at a real job now became doubly welcome.

A few days later, a Thursday afternoon, the two boys were walking home when Max pulled up beside them and said, "Jump in." Upon hearing of the wreck, for which he offered voluble sympathy, Max promised to introduce them to Henry, his stepdad, that night. "Just catch the bus and run on down to Cannon Street after supper," he said, giving them the house number and distinguishing landmarks.

After supper, Buddy said he was going out for a while and left Mrs. Gordon's fastidiously neat parlor with a disapproving glance from her and a soft smile from his grandfather. As he turned the corner beside Mike's house, he found him sitting on the curb jingling two bus tokens.

"Let's go!" Buddy declared, bringing the other boy to his feet.

"You got it," Mike agreed, "let's get this show on the road."

Jumping down at the Cannon Street corner of Rutledge, the boys walked south, passing the degenerating, white, wooden row houses, looking for Max's home. Max had explained that he still had a room with his Mom and Henry, although he used it only for sleep. Tonight he was home, waiting for them.

Making the introductions, Max pointed to a rather over-weight lady in a tight sundress, half-reclining on an old couch, and obviously more than a little worn for wear and alcohol.

"This is my mom, Mrs. Cramer," he said.

"Mom, here's Mike and Buddy."

"How do," Mrs. Cramer answered brightly, then suppressed a hiccup.

"And here's my dad, Henry Cramer," Max concluded.

"Hi!" offered Mike with a smile at the sight of the grossly overweight body and deeply flushed, purple-veined face of Mr. Cramer.

"How do you do?" Buddy put in, successfully repressing a grin.

"Howdy," Henry responded with a broad grin, revealing a natural good humor and an intelligence that realized the world's joke was on him. "I hear you fellas could use some hard money. Right?"

"Yes, sir," the teenagers answered rapidly.

"Well, I reckon I could use two more pair of strong hands to pull the press and stack the papers on Friday and Saturday nights. Ya interested?"

"Oh, yes, sir," Mike answered for both boys.

"It's hard work," Henry continued. "Ya gotta show up around nine and start at ten and work until six in the mornin'. Kin ya handle that?"

"I'm sure we can," Buddy answered.

"What'll your folks say?" Henry queried.

"I think we can talk them into it when money's mentioned," Mike responded.

"Then, okay," Henry observed, pulling a pint of Jack Daniels from behind a chair cushion and taking a swig. Without hesitating he wiped the bottle's neck with his palm and handed it to Rose, Mrs. Cramer, who, in an amazingly ladylike manner, wiped the neck again and delicately tipped the small flask to her upturned lips. This time, she burped, said "Ex*cuse* me!" and held the bottle out to the boys.

Glancing warily out the corner of their eyes at one another, Mike and Buddy graciously refused and begged to be
excused. As they reached the front door and shook hands
with Max and Henry, Henry spoke out, "Tomorrow's Friday.
See you at the *News & Courier* plant at nine o'clock, right?"

"Right! Yes, sir!" the two youths rapidly responded, trip-
ping over each other's words and feet as they made their way
to the street.

"WOOEE!" Mike exclaimed as they ran to the westbound
bus stop.

"A job!" Buddy yelled, startling a sleepy old black man
who was waiting for a bus.

The next morning started unfortunately with geometry
and Coach Stevens. The previous night had seemed that it
would end on a perfect note. He and Mike had, on their own,
gotten jobs. He'd thought his grandmother and grandfather
were going to be proud of him, that they'd see his actions as
evidence of ingenuity and maturity. They didn't, or at least
she didn't, and the row had started before he could even tell
her everything about the job. He'd pulled as usual into
himself, but the night passed sleeplessly.

Now, here he was sitting across from a man who taught
this ridiculous, abstract subject with the same Rotarian, up-
and-at-'em gusto and sarcasm with which he co-coached the
football team—and, according to his uncle, had led a company of the local National Guard through four years of
campaigning in Iceland, England, France, Germany, Austria
and Czechoslovakia. He was as put off by the coach-teacher's
take-charge attitude as by the mysteries of geometry.

The coach taught by drill. Drill, drill, drill. "Read page 25
ten times," he would say. Buddy did, but since he didn't
understand the material the first time, he didn't understand

it after the tenth reading either. Only once did a point get across to him. Suddenly the relationship of one angle to another made sense. Immediately, he not only understood the problem, but he thought of a little light bulb going on over his head—a mental image drawn from the Sunday comics. This revelation of meaning, unfortunately, was not to be repeated in the coach's class and Buddy grew steadily discouraged.

Perhaps he could have borne geometry if conditions at his grandparent's were as peaceful as they had been four years before. They were not. As Buddy had grown up, his grandmother became more and more dictatorial, or so it seemed to Buddy. Actually, she had always been dictatorial, but Buddy had been so much a blank tablet, so empty of all experience, that at first he was willingly cooperative, asking for nothing, refusing nothing, expecting nothing, accepting everything in the manner of one of his grandmother's dozen-odd house cats. As he grew up, learning more, seeing more, Buddy began to develop expectations, a sense of personal taste, an awareness of his own desires, even a tentative sense of identity as Buddy Nighthawk—before age twelve he had no other name—now known as Martin Charles Gordon. The real problem that raised bickering to a constant, highly sharpened art, came then, as Buddy (as he thought of himself, for he never thought of himself as Martin Charles), came to a sense of who he was, although he remained unclear as to what he was.

Every day there seemed to be an argument, although Buddy strove to live by the passive code, to remain silent and to ignore challenges and provocations. It was as impossible to do this with his grandmother, at age sixteen, it turned out, as it had been with his classmates at age twelve. More than this, try as he would, Buddy, or Charles, as they called him though he resented it, found he could no longer repay hard words with silence. He became less and less capable of non-resistance. If there had been forests or mountains near Charleston to lose himself in, vast plains to cross and escape his tormentor, all might have been well. Outside of school hours and weekend work there was no place to move, no hiding place in a small three-bedroom house. Even the backyard was too small to provide asylum. Backed up to a wall, Buddy could only fight back.

Last night, the bitter words, the angry insinuations about Buddy's few friends, about his desire to work the new job, along with the situation of constant harassment and harsh words at home, and his frustration and resentment at the coach and his mechanical mathematics, finally drove Buddy to a decision. If he could not live in peace, enjoy the work he wanted to do in English, history and biology, then he would leave. If there were no mountains near by to flee to, then there were many mountains, many cities, many roads to freedom throughout the vastness of America. Buddy loved all things to do with geography. He spent hours scanning the photographs and maps of *The National Geographic*, the atlas and the globe in the school library. He picked up road maps in gas stations by the dozen. He knew the lay of America's land and decided to see more of it firsthand. So it was that immediately upon completion of the coach's class, the week before the end of his first semester, tenth grade, Buddy ran away. He was not quite sixteen and had only three dollars. He took no bag with him, walking away in his school clothes. What Buddy did have was a body now more than six feet tall, weighing 165 pounds. He could pass easily for eighteen with his swim-conditioned muscles and the deep brown lines already etched into his skin by heredity and many summers spent on the ocean's shore. Buddy rode the public bus to the last stop at the city limits and stepped onto the dual lane highway that ran west, crossing the north-south U.S. highway at Cairn's Crossroads twenty miles away.

After hitch-hiking all night, Buddy cleaned up in a gas station washroom in Columbus, Georgia. Then, walking with head high and back straight, he dodged the milling cars in Columbus' narrow streets and sought out the army recruiting station. The sergeant there, low on his quota of recruits for the month—it was 1949 and volunteers were few—greeted Buddy like a childhood friend and bought him the blue plate special at the cafe next door. Despite the absence of a birth certificate (Buddy didn't have one), the sergeant thought his enlistment would present no problem.

"We'll just have some relative or friends who've known you all your life go to the Charleston county courthouse and make a deposition, and Charleston will issue you a birth certificate," the soldier explained. "Who can I phone in Charleston to set the ball rolling?" he went on to ask.

Buddy's face fell.

The sergeant insisted on phoning Buddy's home and that was it. The army man found it hard to believe Buddy wasn't quite sixteen, but deferred to the grandmother.

"Come back in a year, kid," he said, patting Buddy's arm.

And, although he hated to do it, the sergeant called the local police and reported a runaway, with the silent Buddy standing right there. The policeman who came was a kindly man who drove Buddy to jail, got him a hot meal and gave him an empty, unlocked cell to sleep in. In the morning, back on duty, the same elderly policeman drove Buddy to the station, got him a ticket and put him on the bus to Charleston.

That was round one.

Round two followed almost immediately, the points going to Buddy because of the forbearance of a less righteous but more understanding relative, the rapidly self-destroying Uncle Buster.

Buster's drinking grew to be a larger and larger part of his life, and whether this addiction stemmed from his traumatic experiences in Europe or from the wild days of Prohibition in Charleston that formed his young adulthood, the effect was the same. More and more often Buster was stopped for drunken driving, in spite of the tolerance of most of the police who knew him, had served with him and liked him. On one occasion, an old acquaintance stopped Buster's jeep as he drove, alone, down King Street on the wrong side. "What's up, Buster?" the policeman asked as the big man hung over the wheel.

"Huh!" Buster replied. "Bob, you get in the back and start "Twenty-nine Bottles of Beer" with the other guys. I'll drive us cause I'm too drunk to sing."

Thanks to Bob and many others like him, Buster avoided jail and generally was helped home to bed, or at least to the front room couch.

Buddy's Aunt Lydia worried and fretted, and constantly searched for Buster's stash. Buddy overheard her tell a neighbor that she had found bottles stuffed in every chair and couch, under every bed and in every closet in the house.

But Buster never neglected his military duties and, as a master-sergeant, was present for drill at the Sumter guards every Thursday night. On Thursday morning, after being sent home by the army, Buddy cut school and took the bus to downtown King Street, going upstairs over a clothing store to the drill hall of another National Guard unit, the Washington Light Infantry. Buddy thought he might make his escape that summer, if he could go to summer camp with the WLI. He'd avoided the Sumter guards because he felt Buster might, or almost certainly would, be at that armory, and might put a stop to his plans.

Buddy was lucky; the captain of the WLI was in his office that morning and welcomed his interest. Captain Ramsey was an insurance agent and drove around town collecting premiums from elderly white ladies and poor black families. He liked his job because he could take all the time he wanted to do what he really loved, soldiering.

"Why sure, boy," Ramsey had said when Buddy approached him about joining. "We'd be happy to have you," he continued, getting up and walking around his desk to pat the boy on the shoulder. "I know your granddad. You're the type we want in the WLI. You know that damn federal gov'ment is making noise about us having to take blacks—and we sure as 'ell ain't gonna do it, ya know? We'll all of us resign if Washington tries to force that!" and he again patted the boy's shoulder as though assuming his unconditional allegiance.

Buddy didn't know what to say to all this; the whole idea of race relations, of black and white, was not something he'd thought about, although his experiences in the city made him secretly sympathetic with blacks. However, he wasn't foolish enough to volunteer that he had a little nonwhite blood himself. He just wanted to join up. "Yes, sir," was the extent of his reply.

"You meet the company here at 1900 hours, that's 7:00 P.M., tonight, son, and we'll send you over to the Fifty-first Medical Company with some other fine lads who've volunteered."

"The medical company, sir?" Buddy asked. He knew Uncle Buster hung out with the elderly sergeants in that unit and was uneasy about going there.

"Yes, son. Ya see, ya gotta pass the induction physical, just like regular army, only we do it ourselves. 'Cause we got a medical company right here in town. You'll have no problem. I think the medics'll be at the Sumter guards tonight."

"Yes, sir," the boy responded, figuring he'd take a chance.

"Now, shouldn't you be in school?" Ramsey suddenly asked.

"Yes, sir, I cut today 'cause I wanted to join up."

"Well, that's very commendable, my boy, but I've got to drive up Charleston High way anyhow. Let me give you a ride and you can get to class late, okay?"

"Yes, sir," Buddy responded, not knowing what else to do. He just hoped Buster would be too drunk to go to drill tonight. "What's the time, sir?" he asked suddenly, hoping that at least he might miss geometry and the coach.

Sometimes the breaks come, sometimes they don't. Buddy pretended to be going to a basketball game and left home early, riding the bus to the armory with a classmate who got on in uniform, the uniform of a musician in the Salvation Army, and who asked where he was going.

"I'm gonna join the National Guard tonight, Ted," Buddy replied.

"Really? Which company?" Ted asked.

"The WLI."

"Well, ain't that somethin'?" the other boy exclaimed. "I'm in the WLI, too! That's where I'm goin' now."

"You are? But aren't you in the Salvation Army?"

"Yeah, but the hours don't conflict," Ted said, smiling.

"But don't they kinda contradict each other?" Buddy queried, truly interested in the other guy's neat balance of war and religion.

"They both pay money for only a few hours' work," Ted replied with a wide grin.

"I can see that," Buddy offered, grinning right back.

At the drill hall Buddy and some half-dozen other recruits were formed up, marched haphazardly down a broad, steep set of stairs to the street and loaded on an olive drab school bus. Soon they were herded into the Sumter guard's armory, directed to a large office, and set to filling out forms and answering questions put to them by bored older medics. A doctor appeared, gave each a primitive hearing test, and had each read an eye chart taped up across the room. As all were healthy teenagers, the medic simply checked off most boxes on their forms, scribbled down 20/20 and looked even more bored.

"Okay, boys, line up and drop your drawers," a staff sergeant commanded, with a large grin on his face.

"Drop our drawers?" one fellow asked.

"Get your pants down and your skivvies, too," the NCO repeated, "then bend over and catch holda your ankles. You need a proctological exam."

"A what?" a red-haired kid expostulated.

"The doc needs to look up your ass, kid," the soldier replied, grinning again.

Buddy hadn't realized joining up would mean doing this, but he was almost through the process, so what the heck, he undid his belt, let his trousers slip down and pulled down his boxer shorts. Leaning way forward, he felt for his ankles, which, at six feet three inches, were pretty far away. Leaning like this, his head turned to the left toward the office door, he saw a stout man in khaki enter and stop. Although he could see only as far as the middle of the man's chest, he recognized his Uncle Buster. Suddenly the physician's bony finger probed his fundament, then was gone.

"Ya can stand up, now," the sergeant said, laughing.

Buddy straightened up and looked squarely in the face of master sergeant Buster Bergson. Buddy stood at attention and kept his mouth shut. Buster stared at Buddy, then at the other recruits, and without a word turned nicely on his heel and left the room. Buddy passed the exam and was sworn in by the captain later that night.

Everyone in the family was not as understanding of the jigs and jags, the twists and turns that human beings make in trying to grow up. Buddy came to think of Buster's nonaction as part of the Code of the West, the Conspiracy of Silence that is the real ethic of the military, the willingness to live and let live that characterizes those who know firsthand the fragility of life, the weaknesses of the flesh. But sometimes, too, he wondered if perhaps those who carried their so visible wounds etched in their faces were not, because of their own pains, their own fears, more sensitive to the pains, the fears, of others. It was not a question Buddy could really ask anyone, so he never asked it.

The upshot of the rebellion was twofold. First, his grandparents took Buddy to the courthouse and made a deposition which resulted in the issuance of a birth certificate in the name of Martin Charles Gordon and stating that he was born alive in Charleston, South Carolina, on March 13, 1933, and that his race was white. She saw to it that Buddy's school records were changed to reflect his new name and race, too. Second, Buddy was enrolled in confirmation class, something he had avoided up to now.

Buddy spent two afternoons a week studying Luther's Catechism, the Service Book and the Bible with youngsters two and three years younger than himself. Although upset about many things, this religious study was surprisingly pleasant for Buddy.

Gloria Rhinemann was only a year younger than Buddy. She was dark, tall, with breasts larger than some of the married women in the congregation, and with a face best described as sweet. The first time he really saw her, actually noticed her in class, and noticed her noticing him, he broke into a sweat and nearly passed out. Something he hadn't given much thought to up till now, sex, became painfully present for him now.

The juices of life surge in sixteen-year-old boys and that rising tide is shared equally by healthy teenage girls. For Gloria and Buddy, that tide broke every dam before it and their youthful lives mingled as often as lie, excuse and artifice could arrange.

Gloria was an only child, and both parents worked. Her house was only eight blocks away from Buddy, who wished to flee the hours of advice and moralism his grandmother now directed at him daily. He would have walked away just to be alone. To be with Gloria, if the occasion would have arisen, he would have battled the police.

Drifting down to Gloria's was as easy as going to school. She gave him her address, phone number and the exact hours her parents were away, every day until six o'clock, except weekends. The first day they talked and soon were hugging and kissing, in tune to their developing bodies. Life looked a great deal better now to Buddy. Despite the growing disaffection he was experiencing with school and the neurotic tongue lashings that marked his home life, for the first time, Buddy experienced not passive satisfaction, but positive, active happiness. Gloria's mouth and hair, under his lips and hands, meant being alive. For the first time, he began to look forward to tomorrow, to live in hope and with its constant companion, dread. He now lived day after day in joyous expectation of feeling her body next to his during the day. At the same time, the dread that someone might find out, that someone or something might take his one friend, his love, his sense of completeness away brought real fear.

Whatever gods prevailed on this hot, green jungle coastline, whether those of coastal Santee or inland Choctaw Redmen, dark African Gullah or golden Guinea, blacks, Irish Catholics, French Huguenots or German Protestants, they were not averse to Buddy's happiness. He and Gloria were together through the rest of that tumult-filled year. Only school, his nocturnal wanderings with Mike, ending in their all-night shifts at the *News & Courier* on weekends and his Thursday night drill practice at the upstairs room of the WLI armory occupied more of his time.

The Year of Buddy and Gloria ended on Palm Sunday, in the high southern springtime, when the azaleas bloom in their almost supernatural beauty, peak for Easter and then simply disappear. Palm Sunday was the promised day of Gloria's and Buddy's confirmation. Parents and grandparents, uncles and aunts, all were generous with gifts for the young people, starting with clothes and ending with Bibles and watches. This rite of initiation into the outer circles of adulthood, admission to the Holy Communion and the receiving of their own offering envelopes was highly regarded by the young people themselves, as well as by their elders. Many were happy to be confirmed, "Just for the presents," as they honestly put it, and others were just happy to have it over with. Buddy and Gloria, ironically, chief among sinners, active flouters of the Ten Commandments' more subtle legislation, were—or tried to be—deeply interested in the event itself.

Gloria's parents presented her with a beautiful white dress, white gloves and all the trappings. Buddy's grandparents and his several aunts outfitted him in a dashing blue jacket and snowy white trousers, immaculately fitted to his physique. Decked out in this combination, with a matching tie and black shoes, Buddy looked like a groom, as Gloria looked like a bride. They remarked on the likeness to a wedding to each other in whispers. Many others made the same remark aloud.

This happy pair, whose bond was daily becoming more apparent to those around them, continued their private dates and moved, in public, from making cow eyes at one another to, courageously, holding hands. Gloria's father noticed this on that bright Palm Sunday and started to investigate. He didn't like what he feared he'd uncovered when an elderly lady, two houses from his own, mentioned Buddy's daily visits to Gloria in an otherwise empty house.

Holy Week followed Palm Sunday, then Easter, when once more the confirmands appeared in the church wearing their ritual clothes and sat together to commune, this one time, as a class. As they marched down the aisle together and sat side by side in the front pew, Buddy looked lovingly at Gloria and thought that they truthfully were one.

Buddy's attention was drawn back to the service by a surge of the organ, and he followed the liturgy gladly in his baritone, delicately holding the hymn book in partnership with Gloria. He kept his mind on the proceeding until the pastor mounted the pulpit. As he looked at an oblique angle, the angelic, creamy features and brunette curls of Gloria intervened between his eyes and the sweating preacher's bulk. Buddy soon found, in a choice between such an angel and God, that he was, without reserve, on the side of the angels.

The week after Easter, rain fell, washing the striking azaleas away in red, white and purple creeks that paralleled the curbs and stood in shallow, faded-colored lakes at street corner drains. Buddy, deterred by nothing, trudged up Rutledge Avenue to Gloria's cross street on Easter Monday, and like a husband home from work, let himself in.

"Hello, Buddy," a deep voice greeted him from the darkened living room. "I thought you might be dropping by," Gloria's father continued.

Mr. Rhinemann was rather old to have a daughter of fifteen, almost sixteen. In his sixties, he was a tall, slender, straggly-wristed man, with a brisk, white military mustache. His full head of hair was close cropped and never out of order. As a young man he had come to the United States from northern Germany and joined the U.S. Cavalry, when the cavalry still rode horses. Buddy wasn't afraid of the man, but, quite the contrary, rather liked the old gentleman and his stories of life on western army posts that he told at every Lutheran Brotherhood fish fry and Ladies Aid covered-dish supper. Right now, however, the old man was throwing that position of respect away.

"Buddy," Rhinemann began, "Gloria, up to recently, was as bright and shiny as a box of cellophane-wrapped crackers. Now, thanks to you, she's spoiled. You took your nasty fingers, and God knows what else, and tore the wrapper on the box. All sort of dirt has gotten in. I don't know how I can repair the damage."

The old man stopped for breath, his face beet-red behind his bushy white eyebrows and trimmed mustache.

Buddy looked, and felt, shocked. Not at the old fellow's anger. He expected and could respect that. Buddy was shocked at the terms Rhinemann applied to Gloria. He was amazed at the value, or lack of value, this father put on his daughter. Even being thought of as a nigger Indian was more human than being considered crackers packaged for the advantageous sale.

"I ought to whip you, boy. And boy, I can still do it. But I'm just telling you to get out—and to keep your nasty mouth shut. Don't ever mention Gloria or this conversation to anyone. I'm going to try and cover this over and save my girl's reputation. I wouldn't want anyone to know just how stupid she is, and what poor taste she has. You just vamoose and never come smelling around Gloria again. Find one of your own kind to rut with."

Buddy stood, face frozen, tight lipped, immobile. Then his right arm struck out, the side of his palm struck the old man on the bridge of the nose. A geyser of blood exploded from Rhinemann's mouth and nostrils. He began to crumple backward. As he was falling, Buddy's hand caught Rhinemann a second time, across the mouth. His skinny throat emitted a wet gurgle and the old man toppled backward.

Buddy turned sharply and walked out, not looking back. He walked quickly home.

When Buddy entered the Gordon house, his grandmother, seated in an arm chair listening to the radio and smoking a cigarette, began to harp at him on some real or fancied infraction of her house rules. Buddy walked by, in deep silence, wanting only to go to his room.

"I know you. I know the trash you come from. I know you're up to no good," the old woman shrieked.

Buddy turned at the hall door and quietly said, "Go to hell, you old witch." The old woman gasped, flushing red, then swiftly going pale. Buddy walked to his room, got his red sweater, stuffed a few things in his trouser pockets and passed his grandmother, still sitting speechless, on his way out. Round three had begun.

At the corner, Buddy caught bus four and rode in raging quiet to the county courthouse on Broad Street. He chanced to find the marine corps recruiter working overtime, filling out reports, in his basement office.

"How can I sign up?" Buddy asked the florid-faced staff sergeant.

"You can begin by filling out these papers," the marine replied, digging some mimeographed forms out of his desk. "Ever been arrested?"

"No," Buddy replied. "I ran away once, but they just sent me back."

"No problem," said the sergeant. "Ever been real sick?"

"Not really," Buddy answered in a surprised tone.

"You as strong as you look, kid?" the marine went on with a grin.

"Sure," he said.

"How old are you?"

"Just turned seventeen!" Buddy half-shouted with a deep

sense of satisfaction.

"Hell, we get one parent's or guardian's signature and you're in, man."

"What if a guardian won't sign?"

"Then we'll just make you a year older on the papers," the sergeant blandly replied.

"Let's do it," Buddy said and sat down to fill out the papers.

By the next afternoon, the smooth-talking sergeant had Buddy's grandmother's signature on the enlistment papers and made Buddy a year older anyway, just to be on the safe side. The morning after, Buddy, by courtesy of a Reserve officer making the trip, was driven to Columbia to be sworn in. As they drove, in companionable silence, toward the state capital and the chief recruiting office of the navy and marine corps, the thought crossed Buddy's mind that he had fought hard for three rounds only to knock his own self out. The dread that follows every giddy foray into a new adventure asserted itself and he was afraid.

II

Headed East

4

Mr. Rhinemann narrowly escaped a broken neck in the exchange with Buddy. He might have drowned in his own blood, in any event, had it not been for the arrival of his wife, who left work early that day out of anxiety over the showdown with Buddy. She found the old man on the floor, called an ambulance and got him to the emergency room. When questioned by the police the next morning, Rhinemann lied and blamed his injuries on a black burglar, whom he claimed to have discovered in his house when he returned home to get a second pair of glasses. Buddy knew nothing of this.

Instead, the farce that had taken place when Buddy tried

to enlist in the army was in part replayed with his enlistment into the marine corps. First, his falsified age of eighteen that was typed on his papers became official. The recruiting sergeant, in a burst of clerical overkill, had Buddy's grandmother officially sign the enlistment papers as guardian. He had left Buddy in the courthouse the next morning and driven to Mrs. Gordon's, returned with her signature and no explanation as to how it was obtained. While at the time neither of these incidents seemed earthshaking in importance, several months later at the invasion at Inchon, when all seventeen-year-olds were not permitted to go into combat, the actions of Buddy, the recruiting sergeant and Mrs. Gordon would become painfully clear.

But before there could be adventure, dues had to be paid. For Buddy and the other enlistees, "the dues" was called Parris Island. Buddy was given a ride to the main recruiting office in Columbia by a professor at the university who was also a reserve officer. Buddy spent the night in a tiny, roach-filled room in a second-floor flophouse on Columbia's Main Street and ate in a third-rate hash house—the only places nearby that would take the "chits" or passes given to him by the recruiter. In the morning, he caught a Greyhound bus for Yamasee, South Carolina, the gateway from civilian life and liberty to the closed society of Parris Island.

Buddy had heard about the marines and Parris Island all his life. Even Big John had been through, and graduated with honors, to hear him tell it, those hallowed halls in their first year of operation in the early days of World War I. In those first days they had lived in tents on the sand flea–mosquito infested island. He had served in the Fifth Machine Gun Battalion in France, 1917-18, suffering a broken arm when his machine gun had exploded during the fighting in Belleau Wood. Buddy's early childhood was filled with evenings around a wood fire, hearing of these adventures. And during

World War II, Buddy's half-brother, Bob, had gone to the Pacific with the marines. He was killed in action on Saipan. Perhaps it was an unconscious reaction to the memory of Bob's death that prompted Buddy to first try to enlist in the army, a less mortality-oriented service than the self-consciously reckless marines.

But, having no one to blame, and being fully warned, here Buddy was, getting down from the bus in the dust of Yamasee, the recruit reception point, being cursed and abused by a disreputable-looking sergeant and thinking much too late that he might have been foolish in his choice.

He had heard about this demeaning treatment but had paid little attention. The next morning, on the marine bus into the base, he was reminded of the shaved head he would soon have as a fellow recruit. He suddenly remembered all of the stories and did the only thing he could do. He steeled himself for the humiliation that was to come and kept his mouth shut. Silence did little to ease the panic that was churning in his gut.

The marine green bus passed down the narrow road that skirted the southern edge of Beaufort and turned right into the causeway that led across the swamp to Parris Island's main gate. Driving to the reception center, the bus stopped, and like guards driving convicts condemned for life to Devil's Island, the drill instructors cursed and cuffed the confused "civilians" to line them up, single file, before a huge door. The men walked in with hair of various lengths and walked out with haircuts precise in their likeness, bald. With this haircut the deflation of their ego, the wrecking of each young man's self-image, was successfully begun. Each of the young men, Buddy included, started to grin and joke about the new haircut but were shouted into silence. Standing in the increasingly humid air, each one of the young men seemed to visibly shrink a bit, like an inflated toy with a slow but persistent leak.

A long hall with bright steel tables was their next stop. A particularly vicious NCO demanded that they strip off every stitch of clothing, or as he called it, "Your pogey bait rags," then tear a sheet off a roll of heavy brown paper that stood on one table, wrap up every damned civilian thing they owned, except their watches and wallets, and tie the packages with the heavy twine that was piled next to the paper. Then, with a tone of total disgust, the NCO shouted, "Address the damned things and put your name and 'Marine Corps Recruit Depot, Parris Island, S.C.' as your return address. And that's NOT 'PARE ASS' as in France, it's 'Pare Ass' with two *R*s. Just like hell's got two *l*s, we got two *r*s. Otherwise, the two are just alike, hell'n here. You savvy?"

"Yes, sir," a few called back to him, having already begun to adopt the prisoner's mentality.

"I CAN'T HEAR YOU!" he screamed, red-faced.

Buddy and the rest jerked up straight, the way they had seen men do it in the war movies, and yelled at the top of their lungs, "Yes, sir!"

"Pile 'em on the table nearest the hatch," the NCO commanded, pointing to the door, "and line up."

They were next run naked through a large room fitted out with showers. The floor was panlike, holding an antiseptic-smelling liquid that reminded Buddy of a hospital or high school swimming pool. "We don't want any motherfuckin' crabs or cooties on the Island, you swamp-suckin' SOB's," a red-headed, red-faced PFC screamed at them from the door. Buddy had suffered from cooties, head lice, several times as a child and remembered the usually useless hot oil treatments, the medicated shampoos and the small, fine-toothed combs used to defeat them, but he'd never had "crabs" and didn't know what they might be. A whisper from a more sophisticated city kid told him graphically what crabs were.

"And they really look like crabs?" Buddy whispered back.

"Yeah. They do," the northern boy replied, looking at the southern boy disdainfully, wondering where he'd been.

After drying off the "fresh meat," as they were now referred to, they were run into a giant quartermaster's office that had shelves fifteen feet high or more, each shelf covered with marine utilities and personal gear. Each "man" (most were oversized boys), was eyeballed by an alcoholic-looking master sergeant. He shouted out, with remarkable accuracy, if not an almost imperceptible slight slur, "bring a large trousers and extra-large coat, utility" or "a size seven dungaree cap and a medium belt." The sergeant's face fell, however, when Buddy and a few of the other tall men moved up in line. As he looked up at Buddy, he choked out almost apologetically, "You guys will have to make do until we special order some gear that will be the right sizes for your arms and legs." He added, with a genuine note of apology this time, "I'm afraid you'll also have to wait on your dress blues. They'll need to be special made. Go stand over there and let that corporal take your measurements."

Buddy and several other outsize recruits did just that, then slipped on utilities that didn't quite fit. "Just wait," one Tennesseean said, "we'll have the best damn lookin' set a'dress blues on the base." He wasn't much of a prophet. Buddy was never to see a full set of dress blues. Reality got in the way of playing soldier, as it had such an unsettling way of doing.

Buddy had lived two very different lives, country and city, extremely poor and moderately secure, Indian and white, but in the conservative, traditional societies that both lives embraced. He remained naive. Sophistication, or at least awareness of alternative lifestyles, or of different ways of looking at the world, only began to painfully become part of him at age sixteen. As with most children of his time, the painful awakening was frightening.

Mike and Buddy had taken Henry Cramer's invitation to present themselves at 9:00 P.M. on Friday at the *News & Courier* plant in downtown Charleston, walking from the bus stop through a huge, dark parking lot to the warehouselike structure, where trucks sat backed up to ramps. Entering a large, noisy room, they found Henry, who saw them enrolled as weekend workers.

"Here, boys, put these rubbers on your fingers," Henry said, handing them small, rolled-up latex tubes designed to fit on the thumb and forefinger.

Mike laughed and jokingly asked, "What exactly are we gonna do to the paper?"

Buddy was at a loss, yet laughed anyway since he assumed there was a hidden meaning that he ought to know.

"Well," Henry continued, "you see that rack there, with the wires running up through the floor and back down again?"

"Yeah," the boys responded.

"Well, when the presses down there start runnin', and the foldin' machine starts operatin', pretty soon now, then the complete newspaper is goin' come up them wires, one after the other, with every twenty-fifth paper bumped a little sideways so it sticks out. Ya got that?" Henry asked, looking sternly from one boy to the other.

"Yeah, yeah. We got it," they answered.

"Well," Henry continued, "You've got to grab hold of twenty-five papers at a time, give 'em a whack on this counter to align them, and stack them over there." He turned to point to another metal table.

"Okay," Buddy responded.

"Then, ya gotta' do it again, and again, and again, until

somebody relieves ya to piss or go eat, 'cause the presses just keep on rolling once they start, if there ain't no mechanical breakdown, that is." Henry made it clear that press pulling wasn't easy and there was no room to "mess up."

After that, Mike and Buddy took turns pulling the press and stacking the papers in neat piles of one hundred, alternating the work, never stopping, except when a swingman came to relieve them and they hit the toilet, or walked through the dark streets to an all-night pancake house for breakfast at two or three A.M. This was their weekend all through Buddy's sixteenth year, pulling the press, then church on Sunday. The hours Buddy spent matching his own speed with that of the tireless machine seemed to build his endurance, as well as his active imagination. He thought of Gloria, of escape, of freedom, of fantastic powers and events and places he'd read about in comic books. And he endured.

Press pulling was also, as he later found out, not a bad background for Parris Island. The constant, repetitious motion and monotony of the one was not unlike the other.

Yet, endurance was not sophistication. Unfortunately, in Buddy's world sophistication was generally thought of in terms of sex, drink, and whatever else was thought to be "adult" activity. Mike, totally a man of his time, took it upon himself to be Buddy's guide to this new country that superimposed itself on the streets that he knew so well by daylight.

"Be careful when you go to the john," he whispered. "See that old guy over there?"

"Yeah," Buddy answered dubiously.

"Well, he's queer, and he'll get you in the bathroom if you aren't careful!"

"What?" Buddy spoke out loud, dumbfounded.

"Watch it, he's watchin'. He'll hear you," Mike hissed back.

"But why?" Buddy wanted to know.

"You don't wanna know, man!" Mike assured him.

Heeding Mike's worldly advice, Buddy became too afraid to go to the bathroom when he had to. He would fight the urge until it was no longer controllable, then he would race in and out of the stall as quickly as he could.

Walking to the all-night restaurant, Mike would catechize the boy on the dangers of homosexuals. "Don't never go in that street, they hang out there, you know," Mike would say knowingly.

"Right," Buddy would answer, equally knowingly, and walk a little faster.

Despite his paranoia, Mike was not altogether wrong. The old man at the plant did corner the boys, at different times, trying to proposition them. Mike screamed, "Get away from me, you old homo!" and the man blanched and forever after stayed away from Mike. When he was approached, Buddy, on the other hand, kept silent, turned and ran away, returning to work five minutes early, and began to pull the press with shaking hands.

The boys found that late-night sex came in many forms as they walked the two A.M. streets of Charleston. Street walkers, white and black, old and older, were a regular sight. These women, usually rum-marked and overweight, caused no erotic tingle in these two hormone-pumped boys.

"Man, they sure ain't out here selling it 'cause they're pretty, are they?" Buddy remarked.

"Those drunk swabbies ain't lookin' for looks, they lookin' for relief," Mike shot back.

"I hope I don't ever get that bad off," the younger boy replied.

"Then don't never go to sea for six months," Mike advised him.

The boys found out too that drinking and newsprint seemed to go hand in hand. Not just up in the editor's office but down in the bowels of the plant and out into the yard and on the loading docks, where newsprint-smudged hands tossed the bundles of the early edition into dark painted trucks.

"Have a swig, kid," the loading foreman offered, smiling genially at the two exhausted boys sitting on the ramp's edge.

"Don't mind if I do," Mike replied, taking the pint carefully from the blue-blackened hand.

"You, too, boy," the older man added, nodding to Buddy.

"Don't mind if I do," he rejoined, drinking too quickly, spluttering, drops flying over his shirt, as he thrust the bottle back to the laughing man.

"You need to grow some hair on your balls, boy," he advised, not unkindly.

Sophistication, it seems, comes to some with birth; for others it never comes. However, for most, the grace of balance, which in all events may reside at the heart of life's varieties, comes hard. Buddy, in spite of Mike's tutelage, remained not innocent but dumb.

Parris Island, when Buddy arrived, was all it had been reported to be and more. The object of this three-month training cycle was to break down every defense, every personal idea of the recruit, to render him psychologically defenseless and absolutely obedient to command. Then, when the basic marine was so disoriented, the training sought to build up in the recruit an inordinate pride in himself as being part of a team, a member of an elite group, the marine corps. The system was, and is, sadistic and undemocratic, but it worked.

The lengths to which the drill instructors would go to instill obedience and teach the basics of soldiering to the "ladies" of the platoon were famous, or rather infamous, and most of even the most improbable stories that passed through the recruit grapevine were true. The creativity in cruelty and humiliation of these rough men surpassed the imagination of Buddy and surprised him when it targeted him as victim.

If any one of them made a mistake in "troop and stomp," drilling, he could count on being pulled out of ranks and made to run around and around the platoon as it went on with drill. Sometimes the DIs would then have the platoon double time, so the unlucky recruit had to attempt to run around a block of running men. Buddy found himself on such a muscle-straining mission several times.

Parris Island was a low-lying, swampy barrier island infested with insects. Of particular aggravation to the men outside in summer, and recruits were almost always outside, were the sandfleas, tiny insects much like the "no see 'ems" that make river fishing miserable. Standing at attention for long periods, a frequent activity on the parade ground, made the men subject to the itchy, often painful, attentions of these miserable insects. If a man was so disturbed as to swat a sandflea when he was supposed to be immobile, eyes front, and a DI saw it, a bizarre ritual could begin.

Buddy was standing in the rear rank. The platoon had been drilling in a very hot sun for a long time. Perhaps to give himself a rest, the DI called a halt, a "Left face, huh!" and told them to stand at strict attention. Many uncomfortable minutes went by, which grew more miserable as the sandfleas and flies found this huge tonnage of human flesh pan-frying on heat-softened asphalt. A sandflea began to crawl up Buddy's right nostril. He wriggled his large, Roman nose just enough to deflect the bug's path. However, this thwarted flea, or a relation, began to burrow into Buddy's right ear canal. This sensation was too scary, too unsettling to endure. As steadily as possible, the boy reached up to dislodge the sandflea. Sgt. Craven, the DI, saw him, screamed, raced to Buddy's position, and, from his full height of five feet, eight inches, thrust his perpetually scarlet face upward at the boy.

"You, shithead! Did you kill that poor sandflea?" he shouted.

There wasn't any use in lying, the man had obviously seen him. "Yes, sir!" Buddy replied in best bootcamp fashion.

"Well, you mother-murdering pissant, you got to give that poor sandflea a military funeral. You hear me, numb nuts?"

"Yes, sir!"

And, after a long chewing out, Buddy was ordered to report to the DI's room at the barracks just before "lights out" that night.

"Yes, sir!" Buddy cried again, scared as he'd ever been about what might be coming.

The rest of the day passed and finished with the misery of a general cleaning of the squad bay. No mail. No time to shine shoes or write letters. Just screaming from the corporal who seemed, contrary to regulations, a bit under the influence. Buddy cleaned one miserable crapper three times before the man was satisfied.

Just before lights out, shortly after the general inspection was completed, Buddy forced himself to march up to the drill instructor's door, and forced his arm up to knock.

"Enter!" Sergeant Craven bellowed.

"Sir, permission to speak, sir!" Buddy cried as the door opened.

"Speak!" the sergeant replied.

"Recruit reporting as ordered, sir!" Buddy continued.

"Ah, yes," the sergeant said, smiling. "Boy, you see that entrenching tool in that corner?"

"Yes, sir!"

"Well, grab the damned thing! And fetch that matchbox off the table!"

"Yes, sir!"

Buddy was quick-marched back to the parade ground and told to get down on his hands and knees and find "that poor, damned dead sandflea for burial." Dragging the short shovel in one hand he crawled about the still warm tarmac until a sandflea landed on his encumbered hand. Quietly, in the darkness, he swatted this offering of nature and cried out, "Sir, permission to speak, sir!"

"Speak!"

"Sir, I've found the sandflea, sir!" he cried again.

"Good, good," Sgt. Craven chuckled. "Well, get up and put the poor critter in that there matchbox!"

"Yes, sir!" Buddy screamed, rising, laying down the shovel and reaching for the matchbox in his jacket pocket. He carefully opened it and put the squished bit of matter inside; he closed it with a small sigh of relief.

"Asswipe! You get that entrenching tool! You gotta bury that fella now!"

"Yes, sir!"

Sergeant Craven quick-marched the rattled youth to the tiny strip of grass behind the platoon's wooden barracks. Calling a halt in a little patch of light that fell from the lower windows, Craven observed quietly, "Now, don't tear up the grass, idiot. Just dig a neat little hole, a foot deep and put that critter down there!"

"Yes, sir!"

Buddy carefully gouged out a circle of sod, dug a twelve-inch-deep hole, and kneeling, placed the flea's coffin at the bottom.

"Cover that little fella up, boy," came a shout in the darkness.

Buddy replaced the dirt with his hands, tamping it down with the folding shovel. He placed the circle of sod back carefully and stood up.

"Now, the poor guy needs a twenty-one gun salute and taps!" Craven said quite reasonably.

"Sir?" Buddy asked, startled by this development.

"You do 'em!" the sergeant ordered.

"Yes, sir!" the now embarrassed boy responded, and began "BOOM, BOOM, BOOM..." Buddy almost lost track but got twenty-one "BOOMs!" out without croaking or crying. Then, as the sergeant came to attention, he put his cupped hand to his mouth and began intoning," Da Da Da Daaaaa...Da Da Da Daaaaa, Da Da Da Daaaaa!"

When he finished, he dropped his hand smartly. Sgt. Craven gave a final salute and said, "Screw-up, you're dismissed!"

And Buddy cried, "Yes, sir!" and raced back into the barracks, creeping as quietly as he could into the rack. Snickers and muffled laughs rose from the ranks of the supposedly sleeping men who, a few moments before, had sneaked to the window to enjoy The Sandflea's Funeral.

He hated the slop he was given to eat, hated the loss of sleep, the stupid, sadistic games of burying sandfleas in matchboxes, and the lack of the company of women. However, even the marines had a few microscopic aspects that passed for civilized behavior. After a very long day (that was every day), of running, calisthenics, marching, classes, lining up for meals, making beds, cleaning the squad bays, or barracks, and standing stiffly at attention at the foot of their bunks until the drill instructors were satisfied, the "skinheads" of Buddy's platoon might be given a few minutes to relax. They would occasionally be given mail, and allowed to sit on their locker boxes for a short time to read it. Those who got no mail would continue cleaning rifles, shining shoes or sewing rents and tears in their gear.

One midweek evening, Buddy got several letters. There was a second letter from Mike, who was becoming as dedicated a letter writer as Buddy. He maintained that the others on the night shift at the *News & Courier* missed Buddy, after getting over their anger at his "just taking off like a stupid-ass ape," with no explanation. Buddy rather doubted that the rough bunch on the night shift even knew he was gone, although they certainly must have been upset by the hole he left in the work force that first weekend after he joined up. Mike had seen Max, who was sick. Mike hadn't returned to Max's house; his parents seemed kind of "funny" even for Charleston! The letter gave Buddy his first smile of the day.

There was a card from his grandmother. Her tiny, precise lettering said he was missed very much by both his granddad and herself. Buddy felt a twinge of guilt and resolved to write during free time the following Sunday.

The last letter was an official government envelope that surprised him. It was an honorable discharge from the South Carolina National Guard. The reason for discharge was a coded set of letters and numbers that Buddy guessed meant because of enlistment on active service. The boy felt another wave of guilt in reading the legal-looking document. This was another group that depended on him that he'd walked out on when he enlisted. He stilled his uneasy feelings by promising himself that he'd never let anyone else down again if he could help it.

Buddy probably made every mistake possible in recruit training. He was tall and gangling, and fully coordinated only in the water. Unfortunately, he'd passed his swimming tests the first night they were given. Combat swimming was restricted, normally, to learning to jump from a simulated ship's deck while wearing full field gear. However, somehow he was able to secure permission to swim whenever the poorer swimmers were practicing. Buddy's skill and desire did not go unnoticed. Unfortunately, athletic ability in the water didn't, in Buddy's case, carry over to land. He finally became a precise marcher, learning, in time, the most intricate drills, even the mind-boggling "To the Winds March" in which each marine stepped off in a different direction, but during the first weeks he spent the best part of his drill time trying to keep from falling over his own feet.

Buddy's underage body still suffered from a lack of self-discipline. The marine corps, however, had taken that contingency into account. There were punishments, dreaded punishments, that were designed to make the most undisciplined mind and body willing to cooperate. It was not unusual to see a recruit, his laundry bucket covering his head, squat and proceed to "duck walk" in perfect cadence, then with the bucket limiting his vision, stand and run down the company street guided only by what could be seen of the curb and pavement at his feet.

Buddy had watched more than one of his pals go through that nerve-wracking maze and he was determined to practice and practice so his seventeen-year-old feet would not trip him up. So it was with chagrin that he heard Corporal Garcia scream, "Okay, Gordon, you dumbass! Get up to that squad bay and fetch your bucket!" Buddy had been concentrating so hard on his feet that he missed some move with his rifle during the maneuver.

"Yes, sir!" he once again shouted back and fell out of formation, raced up the wooden steps to the barracks, to his bunk, grabbed his laundry pail and raced back to the street again.

"On your head, stupid!" Garcia cried again.

"Yes, sir!" Raising the pail overhead, he pulled it down to cover his dungaree hat and his face, and then he snapped to attention.

"Duck walk, lady!" the corporal screamed with delight.

"Yes, sir!"

Buddy squatted down, his M-1 at port arms, and waddled along in front of the platoon. No one was brave—or dumb—

enough to laugh. After several minutes, Garcia yelled, his voice sounding far away to Buddy, who felt as cut off from the world as a deep-sea diver. "On your feet, dumb shit!"

"Yes, sir!" the boy cried back, his voice echoing inside the galvanized container.

"Double time, asshole!"

"Yes, sir!" His own voice stabbed painfully at his ears.

Buddy tried to keep the curb at his right side in view as he ran but at the corner he was without a guide, powering along blind until the next curb appeared. He thought he had this figured out until the corporal, who was running along beside him, to his left, shouted "To the rear, huh!"

"Oh, shit!" Buddy whispered to himself, turning about, barely missing the DI.

He ran as carefully as he could but wavered, almost colliding with Garcia, until the corporal screamed, "Double time, halt!" Buddy pulled up, sweaty and confused, waiting for the next humiliation.

"Boy," Garcia screamed, "get that damned bucket off your head and take it to the squad bay!"

"Yes, sir!" the boy responded, running happily to deposit the bleach-smelling instrument of torture at the rear of his bunk.

The sole "holiday" Buddy's platoon was given didn't last long. It was given following a stiff inspection after six weeks on The Island and exemplified all the graceful entertainment that Parris Island brought to mind. They were given the opportunity to run flat out across the parade ground to the PX and buy one quart of ice cream. They were permitted to eat it there standing in the middle of the PX. Twenty minutes later it was all but forgotten as they marched double time in the hot afternoon sun.

Sunday church call and the regular swimming training

were about the only ways Buddy could relieve the strain and restore some sense of his own humanity. Though he and the others were required to march to chapel, it was the one place on the island where he felt as though he were not being treated as a slave. He went every Sunday. At the pool, Buddy found the instructors commanding but not sadistic. Because of his prowess in the water, Buddy soon earned a first-class swimmer's card, which allowed him the privilege of swimming laps by himself. His natural comfort in the water made the special training a joy rather than a drudge. He actually enjoyed jumping, in full gear, off the simulated deck into the water. He had no fear of drowning. The water was his one true friend. He understood it and trusted it.

The end of the training was nearing rapidly and everyone knew it. The one sure sign of closure was the rifle range. They wouldn't let new recruits near one until the end. To Buddy and the rest of the platoon this was truly a treat. They lived in tents near the range, went through combat maneuvers and "snapped in" with the gunnery instructors, who were not DI's and therefore were automatically semi-human. Buddy found the rifle training demanding because he had to twist and fold his long legs and arms in an assorted series of poses to accomplish the different firing positions. In spite of the contortions, he fired well on "record day" and became a Sharpshooter—not the best, but definitely better that Marksman. The one aspect of all this rifle training that bothered Buddy was the bayonet work. The idea of scores of naked bayonets, especially as they were marching, unnerved Buddy. He had never liked a bare knife pointed at him; he believed a knife to be far more lethal than a gun.

Through the marching, drilling, swimming, shooting, the days fled and finally it was graduation day. The platoon marched past the reviewing stand. The men were congratulated, shooting badges were awarded, and each man was promoted to PFC.

After a handshake with the chief drill instructor, Buddy walked away from the crowd of his fellow PFC's, their proud parents and friends, and boarded a bus for Charleston. He had a ten-day leave before he was to join up with the Sixth Marines at Camp Lejeune. He went back to Charleston alone.

5

Buddy entered the company office of the Sixth Marines at Camp Lejeune, North Carolina, to report for duty and found the austere room filled with a frenzy of colorful civilian clothing and even more colorful language. Apparently, there had been an accident in Jacksonville, the grimy eastern Carolina liberty town just off base. Several state and county police officers tried to control the irate civilians who kept pointing toward and screaming at a drunken, disheveled group of marines standing manacled together. While this group was trying to sort out their differences, medics carried in another marine, this time dressed in civvies, on a stretcher.

He had been doing 75 down the main drag out of town on his motorcycle and had missed a curve. Buddy thought to himself that the guy's leg looked like it would be pretty useless for quite a while.

Buddy, in the meantime, had moved over to the clerk's desk and stood, seabag in tow, quietly waiting to report. He went unnoticed for over thirty minutes. The clerk, so occupied with the evening's events, did not notice Buddy until the company first sergeant, a volatile Puerto Rican, his shirt front covered with battle ribbons, came in and began swearing Parris Island style. The "top" squared away Buddy's papers and sent him to Howe Company's barracks where a buck sergeant assigned him a bunk. Buddy then wandered over to the Third Battalion's mess for his first non–boot camp meal. He was impressed and surprised at the life style of the combat ready rifle unit. The men were distinctly informal with each other and in the mess ate large, actually good-tasting meals, family style. During the meal there were huge pitchers of milk and much joking at table, the men held up empty serving bowls for the K.P. workers to refill. Buddy decided he was going to like it there.

The next day he caught a work detail, then was called out to draw his "782" gear, the company issue of pack, shelter-half, tent pegs, entrenching tool, cartridge belt, bayonet, canteen and first-aid kit. He also purchased some more uniform items at the clothing issue office and drew a rifle from the armory. Weighted down with gear, he returned to the barracks and stowed his belongings in his footlocker and wall locker. Buddy felt at home in the sense that he always felt at home wherever he had something to eat and a place to sleep.

Life fell into a soothing routine. In the evenings the men in his squad bay gathered at the base slop chute, or beer garden, and drank a few pitchers. The company mascot, an English Bulldog named Tuffy, lapped up his share as well and fell asleep at the end of the table. During the day, they attended training classes in first aid and in the laying out of signal panels to instruct marine close air support fighters and dive bombers about their positions and the direction of the "enemy." Then, on the sixth night after Buddy's arrival, just as he and his platoon returned from the deep pine woods where they had been on a training exercise that had disintegrated into a snake hunt, they were greeted with a gruff order from the top sergeant. "Pack it up! We're moving out!"

"What?" Buddy asked a companion.

"We're moving out, probably going overseas," the older man said. "Get your gear together."

"Do we take everything?" Buddy asked.

"Sure, all your stuff," the marine replied, "but pack your personal gear in two seabags. We'll probably drop them along the way. Be sure to pack everything you'll need in your knapsack and haversack—that's all you can be sure of taking with you from now on."

"Right," Buddy said as he stood looking at the enormous quantity of gear he suddenly seemed to own. "Help me roll my pack the right way?" Buddy asked in a moment of confusion.

"Sure, kid. I'll watch to see you do it right while I get my stuff together."

Buddy nervously rolled his blankets and poncho together in the horseshoe roll that wrapped over his pack, wondering what was going on.

After Buddy and the men fell out in the company street, wearing packs and carrying two seabags, and rifles, they were put on six-by-six trucks and driven to a large railhead in the midst of the dense pine forest that covered Camp Lejeune. Here Buddy and the others piled their equipment together and went to work loading thousands of artillery shells and hundreds of boxes of hand grenades and ammunition into boxcars. They worked all night under floodlights, breaking for thick sandwiches and coffee around midnight. At dawn, they were paraded with their gear, inspected, and marched aboard passenger cars that were pulled up to replace the freight cars.

For the next five days, Buddy and his companions had no idea where they were going. Buddy slept, played cards, smoked and read in his seat. He and the others were taken by turns to the dining car and fed three meals a day. They sang songs and laughed as they passed through the Carolinas, Georgia, Alabama, Mississippi. In New Orleans, they were allowed to get off the train and do exercises in the empty station. This was the only time they were permitted to get off the train until it reached California. After New Orleans, the officers in charge ordered the windows shut whenever the train stopped at a station. At a station in Arizona, Buddy watched women press against the glass and heard the men go crazy; in New Mexico, vendors tried to sell sandwiches and coffee but to no avail. Howe Company was on a sealed troop train; the men were finally told on the morning of the fifth day that their destination was Camp Pendleton, where they would undergo a short tour of combat firing training, and then go to Camp Del Mar, near Oceanside, where they would cram amphibious training into a few days.

"What then, Cap'n?" a young marine asked.

"Then it's up to Eighth and I," the officer replied.

Several of the newest members of the company looked confused, Buddy among them. Whispering to the veteran marine next to him, he asked, "Eighth and I?"

"Headquarters for the corps," the older soldier whispered back.

The men had been talking about Korea ever since Lejeune, but Buddy, who had no portable radio and read no newspapers, wasn't sure what that meant. He had heard that Korea was invaded while he was at Parris Island, but Buddy didn't know where Korea was, except that it was somewhere in Asia. The *National Geographic* that he had read had little or no information on that faraway place, and Buddy had no maps.

"Now listen up, you men," the captain went on, "you have just had your unit designation changed. You are now part of the First Marine Division, Fleet Marine Force, Pacific. Your current unit identification is now Third Battalion, Seventh Marines, Reinforced."

"Seventh Marines! Combat, here we come!" one skinny PFC exclaimed.

"Stuff that!" a dark-haired corporal replied. "I'm a lover, not a fighter."

At that, a couple of the men started the whistles and jeers. There was even one rather obnoxious fellow from somewhere in New York City, Buddy wasn't sure where, who made an offensive noise that he proudly called a "Bronx cheer." Personally, Buddy though of it as a fart, but, now, he didn't think about it at all. He was baffled, anxious and, at the same time, strangely excited by the travel and this unexpected turn of events. He found he was looking forward to California. As for Korea, that was too mysterious, too far beyond his imagination to worry about, yet.

Even as Buddy and his comrades were receiving their news, the First Marine Division, three disjointed segments plus several other smaller pieces, was being called to service from around the world. One of the Sixth Marine battalions was on board the fleet in the Mediterranean, and was rotated back to form part of the Seventh Marines. The division was to form the spearhead of General Douglas MacArthur's bold plan to repel North Korean aggression by a surprise amphibious invasion at Inchon. The peacetime marine corps was small and undermanned. Troops were called from everywhere. Units were not to meet as a team until the last regiment, the Seventh, was ashore in battle at the Han River and the capture of Seoul in September.

The few days of rifle and machine-gun practice at Pendleton passed rapidly, as did the amphibious training at Del Mar, and Buddy still did not understand the full implication of what lay before him. After a week, the entire unit was moved to the San Diego Naval Destroyer Base. Still in mothballs from World War II, the troops slept on the docks, on top of boxes packed for shipment, or, when it was cold and foggy, under shelter halves strung between packing crates, jeeps and bulldozers. Only the mess hall had been opened for the troops; it was the opinion of not a few, including Buddy, that they shouldn't have bothered. Buddy and the others endured this half-serious Boy Scout outing for a week; then the officers relented and gave the men liberty. Every night, they unpacked their dress greens, shaved in the open lavatories, and dressed in the open, then walked to the main gate and hitch-hiked into San Diego or down to Tiajuana. Buddy, bored with the waiting, went into Mexico every night to sample the gaudy lights and the bottled lightning sold in the "world's longest bar."

Tiajuana was by far the dirtiest town Buddy had ever seen. The crudity of the open sexuality and complete drunkenness that peopled the streets and buildings both fascinated and repulsed Buddy. As he walked these streets and watched these people he became even more aware of his own innocence and inexperience. The Mexicans and the other marines seemed to be a thousand years older than he. Even his own name, Buddy, was the name of a child, not a man going off to the war. If life had been different, Buddy reflected, if he were still on the reservation, he would be called Hawk, the shortened form of his real name. Yes, he thought, as he made his way through the chaos of the border town streets, his name was really John Nighthawk, Jr., not Martin Charles "Buddy" Gordon. With new resolve he would go into this new world with a real name—Hawk.

It was during these walks that he noticed the Indian features that were so prominent among the Mexicans. He also recognized the poverty and exploitation that accompanied those features. One night, after a bottle of Carta Blanca, Buddy stopped at a tamale cart, bought one, then two. He stood there, eating the bland, meatless bean and corn paste tube wrapped in its green corn shuck and tried to speak to the vendor.

"You know, I'm an Indian, too," Buddy said in a thick voice.

"*Qué?*" the man asked.

"Me," Buddy said, striking his chest with his right fist, "Me, I'm Indian, too. Like you."

"You?...Me?" the Mexican said. He obviously knew English. "You like me?" he continued.

"Yeah," Buddy said, confused by his response.

The Mexican was five feet tall, give or take an inch either way. Buddy was six feet, four inches. The Mexican weighed perhaps 110 pounds. Buddy weighed 185. The Mexican was brown-skinned with coal black hair. Buddy's skin, though suntanned, was distinctly white. The Mexican's brown eyes lit up, and looking squarely into Buddy's grayish blue ones. He laughed. Buddy was cut to the quick. Not since he was ten years old had he been so thoroughly rejected by an Indian. At least, back then in North Carolina, the tribe had been more accepting and tolerant most of the time. He turned in embarrassment and shuffled away.

At the end of the week, once more at evening, the word to "Roll 'em up, move 'em out" came down. A personnel boat pulled up to the dock and took Buddy's platoon aboard.

"Just take your packs on the ship," the transportation officer said. "Leave your seabags in the lighter. They'll be stored in the hold."

Buddy and his fellow marines clambered over the side of

the small boat and onto the inner deck of the Landing Slip Dock (LSD), for the smaller boat sailed right inside the larger ship, which opened its huge bow doors like the mouth on Jonah's whale.

As soon as Buddy's unit was embarked, the ship got under way and sailed west into the Pacific. He and his unit were sent down to the troop quarters deep in the bow section of the ship. The racks, or bunks, were six to eight levels high. Right under Buddy's tier of racks was the ammunition locker for the ship's five-inch gun. Every time the gun crew held practice, Buddy's rack was collapsed up against the bulkhead. He and the other rudely awakened men scrambled to get out of the way. The LSD 17, the U.S.S. *Catamount*, was a strange yet well-designed ship, but life aboard her was anything but comfortable—especially for Buddy, who, in ignorance, left not only his two seabags to be stored in the hold, but also the new sleeping bag issued to him at Camp Pendleton. Buddy slept cold crossing the North Pacific.

Physical exercises were held on deck every morning. Rifles were cleaned, clothes were washed in buckets and tied to the rail with short lengths of string. Otherwise there was plenty of free time on the thirty-five day crossing. Buddy soon found a place to escape, in the rope locker, located deep in the extreme forward section of the bow. An old chief petty officer ruled this area and allowed Buddy to sit on a huge coil of rope in the cool, quiet space. The old man even taught this youngster to splice rope and tie useful knots. The quiet peace of this place and occupation soothed the young man's anxiety. The old navy chief reminded Buddy of the elder, Longleaf. When not trying to learn to tie knots, the boy would write letters that would wait weeks to be mailed after censorship.

It was always with regret that Buddy would look at his new Timex, bought in the ship's store, and see that it was chow time. He would climb the tall ladder up into the blinding sunlight and continual chatter of his fellow marines, some of whom would fish over the side of the ship, pulling strange fish aboard, most of which Buddy had never seen before. As the days passed, Buddy, the newcomer, came to know his fellow marines. There was Juan Noriga, an Apache from the Southwest, tough, honest, and foul-mouthed. There was Master Sergeant Richard Maye, profane, barrel-chested, and mean to the extreme. Lieutenant Harry Colliers, a Washington State reservist hastily called up, who joined them in California, served as executive officer of the company. Colliers was a large man, tall with a beer belly, an engineer in civilian life. There was Jean Paul Luc, called Lucky for short, Buddy's squad leader, a dark-featured French Canadian lumberman from Maine; Bill Knight, a skinny bean pole of a man in his late thirties, a veteran of World War II army service and the oldest private in the company. John McNair, a devout Southern Baptist who neither smoked nor drank and didn't use profanity, became a close friend. Dan Conover, a wacky, comic-strip version of a marine, carrying a sharp combat knife stuck in his yellow leggings, became a great and good friend to Buddy. Conover talked about combat and of how he would kill the enemy, constantly. Many of the men were put off, including Buddy, by his sea stories and verbal heroics until the captain let it out that Conover had actually fought on Iwo Jima as a youth and won a medal there.

Brown, Simons, Gibowski, and Bill Pearch, a German immigrant, were members of Buddy's squad who peopled his tiny world on shipboard with familiar and generally friendly faces. But one man stood out from all the others, although retiring, shy and even gentle in his infrequent appearances up on deck. This quiet man was Captain Fred Hammond, the company commander.

Captain Fred, as he was called by his men, had fought as an enlisted marine in World War II. Behind him lay service in three major combat invasions. Hammond had been wounded on Okinawa, and the scar of that wound could still be seen, suffused with blood and sometimes throbbing, on the left side of his neck, running down to disappear in the heavy green material of his dungaree jacket.

There was no posing, no mock heroics about Captain Fred. Unlike the younger Conover, who was slightly unhinged by the terror of the Pacific War, 'Cap'n Fred' had turned more introspective and self-contained rather than aggressive and crude. He dressed as a private, his double silver bars worn on the underside of his dungaree jacket, a token of combat days, when such flashing insignia of rank attracted sniper's bullets. His jacket was emblazoned only with the stenciled marine corps eagle, world, and anchor device over his left breast pocket. Fred wore a pistol belt and holstered .45 automatic, as demanded by his rank, and had only one affectation: he wore, additionally, a shoulder holster on his left breast, with a second .45 automatic pistol. Buddy heard the captain mention that this second pistol had been carried by his father in World War I and by himself in World War II.

As discussions on combat tactics were held on deck, with all the men wearing their web gear and carrying weapons, the men saw that Lieutenant Colliers also carried a reserve weapon, a .38 combat masterpiece pistol in a black leather holster on the left side of his khaki dungaree trouser belt. There were other bearers of personal weapons among the troops, sergeants and corporals who carried everything from wicked-looking knives to revolvers to captured Japanese automatic pistols. A large percentage of even the lower ranking NCOs were veterans of the Second World War, one or two having fought on the wrong side. A Lithuanian corporal had served in the *Wehrmacht*, a very German PFC had been a submariner in the *Kriegsmarine*. A cherubic-faced alcoholic from New

York City had spent eight years in the Merchant Marines before joining the corps. All these different sorts of men brought their own peculiar expectations, weapons and talents to the as yet unspecified task that lay before Buddy's Howe Company.

No one noticed as they passed from one day to another and from one world into another. No ships were sighted and only the occasional pod of playful whales would remember their passage. Flying fish leaped beautifully into the air, the blueness of the huge sky swallowed the world and even the vast ocean. The sun bore down, browning everyone while they marinated in the growing realization that danger lay on the other side of the horizon. Some thought of home, others of God, but most turned to gambling.

Many of the troops played wild games of poker in the troop compartments every night. The older men knew that their U.S. currency would soon be taken away and replaced with script, a kind of play money useful only in Occupied Japan or in the PX and enlisted clubs run by the military. The better players knew, too, that everyone would think, even if they didn't want to, that these could be their last days, giving money a distinctly unimportant value. A few family men planned to win as much as they could, then try to mail it home to mothers, wives and children before going into combat.

A few, however, refused to gamble, Buddy and John McNair among them, as their rearing made gambling a wasteful, even sinful, pastime in their eyes. What surprised McNair, whose religion forbade poker, and Buddy, whose grandmother's teaching had made cards seem as illicit as whoring, was the reaction of Conover. He refrained from gambling, too, without any explanation. Buddy now knew that Conover had been underage when he served at Iwo Jima, going through the same struggle to move from childhood to manhood that he presently suffered himself. He wondered, secretly, if Conover was not still, in his own mind, sixteen and facing that age-old struggle over again. Even though Buddy had never heard of regression, he knew it when he saw it.

So it transpired that Conover, tall and broad shouldered, decked out with knives at belt and in his right-hand legging, McNair, in white undershirt, and Buddy, in utility coat, sat on deck in the evening, night after night, playing Hearts, a childlike game, solely for points, while thousands of dollars changed hands in other, more serious games.

"He's gonna shoot the moon," Conover would cry, when McNair started taking tricks. "Who's got the queen?" he'd ask in despair.

"It's only a game," Buddy would say.

"Only a game? *Nothing* is *only* a game!" the distraught veteran would moan.

And one or the other would shoot the moon until the moon rose and the light was too dim to read the spots on the dirty cards.

6

After more than a month at sea, the wallowing LSD-17 docked at Kobe, on the inland Sea of Japan. This port of call was made only to load more ammunition and supplies aboard the already combat-loaded craft. Instead of liberty, the crew and their marine passengers were given work details loading the ship. Only one person was allowed ashore: Hawk, through an unexpected exchange at morning roll call on the day of the Kobe docking.

The ship's captain asked Captain Hammond for a guard for the bridge, once they left Kobe for the Combat Zone. He specified a big man, energetic and trustworthy. This request came to the company commander and was passed on to the first sergeant, who translated it into realistic terms.

"Who," the Hispanic NCO asked himself first, and then asked the platoon sergeants, "fits this bill and can be safely spared?"

The NCOs wouldn't willingly give up a vital man, only one they could effectively do without. The choice fell on the youngest, newest member of the unit: PFC Gordon.

So Buddy was ordered to dig out dress khakis (he had one pair in his pack, including a tie), and to report to the bridge. He did so, even as the sailors of the deck gang were hurling heavy ropes to the short, scurrying Japanese laborers on the dock. Buddy couldn't help noticing one Japanese worker, sitting on one of the pilings, eating what looked like a whole squid. He was drawn, against his will, to the slanting, al-mond-shaped eyes of this skinny, ragged laborer.

The ship's captain looked at Buddy, said "You'll do," and amazed the boy by saying, "You aren't needed now. You can go ashore for the afternoon." That was how Buddy came to be dressed and free on the one day Howe Company landed in Japan.

Drawing a liberty pass from the master-at-arms office, Buddy hurried off the ship and through the high gates of the naval docks. He emerged on to a lovely, tree-shaded street, which ran on each side of a classic Japanese park. Turning in to the greenery of the park, Buddy saw a curved bridge, the mirror image of similar old bridges that he had seen in prints and in *National Geographic* pictures.

Buddy approached the bridge and at once entered a zone of disquiet, of strangeness. He suddenly felt outside himself, as if he were watching his own actions, knowing what he was about to do and see before it happened. A new and unusual sensation gripped his entire body and seized his thoughts. He felt as though he were coming out of a fainting spell but without the weakness. The spell was not unpleasant nor was it frightening. In some way, he had never felt more alive, not even in the surf or diving into the breaking waves of the Carolina shore.

The young marine "knew," if that is the word, that he would see a leper on the other side of the bridge, although he had no clear idea of what a leper looked like. Lepers were, to him, unfortunate people in the Bible stories he'd heard in confirmation class and sermons. Yet, when he walked down the other side, he saw an old woman seated on the ground, crumpled up like a pile of old rags. When she raised her head, Buddy saw only a shallow, dark hole where her nose should have been. "So that's a leper," he thought, and hurried on. He knew exactly where to walk without knowing why.

The strange feeling didn't leave him. He knew there was a gift shop across the street that bounded the other side of the park, just as he and the others on the mountain many years before had seen what was to lie ahead in their visions. He knew that he would buy presents there and meet a girl. His foreknowledge was perfect.

Crossing the street, Buddy entered a bright shop full of statues, fans, chess sets and tablecloths. As he selected a tablecloth for his mother, another shopper, a young girl, walked up to Buddy's counter and offered, in English, to help in the bargaining. Buddy welcomed her assistance. She introduced herself as Koito. He, in turn, introduced himself, both panicked and pleased. Quickly, purchases were made, and with Koito's help, they were packed, addressed, and made ready for mailing by the shop to the States.

"You bought your mother something nice, eh?" Koito lisped in an endearing way when Buddy looked up from the glass counter and saw her standing near.

"Uh-huh, somethin' for my mother and somethin' for my grandmother," Buddy replied, staring at the lovely girl with fascination.

"You seem like a nice boy," Koito ventured. "Not rough like so many soldiers."

"I hope I'm nice," Buddy said, smiling, feeling his face beginning to tingle. "I could never be anything but nice to a girl like you," he added, blushing to a deep red.

Five minutes later, Buddy and Koito left the store to walk aimlessly through the streets. An hour later, they were seated in the last row of a movie house. The film was French, and the sound track pattered on in romantic syllables Buddy didn't understand. At the bottom of the screen, a Japanese text was printed, but Koito was too busy talking to look up and read the translation. Neither knew what the movie was about and neither cared.

Listening to Koito, Buddy found her to be overwhelmingly beautiful. He also found that they had more in common than either could ever have imagined. She was about Buddy's own age, and a loner, forced into a double life, neither Japanese nor American. Orphaned in 1945 when most of Tokyo was burned by American B-29 bombing raids, Koito was taken from a Catholic child care center in 1947 by an American brigadier general and his wife, who were now like parents to her. Part of two worlds, Koito belonged fully to neither, having no dates with the sons of other American officers and forbidden to date enlisted men, who generally thought of all Japanese women as unworthy of their respect. All this came out as Buddy and Koito walked through the city, and later sat in the movie, both talking as they had never talked before. He, too, shared with her the double life inflicted on him, similarly caused by misplaced human kindness. He, too, was warmly accepted in his loneliness by Koito. For both, it was love at first conversation, and it was with regret and a downcast expression that Koito told Buddy, "I must go home before it gets too late."

"I know," he replied, wanting but fearing to call her something sweet and dear and personal. "I've got to be back on that ship by midnight myself."

"You take me home, or near to home?" she asked.

"If it's not a hundred miles away, sure," Buddy answered.

"I live in the general's house, with him and his wife. As I told you, I'm their ward." She looked away from Buddy's face as she said, "You must be careful if you come to see me. The general does not like enlisted men."

Smiling, Buddy responded, "I'll bet on that!"

"You're not angry?" she asked.

"No, I wouldn't like enlisted men if I were him and you were my daughter either," Buddy said, drawing her near, gently kissing the top of her head.

"My home is a twenty-minute train ride from here. Can you do it?" she asked.

"Sure. I can get back here by midnight, if you'll tell me how to recognize the train stop by the docks."

"I'll show you," she said, smiling at him as though he'd just given her a wonderful Christmas present.

"Then, let's go," Buddy said, feeling both awed and touched by the joy with which this lovely young girl responded to him.

Together they climbed the high wooden structure that housed the inner-urban train station. They stood in the shadows kissing until the train arrived. Koito pointed out a sign Buddy could recognize on the way back. The train was crowded, so they stood together in silence, Buddy looking down into Koito's lovely dark eyes. Some eight stops later, they got off and walked along a road running up a steep hillside, between large, rich-looking, western-style houses. Koito's house, from the top of this road, overlooked the rest.

The house was dark, and they circled around inside its

fence to the back door. "Shhhh," Koito said. "No noise. I'll wake the cook. She's a good lady, who'll let us in and not say anything."

"Okay," Buddy replied, for the first time since their meeting feeling uneasy and more like the youthful boy he was than the manly marine he wanted to be.

Koito rapped lightly on the door panel for some time before an older Japanese woman opened it, staring inquisitively into the dark. She let them in to Koito's room, a small square marked off for privacy by sliding screens. The old woman made signs for the young people to be quiet. From the way she kept pointing to the front of the house, Buddy gathered that the general was home.

Just then shadows moved on the right-hand screen of Koito's room. At the same moment, the left-hand panel slid back, and the cook ran in to tell Buddy to hide. "The general comes," she declared.

"Go with cook, Buddy. Come back soon," Koito whispered anxiously.

Buddy left the room with the cook, who put him in a narrow broom closet in the American-style kitchen. He stood there rigidly while hard shoes walked by the closet door. An old man's voice mumbled something to the cook he didn't understand. Then the water tap was turned on, turned off, and the footsteps moved away.

In a moment, the door was thrown open by the cook and Koito. "All okay," they nearly shouted at the pale boy standing at rigid attention with the brooms.

"He only came in for a glass of water. Now he's gone to bed. You better go to your ship, now," Koito said anxiously.

"Right," Buddy replied, feeling weak all over.

"Here's my address," Koito said, thrusting a piece of paper in his hand. "Please write to me, Buddy."

"You know I will," he replied, holding her tenderly for one

last kiss good-bye.

"Take this and wear it around your neck," Koito whispered, handing him a small wooden doll. "You'll remember me by it. She is Kuan-yin, the bodhisattva. She is full of compassion for all living beings and has vowed not to become a Buddha until she saves everything that lives. She will protect you in all that is coming."

He shoved the doll into a front jacket pocket. Later, as he rode the train back to the dock area, he fastened the small charm to his ID chain. As it fell back around his neck and slid down beneath his shirt, he felt the comforting touch of the smooth wood and thought of Koito.

Buddy had no trouble getting back to the ship. He found the gate locked at the head of his dock, but simply climbed over the fence. The sentry at the gangway looked at him enviously as he ran up to the deck, saluted the flag and asked permission of the watch to come aboard.

The next morning, already steaming through the Sea of Japan, Buddy began standing guard on the ship's bridge. While he found it interesting, he also regarded it as useless. Nonetheless, he wore the pistol issued him by the master-at-arms and stood around looking as stern as a seventeen-year-old can.

Several days went by. Then, one afternoon, the captain mustered all the marines on the foredeck. Buddy was relieved from bridge duty to go.

"Men," the captain began, "it's time to cut you in on the scoop. We have been mounted out from the States and staged in Japan for an amphibious invasion."

'Wow!" "Great!" "Man, I knew it!" "Where?!" Exclamations involuntarily burst forth from the ranks. Everyone, including Buddy, looked more pleased than common sense would warrant.

"Just a minute. Hold it down! I'm coming to that!" the captain barked out at the troops. "You gung-ho people will get all the action you want. I can guarantee you that," the captain continued with a deep frown. The scar pulsed on his neck, reminding him and all who saw it of the real price of adventure.

A hush spread over the men, who shuffled their feet and looked silently at one another.

"We're going to attack behind the enemy's lines, strike him in his rear, cut his lines of communications and supply and roll him up against the forces holding the Pusan perimeter," the captain began.

"The where of our attack is Inchon, the port city of South Korea's capital, Seoul. This is a tricky landing, as Inchon Harbor has extremely high tides and great stretches of mud flats that are uncovered at low tide. There's only one channel, really only a ditch through the mudflats, that can accommodate large boats, except at high tide. It seems Inchon has one of the biggest spreads in water depth between high tide and low tide of any spot in the world.

"You can see, then, that this operation has to be timed just right.

"And another thing, you older NCOs who were at Tarawa will understand this problem—there's a sea wall."

Loud groans came from several senior NCOs.

"Yep. I know," the captain continued. "A sea wall. Pretty substantial, too, I'm told. The assault wave will have to climb over it using ladders."

"Ladders?" a shocked and incredulous gunnery sergeant exclaimed.

"Yes, Sergeant Comstock, ladders. The navy is to provide the first assault wave with fire ladders from navy base fire stations in Japan."

"Good God!" Comstock rejoined. Other veterans looked

disgusted and shook their heads.

"My sentiments, too," said the captain.

"Yeah," Hammond went on, "this one is tough. General MacArthur outdid himself this time."

"Old Dug-out Doug," someone called out.

"Enough of that!" Hammond continued. "We're not too badly off."

"How's that, sir?" Lieutenant Colliers, no longer able to restrain himself, put in.

"Well, we drew floating reserve," Hammond responded. "We stay aboard ship, out at sea, away from harm, while the First and Fifth go in. We'll be sent in if any kinks develop in the assault."

"Wow!" "No way!" "I like it!" "I don't like it!" and other mutually contradictory exclamations came from the assembled troops. The ship's deck pitched roughly as the LSD moved as fast as her engines would allow.

"What are we going to do? What action are we going to get?" the top sergeant asked desperately.

"Well, Top," the captain said smiling, "that's the sharp part. We pass through the Fifth, after the landings, and strike forward with the Fifth and First to cross the Han River and capture the capital city, Seoul."

"That's more like it," the Top exclaimed, secretly relieved for his men.

"Hot damn!" Buddy cried out at the thought of taking a capital city.

"There you go!" a relieved staff sergeant said quietly to no one in particular.

The marines dissolved into common back-patting at the announcement: the youthful and ignorant were exalted at the idea of marching into and taking over a city; the experienced hopeful that it would merely be a cleanup operation. No one noticed the spray that broke over the starboard rail.

"We'll go over the tactical plans beginning now," the captain broke in. "But first, as D-Day is tomorrow, all you people must check your weapons and draw live ammunition and grenades." Hammond turned to the top sergeant, "Top, get these men armed. And see that no pogey bait marine shoots someone or blows off his own hand with a grenade!"

"Yes, sir!" the Puerto Rican answered brightly.

"You, marines! Listen up! Form up by squads to draw ammo. And keep safety in your heads! You don't want to die by accident, only in battle!"

"Yeah! Yeah! Yeah!" the company cried, pumping themselves up like a football team in the huddle, and fell into formation, lining up before the green metal ammo boxes and larger wooden crates of hand grenades. For every man whose heart beat faster with the sense of adventure, another, wiser soul felt his spine turn cold in apprehension of what was to come.

Buddy felt as though he were at a Saturday afternoon war movie, double-feature. He was issued clips of 30-caliber ammo for his web cartridge belt and then given three thin, khaki bandoleers filled with more rifle ammo to wear around his neck and shoulder. He had to pull the heavy weight of the rifle rounds up under his left arm. Added to this, he drew four hand grenades, to be carried in the big patch pockets of his field jacket. The ammo and gear weighed a great deal, and he was glad to go below to stow it on his bunk.

When he climbed the ladder back to the foredeck, he saw his platoon leader, Lieutenant Newton, called "Fig" Newton, the top sergeant and Captain Hammond holding a conversation. He was startled to be called over by the lieutenant.

"Say, Buddy," Newton said, "how'd you like a special job ashore?"

"Special job, sir?" Buddy was genuinely interested. "What kinda job, Lieutenant?"

"To be the company runner. To carry Captain Hammond's messages," the young officer replied.

"I'd like that, sir. Yes, I think I'd like that fine," Buddy answered.

"Then it's settled," the captain said. "Buddy, you'll be my runner and carry the word to the platoons when we hit land."

"Yes, sir!" Buddy half-shouted, feeling that he'd received a promotion. He was still young enough to look up to older men, and had a special respect for the gentle-voiced Virginian, his captain. He looked forward to Hammond's company, not realizing that messengers, runners, were men who squad leaders thought were expendable, not really needed, and not knowing that a runner's life, in battle, was often short.

"Get your gear and move in with me now," the captain said. "You'll be staying close to me from now on. You'll be my bodyguard, too, so I'll give you one of my pistols."

"Yes, sir!" he cried, snapping to attention. As with every young marine, Buddy literally coveted a .45 pistol. More than the service rifle, it was somehow seen as a symbol of manhood.

Buddy moved his gear to the compartment where the captain, Lieutenant Colliers, the top sergeant and the company clerk were bunked. While the ship approached the invasion area, the clerk helped him to learn the typewriter keyboard.

"Hey, do ya think I could type a letter home?" he asked Corporal Dalego, the company clerk.

"Sure, why not? Just watch those keys, they stick," the corporal replied.

"Let's see. U.S.S. *CATAMOUNT*, LSD 17, FPO, SAN FRANCISCO," Buddy laboriously typed out, one capital letter at a time.

"How's that look?" he asked Dalego.

"Okay, kid, but if you don't mind I'm trying to read."

"What ya reading?"

"H.G. Wells's *War of the Worlds*," the corporal answered.

"What's that?"

"Science fiction. Really old, classic stuff. It's an armed forces edition I got in the ship's library," the clerk explained.

"Can I read it next?" Buddy asked.

"Sure, type your letter. I'll give it to you tonight."

The next morning, the 17th of September, 1950, the company was roused from its bunks at 3:30 A.M., trooped to the galleys and offered a breakfast of steak and eggs, the traditional marine corps preinvasion breakfast. After eating, the men assembled at the huge cargo nets hanging down each side of the ship, put on their packs, and scrambled down into the LCUs, the smaller landing craft, for the run in to the beach. The First and Fifth marines had landed under fire on September 15th, securing a beachhead and driving inland, so this was an "administrative landing," a "dry landing" or one made without opposition.

It was still dark, very dark, and marines stumbled over each other and the gear stowed in the heaving boat. In the wet, chilling cold, Hawk had gone down the net with the captain and lieutenant, carrying, in addition to his own gear and ammunition, an SCR 536 radio, handie-talkie, and wearing the captain's extra pistol in a shoulder holster. Hammond had drawn a carbine and slung it around his neck, saying, "A pistol isn't much good at any range." Buddy didn't care. He was proud to have that pistol.

The landing craft began to make large circles round and round the ship, waiting to be called in to the beach by the navy beach masters. On one circle around the boats broke off and started roaring in but were warned off by a signal flag, and began again to circle. When everyone was wet through and through, their nerves frazzled completely, and exhausted, the coxswains got the word and ran the LCUs on in to the beach. Buddy's boat beached on fortified Wolmi-Do Island, the scene of heavy fighting on D-Day, but it was now dark, quiet and deserted. Numerous artillery emplacements, as Buddy got a closer look, were splattered with bullet marks, gun barrels pointed uselessly upward at odd angles.

In the dark, the platoon was assembled on the beach of splintered rock by a Shore Party marine and told to lie down and rest. Buddy took off his helmet, used it as an uncomfortable pillow and fell asleep, as an old man, a beach master chief, murmured, "You guys get some sleep, you're perfectly safe here."

Buddy awoke as Lieutenant Colliers shook his shoulder. "Hey, kid, get up. Let's go, we've been asleep an hour."

"Yes, sir. Right now," Buddy responded. He tried to rise and found that his whole body was stiff from sleeping on the cold, wet stone. At last he made it up and fell in beside the captain and the others of the headquarters' staff.

"We walk from here, men," the captain boomed out over the beach. "Mount up, move out. Follow me."

The company formed up in a rough double column and flowed over the rocky beach and down a hillside, then, walking out of step, along a long causeway that linked Wolmi-Do with the mainland. "Watch your step, you jarheads," the top sergeant called out. "There's deep water on both sides of that thing."

The men reached the mainland. The bullet-pocked sea wall showed in the growing light to their right. They spread out and followed the captain in a long, open line. They marched through city streets littered with rubble, past a large brick building hit squarely to its front that turned out to be a Roman Catholic church, and tramped on beyond town to a broad highway. Buddy could not help but think that it would have seemed so peaceful if the dawn-streaked sky hadn't been split by the constant firing of the sixteen-inch naval rifles of the battleship U.S.S. *Missouri*, which lay in the harbor, pounding the Korean capital miles away.

As the day fully broke, the air suddenly filled with aircraft flying from the carriers that stood farther off the coast. Flights of F4U Corsairs, gull-winged marine fighter-bombers, came over, carrying bombs and rockets to Seoul. The troops soon became accustomed to the deep booming of the naval gunfire and the droning of the airplanes but they continually gaped at the sixteen-inch shells which could be easily seen, and in Buddy's opinion seemed to float overhead and on over the horizon toward their distant targets.

"That SOB is as big as a Cadillac," one man shouted.

"It's a big momma, for sure," another agreed.

The day grew hotter as the men labored under the weight of their packs and weapons. The company moved on until it reached a junction in the road where a convoy of marine six-by trucks sat along the roadside, with motors idling.

"Here we are, men. We ride from now on," the captain announced.

"Hooray for that!" someone cried out, as many of the men laughed with relief.

With a wry smile the officer turned to greet three marines who emerged from behind one of the trucks. "Howe Company here for motor transport," Hammond announced.

"Very good, Captain," a middle-aged warrant officer answered. "Please get your men aboard the trucks."

The captain nodded toward an NCO standing near. The first sergeant snapped to attention and bellowed, "Aye, aye, sir. Mount up, you men. Squads keep together." The captain moved toward the lead truck with Buddy in tow.

Buddy got into the truck cab with the captain. It was a tight fit with all their gear. Packs were shucked and thrown in the back with the troops, but weapons, the radio, the captain's map case and field glasses all took up space. Squeezed between Hammond and the lieutenant, Buddy flashed back to Buster's truck, riding cramped between Steve and his uncle, and the stench of shark. An uneasy thought forced its way into his mind, and he wondered how many sharks were in this truck, too.

Five minutes after the trucks started, both Buddy and the captain were asleep. They missed the scenery, the scarred airfield at Kimpo and the overturned, burnt-out vehicles that littered the roadway, as they were rapidly driven to war. The dust billowed out behind the motor transport column, trailing like the shadows cast by a giant bird of prey. These clouds of gray sand flowed backward in an inverted V, like a double shadow, one for the living, one for the dead.

III

The Crossing

7

The dirty, dark green trucks unloaded Company H at Yongdong-Po, a battered industrial town on the Inchon, or south side of the Hang-gang, the broad Han River. The area where the troops dismounted was flat and sandy, without cover. A few dried-up cornfields stood in the east. Several damaged factories marked the southwestern edge of what the company came to call Yellow Beach. Along the riverbank, a number of junks lay beached, tilted on their sides. Few, if any, other features could be made out.

In the distance, to the right, the destroyed span of a railway bridge was visible. To the front, the tidal river,

marked with dirty waves, stretched almost a mile wide across
to a narrow beach, backed up slightly to the left by an electric
plant with tall smokestacks. The river itself flowed swiftly,
tumbling hundreds of dead Korean bodies west, down to the
sea. These bodies were bound together by barbed wire, four
to a grotesque "raft." This floating carnage had been executed
by the North Koreans who had captured the city and were
now losing it. Among the rafts of dead civilians were the
individual bodies that floated down the river like logs, jam-
ming together, momentarily blocking the flow, then breaking
apart under the increased water pressure. These were the kill
of the equally vicious South Korean marines who were, even
as Hawk and his fellow marines were standing for the first
time amidst the ruin of this new war, attacking the enemy to
the company's left.

The troops moved forward toward the river on foot. A
huge man named Roberts, a reservist who'd been recalled
from his post office job, became Radio Man, carrying the big
SCR-300 on his back. Cheerful and forbearing, the World
War II vet didn't seem to mind. He'd been a communicator in
Saipan.

In their approach to the river the company got into brief
skirmishes and one intense firefight. This move forward,
stop, move sideways, then forward again motion reminded
Buddy of the chess games he'd watched in school. Just before
the river the headquarters section tramped through a rice
field, sticking to the low banks of earth that divided one
paddy from another. These dikes were the usual trails followed by the locals although they undoubtedly knew where
they were going. One stretch of dike was spongy and damp;
the ground sank a bit as each man passed over. It held until
Roberts, the two-hundred-plus-pound radio operator, took a
step forward and began to sink into the earth. Buddy and the
rest who had already marched over the dike heard his startled

cry and turned to see Lieutenant Colliers running back toward the huge man struggling up to his knees in muck. By the time Buddy and the others got to him, Roberts was mired up to his armpits in a noxious, watery mess.

"What is it, Lieutenant?" Luc asked his superior in astonishment.

"A honey pot," Colliers responded. "You two, there," he continued, pointing over to Buddy and Conover, "help that man out."

Conover wrinkled his nose. "Excuse me for sayin' so, Lieutenant, but that ain't no honey, tha's shit, sir." He wrinkled his nose again and said, "Do we have to, sir. Get 'em out, I mean, sir?"

"Get to it, you two," Colliers commanded.

It eventually took four of them to pull the man free with a rope that they had passed beneath his armpits. When he was once again standing on solid ground the rest of the four men backed away as a staff sergeant said, "At least you don't have to carry him."

Cursing at the laughter around him, Roberts soldiered on, the slimy mess drying in the glaring sun, leaving a nauseous coating over his body, clothes and equipment. "He's the only one here who's properly camouflaged," Captain Hammond remarked, sending Buddy into a fit of laughter that forced tears from his tired eyes. The radio, also properly camouflaged, had stopped working. As company runner he would now have to do the radio's work, too. Buddy stopped laughing.

Overhead, the sky was filled with the seemingly slow-moving rounds from the battleship *Missouri*'s sixteen-inch guns and flights of aircraft carrier fighter-bombers, which darted in—suddenly appearing larger than life—to strafe and release their rockets. The most dramatic-looking planes were the F4U Corsairs of the First Marine Air Wing. Buddy and the troops cheered as napalm canisters peeled off from beneath their wings and splattered fire on the gray, almost silent city.

As the battle for Seoul continued and the company awaited amphibious transport, Buddy and Conover were detailed to stand watch overnight at an LP, listening post to the east of Yellow Beach. This was an outpost on high ground, out beyond the MLR, the main line of resistance—better known as the front line. The LP was at the top end of a fingerlike ridge that stretched toward the enemy's last known positions. Conover, still bloodthirsty, was glad to go since the LP contained a machine gun as well as several cases of fragmentation grenades. Before the two crawled the last hundred yards up to it, in the near dark, they were told that division expected large numbers of the NKA regulars to attempt either to slip away through the ravine that lay below the LP, or else to move through it, wheel and attack the battalion from the rear. Unlike Conover, Buddy didn't really want to go. The thought of two of them and hundreds of "them" out there in the dark was too damned real to be adventuresome. He wished he could be excused.

"If you hear men moving down there, then empty the damn gun on 'em and pitch every hand grenade you got over the side," the sneering top said, grinning wickedly so that even in twilight his large white teeth were easily seen. "That's why we've sent so many grenades out there," he continued. "You do know how to throw 'em, don't you?"

Neither Buddy nor Conover bothered to answer but started crawling toward the LP and the most dangerous part of their assignment, getting themselves recognized by the two marines they were sent to relieve.

Somewhat short of the hole they were stopped by a sharp, whispered challenge: "Halt, who goes…?"

"Relief!" Conover whispered back.

"What's the password?" the disembodied voice responded,

punctuating the question with a loud snick! as he closed the bolt on the machine gun. As the forward action primed the .30-caliber for firing, Buddy decided that the slap of milled steel on steel was the most terrifying, loudest sound he'd ever heard.

"Abraham," the boy whispered.

"Lincoln," the voice returned. "Get your asses up here in this hole!"

Once the two guards had familiarized the new men with the routine of the LP, they crawled back toward the line, leaving Buddy and "Combat" Conover in charge.

"I'll watch the first two hours, while you rest," Buddy said. "But don't go to sleep. This is a hellofa spot."

"Check," Conover said and slumped against the side of the large, deep hole.

Noises can always be heard in the night, anywhere, and Buddy heard them, or thought he heard them, here. Yet nothing really seemed to be moving in front of them, or more importantly, below them, where the ravine snaked by before bending back toward the river—a natural subway to the rear of Howe Company's line. Buddy woke Conover, for he was asleep, and watched him take his position, standing behind the mounted automatic weapon. Buddy then lay down and tried, as much as possible, to rest. He, too, dozed until Conover's finger tapped his helmet and he unwrapped his limbs for another tour on watch.

Buddy's dreams had not been comforting and his nervous system was wound tight. He almost thought he could see through the deep darkness, see hundreds of the enemy silently crawling through the gash in the earth below, bent upon destroying Big Ben, the captain, Fig Newton and the rest of the guys. He saw nothing, of course, and the dream floated up into his conscious mind, a dream that depressed him.

He was walking through a mountain meadow, the sun at

ten o'clock. His long shadow stretched to his lower right, or four o'clock, curiously paralleled by a shorter shadow directly at three o'clock. Immediately, he found himself upon a wide sand beach, walking in the same relation to the sun. But this time, his shadow at four o'clock was almost gone and the unnatural shadow straight out at three o'clock was long and dark.

Before he woke, he saw himself in helmet and utilities, armed, walking through a stubbly corn field near the River Han. The sun hung motionless at ten o'clock, the sky bright, so bright it seemed to blind him, for, glancing about, he found he threw no shadow. "I am disappearing" formed upon his lips as the rough knock of Conover's finger struck his helmet.

A rolling stone, almost directly below him, brought Buddy reeling out of his thoughts. He tensed and focused all his senses. He half-turned and kicked the prone figure behind him and stage-whispered, "Up and at 'em, Combat. You gonna get your wish!"

Conover rose, listened and spoke directly into Buddy's right ear. "It's them. Ain't nobody out there but the NKA."

"Afraid you're right," the boy hissed back. More stones rolled; scraping sounds came through the darkness. A number of bodies were passing their position.

"Let's do what the man said!" Conover said softly. "I'll take the gun, you do the grenades! Okay?"

Depressing the barrel of the light machine gun as far as possible, which was probably not far enough, Conover opened up, a red stream hosing downward in an arc as the red tracer bullets inserted at intervals in the ammo belt showed the direction and fall of the rounds.

Buddy pulled a case of grenades, already removed from their individual containers, to the edge of the pit, pulled each round ring carefully and pitched them over the side, hearing them roll down the ridge side until they exploded in a geyser of red- and blue-streaked white below them. Throwing them faster and faster, the explosions illuminated the ravine floor. The glare exposed Koreans, a ravine full, now terrified and throwing themselves down at all angles, all the while screaming in fear and pain. He exhausted a full case, grabbed another, found its top was loose and pulled out more bombs. These had been made safer by having tape that had sealed each individual container used to bind the "spoon" or handle to the body of the grenade. He lost time as he unwound this tape, pulled on the ring that armed the weapon and threw it, straight armed, standing up, down into the panicked, doomed unit below.

Suddenly, Conover stopped firing. "Need ammo?" Buddy whispered.

"No. I think that's it, that's all," the other replied. And listening intently, since the harsh clatter of the gun and the slam of the grenades had deafened them, they noted, after a time, the silence below them. "Nobody's movin' down there now," Conover observed.

"I can't hear too good," Buddy replied, "but I don't think so, either."

"Well, we done kilt 'em or scared 'em off," Conover offered.

The remainder of the watch was tense to the point of disabling neckaches for both men, but no enemy returned. As the sun came up and the light strengthened, the amazed companions found that Conover had been right. They had killed a large number of North Korean troopers and scared the rest away from the sunken highway they had followed to escape or to sneak attack.

When they were relieved and snuck back to the beach bivouac to report, the only comment they received from the top soldier was, "You used up almost all of them grenades?"

• • •

The company's mission was to cross the river from Yellow Beach and seize the electricity plant and a range of low hills just behind it, on which many ruined shanties stood. The question was how, as the amphibious tanks and amtracks, or amphibious troops carriers, were delayed in arriving. In fact, a detachment of the marine Shore Party, charged with setting up a ferry over the river, once the other bank was seized, arrived immediately behind the infantry. They, too, were at a loss as to what to do since their heavy equipment, including pontoons to build ferry barges, had not yet arrived.

Three hundred men lay burrowed in the sand, as the North Koreans had Yellow Beach under observation and dropped several rounds of heavy mortar fire on it every few minutes, and tried to figure out how to cross the river without equipment.

"We sure can't swim that river with our weapons," Lieutenant Colliers observed. "What's holding up the amtracks?"

"No, we couldn't get the machine guns and mortars over that ditch, and probably couldn't get all the men over either, even though they're supposed to be good swimmers," Captain Hammond replied, adding, "I don't know where the amphibs are."

"We got to wait on them amtanks and amtracks," the top soldier put in. "I'll get the men to dig in."

"Okay, Top. Do that. And I'll suggest to the Shore Party officers that they do the same." The captain agreed and asked Buddy for the hand-held radio.

Sand drifted in the air over the area as hundreds of holes began to appear all over the riverbank. The battery of heavy Russian mortars and rockets which came to be called "Foxhole Charlie" settled down to serious work.

Buddy helped the fireteam from the first squad, second platoon, who had been detailed to dig a large fighting hole and fortify it for use as a company command post. Soon, they had a large, rather shallow oval dug in the sand, with their packs stacked around the edge facing the river. There were no sandbags available to protect the command post. Buddy found that he had just opened an office that would keep him perpetually busy, as one errand after another needed to be run for the captain. A defense perimeter was set up, and, in the absence of communication men, it was tied together by the squad's handie-talkie, not very good at any distance or if a ridge intervened between the sending and receiving sets, and by runner, which was Buddy. When night fell, the company and the Shore Party section were dug in.

Twilight brought, not peace, but a terrible pounding from the huge Russian rockets the North Koreans often used as artillery. Big holes were scooped in the sand as these rockets fell, and the resulting shaking of the ground caused the sides of most gun pits, fighting holes, and even shallow foxholes to cave in. There was no sleeping done, and even when the bombardment was lifted, a seventy-five percent alert was ordered—only one man in four was supposed to sleep. Toward eleven P.M., strange noises were heard in the dry cornstalks to the company's right. As the moon slipped in and out behind scudding clouds, shadowy shapes were seen flitting toward the right flank.

"Infiltrators," a platoon sergeant whispered. "Pass it on."

"Infiltrators," men whispered hoarsely to one another.

The word reached the C.P. where the two officers were sleeping. The top soldier woke them up, kneeling beside each man and gently shaking a shoulder. "We're being flanked by infiltrators. They could be surrounding us. What do you want to do, Captain?" the sergeant reported.

"Don't fire and give your positions away. Keep still. Let's hit them with grenades when they get closer," the captain answered.

"Buddy," Captain Hammond whispered loudly, "get over

to the First Platoon and tell Lieutenant Newton to pound that cornfield with grenades. No firing. You got that?"

"Aye-aye, sir. Grenades, no rifle fire."

"Go," he ordered.

Buddy crawled out of the shallow pit and scurried, half-bent over, for a hundred yards, then threw himself to the ground and crawled toward the right flank's fighting holes. He found the shoulder holster a hindrance, so drew the pistol, flopping forward like a sea lion, .45 in his left hand, M-1 rifle in his right.

"Who goes?" a southern voice demanded in a stage whisper.

"Me, Buddy. Runner," Buddy could barely gasp it out.

"Gordon, that you?"

"Yeah, it's me. Where's Fig Newton?"

"Over here, if you please, Mr. Gordon." Buddy's already flushed features colored more deeply, and warmth spread over his cheeks. He knew he was blushing like a confused kid, but couldn't help himself.

"Sorry, Lieutenant, sir. Word from the captain."

"Yep?"

"You're to take care of the people crawling in the cornfield with grenades only. Don't give away your position with rifle fire."

"Okay, will do. Tell the captain that."

"Yes, sir!" Buddy responded, but before he could crawl away, he caught the slurping sound of many feet running through deep sand. Then the ground around them rocked with incoming grenade explosions and automatic fire.

"Everybody down! Stay here, Buddy!" Fig choked out and despite orders, a firefight developed. The right flank fought for its life.

Buddy jumped into a gun pit with a Browning Automatic Rifle man and his assistant. The automatic weapon ripped though the night, then stopped quickly as the gunner changed clips. Buddy threw his hand grenades toward the burp-gun muzzle blasts that were quite distinguishable from the marine weapons. The North Koreans were so close their weapon's flash hiders didn't mask their muzzle blast.

A surge of automatic fire swept over the hole where Buddy and the two marines crouched. Suddenly, the BAR man grunted and slumped back into a sitting position. It was too dark to know what happened, but it seemed sure he was hit. The assistant BAR man grabbed up the weapon and resumed fire. Buddy began digging clips out of the ammo belt on the BAR man's body and handing them to the gunner. From time to time, Buddy raised up and fired the captain's pistol toward his front.

Twenty minutes later, the engagement broke off as quickly as it started. The automatic fire stopped, and the grenade explosions faded away into silent echoes. Raggedly, the marines all along the flank ceased firing. Even after five more minutes, one or two of the men along the line let off a round or two. Lieutenant "Fig" Newton's voice shouted hoarsely, "Cease firing! Hold your fire!" Silence and a deepening darkness settled on the sandy beach.

Buddy crawled to the side of the gun pit and called to the platoon commander, "Lieutenant, should I go back to the captain now?"

"No, Buddy. Sit tight. It's too dangerous to crawl around out there now. Some marine is likely to shoot you. Cap'n Fred knows we got hit here. He ain't deaf."

"Okay, sir." And Buddy crept back to the gunner, who was feeling the body of the BAR man.

"No pulse. He's gone. We may as well sleep. You go ahead and I'll watch first," the other marine whispered. It was impossible to see either the face of the surviving BAR man or of the marine slumped backward across the side of the hole, obviously dead.

Buddy settled down to sleep, but couldn't stop his mind's racing. His shoulder touched the body of the slain soldier. That didn't trouble him, but in the dark, where he couldn't even see what sort of shadow he cast, he was anxious and tense. "So this is what it's like," he thought. A kind of proud exhilaration mingled with a shaky feeling of aftershock throughout his body. He was still awake two hours later when the automatic rifleman tapped his arm and said, "Take over," in a yawning whisper.

When morning broke, ghostly white with a deep fog rolling in from the river, and it became possible to see, however dimly, Buddy discerned the wet, black front of the BAR man's jacket. As the light came up, a huge hole was visible. He'd been struck squarely in the heart with a large-caliber bullet. His life's blood had literally gushed out over him. Buddy could see some of it splashed reddish black on his own dungarees and on the arms of the sleeping BAR man's field jacket. The dead man's face was slack and gray.

The sleeping marine had "Chet" scrawled in large black letters over his field jacket pocket, so Buddy called, "Chet, wake up," as he touched his arm. Chet opened one eye, looked at the young fellow, and then at the other one who would never get any older, saying, "I'm up."

"I'm going to go back to the C.P."

"Better tell 'the Fig.'"

"Okay," Buddy agreed and once more squirmed out of the pit, through the sand, toward the lieutenant's position.

"Lieutenant!" he said.

"Call me Fig, Buddy. Everybody else does."

"Yes, sir, Fig. Can I go back to Captain Hammond?"

"Sure. Just watch yourself. Some pogie bait marine might shoot your head off in this poor light."

"Yes, sir. Oh, you got a man dead in that hole to your right."

"I got five more I know of, kid. You can tell the captain that."

"Yes, sir."

Less than ten minutes later, Buddy was up to the rear of the C.P.'s pit. He knew better than to crawl in unannounced.

"Top! Captain! It's Buddy! Can I come in?"

"Get on in here, kid," the captain replied with a hint of laughter in his voice.

Buddy squirmed over the lip and rolled into the pit, spraying sand over everyone.

"Watch the sand, kid," the first sergeant snarled.

"The coffee okay?" Colliers asked.

"Yeah. No sand in it," the sergeant replied.

"Let's drink some then," the stout, not quite portly lieutenant said curtly.

The Top was heating coffee in a canteen cup over a can of Sterno.

Buddy moved toward the center of the C.P. "Captain, Lieutenant Newton told me to tell you he has at least five dead, sir."

Hammond looked up at the boy. For a second his eyes took on a sharp edge, then as though to help digest the new information he looked over to the Top and the coffee and asked, "Where'd you get fire like that?"

"I always carry that stuff with me in the field," the Top replied. "I been soldiering twenty years, so I learned a little somethin'. The corps don't always issue exactly what you need."

"Eat the apple and screw the corps!" exclaimed Colliers with a laugh. "That's what we always said in World War II."

"Right," Hammond put in. "Hey, Buddy. You can share this coffee. What did you do, go AWOL last night?"

"No, sir, I got to the platoon on the right flank just in time to be caught in the attack. I helped some, and when it was over, Lieutenant Newton told me to stay."

"Just as well. We mighta shot you in the dark," the Top put in.

"Yeah, nobody needed a runner to tell what was going on last night," Colliers put in. "Get your C-rations and eat, kid. It's gonna be a long day."

With morning, the heavy rockets and heavy mortars opened up on the dug-in marines again. These missiles caused more noise than damage. There was little likelihood of an attack in broad daylight. Even with their weak defenses, the open ground around the company guaranteed an attacker heavy losses. Now the C.P. group could worry about fulfilling their mission, to cross the river.

"Buddy, you go back, back down the road we came up, and look for those amtracks and tanks," the captain ordered.

"Yes, sir."

"Here, leave the M-1 with me. I need it here. You can travel faster with my carbine."

"Yes, sir."

"Still got my pistol?"

"Yes, sir, it's under my field jacket." Buddy opened the tan, lightweight jacket to show the leather holster on his left breast.

"You got any grenades?"

"No, sir. I used mine last night."

"Top, give him one of yours, okay?"

"Fine, sir," the Top said, reaching for his jacket. "Be careful, kid. See, I pressed the ends of the cotter key down," he held one of his personalized grenades up for the boy's inspection. "That's so the pin won't accidentally fall out," he added, and then continued absently, "I seen that happen once." Then looking back up at Buddy, "You got that?"

"Yes, sir."

"Don't call me 'sir.' Call me sergeant!"

"Yes, sergeant!"

"Okay, Buddy. You're no kid to us," the captain said. "You've got a man's job to do. You follow that road all the way back to Inchon, if you have to. Just find those damn tanks!"

"Yes, sir!"

"And if you see any engineers or motor transport people, ask about the ferry equipment for these pioneers with us."

"Who, sir?"

"The Shore Party men. They're combat engineers or pioneers, you see."

"Yes, sir."

"Take off!" Hammond ordered with another laugh.

Buddy leapt out of the hole and took off across the clammy sand as fast as his awkward boondockers allowed. In a short time his feet hit the hard stony soil beyond the beach and he began running faster.

He was not really tired. That he had not fully slept since the short rest on the rocky beach at Wolmi-Do the day of the landing didn't seem to trouble him. He was not particularly hungry, although he had taken only a swallow or two of coffee and a few C-ration biscuits with canned jam. While no fierce fighter, he was not afraid as he moved out to explore the road to the company's rear. The fog had burned off and the sun was coming out. Buddy felt great. His blood was up, there was something important to do. The carbine was light in his hand, and the pistol, heavy on his chest, made him feel like a man. He liked being able to run free across the countryside. Digging and sitting in a hole was boring. He began to trot, keeping his eyes open for North Koreans.

After a mile, he ran upon other units. These were an artillery battery of the Eleventh Marines and a medical unit, set up at a curve in the road. Buddy strode in unchallenged. The marines there nodded or said "Hi." Clearly, the machine gunners had watched him come along the road for some time.

Buddy sought out a lieutenant, saluted and asked if he'd seen the tanks and amtracks. He hadn't. But the officer was willing to help and called a young black marine over.

"Flip," Lieutenant Anderson began, "this young fellow's name, he tells me, is Buddy."

"Yes, sir. How you doing, Buddy?"

"Okay, Flip. You?"

"Flip, here," Anderson went on, "is the best damned jeep driver in the marine corps."

"Great, sir," Buddy answered.

"Flip, I want you to drive Buddy wherever he asks you. He's got to find the tanks and amtracks so the Seventh can get across the river."

"Yes, sir. Where we gonna go?"

"I don't know. Buddy doesn't either, exactly. I suppose you all ought to keep going toward the rear, and maybe spread out, if you see any roads, to the east or west."

"Yes, sir. Them vehicles must have gotten lost," Flip said.

"Maybe so. You two be careful. Get moving."

Flip only drove at one speed, the highest allowed by the governor on the carburetor. He drove the way a big-city taxi driver pushes his cab, to the limit, all the time. First the two passed some bullet-riddled buildings that housed a South Korean hospital. Wounded lay in rows on stretchers in the dusty yard. There seemed to be few nurses or doctors about to help them. They passed many units now, including the remaining two companies of their battalion. When Buddy recognized the troops as "I" Company, he had Flip stop. The captain and major he spoke to thought the amtracks were ahead with Howe Company, and were concerned to learn that they were not. Buddy saluted and took off with Flip again. The major with "I" Company was very excited and said he was sending out other runners to help find the amphibious vehicles.

Flip and Buddy roared down the road to Ascom City, where many units were set up. The amphibious tanks weren't there, but the heavy tanks were. Buddy relayed word to the first tank officer he met that his captain was looking for support.

This time Buddy and Flip were interrogated thoroughly by a lieutenant colonel. He was a tall man, in his late fifties, very serious. Buddy was impressed when the colonel told them, "The trucks with those pioneer pontoons are here. I'll see they go up to the river ASAP." The officer continued, "But if there's a unit of gooks that's big enough to take on your company still loose on this side of the Han, I'm sending the tanks with them.

"Those amtracks and amtanks are very probably on the river east of your position. You two set out to the east now. You'll run into the First Marines. Be careful. Chesty's men shoot first and ask questions afterward. I'm going to write an order for the tankers to follow you. You understand?"

"Yes, sir!"

The light colonel scribbled a note on a message pad and handed it to Buddy, saying, "Well, go now, boy. We've lost half a day. And don't let Colonel Puller shanghai you into the Fifth!"

Flip drove flat out to the east. After being stopped by the First Marines' units and let pass, the two came to a low ridge just before the Han River. Parked on the reverse of this ridge, in a straight line pointed east, they found the amphibious units. Three heavily armored amtanks, called Pigs, were in front, then a company of troop carriers, amtracks, followed by three more amtanks. A platoon of Ducks, amphibious trucks, was parked to the side. The dust raised by Flip's jeep attracted the enemy's attention, and mortar rounds started falling. The young men leaped out of the unarmored jeep and rolled to the side of an amtrack. A number of men were sheltered behind the vehicles.

"What's the problem?" Buddy cried.

"We're getting the crap shelled out of us," a warrant officer answered testily. "You better get yourselves covered, too."

"Yes, sir. You bet, sir," Buddy answered, over his shoulder, as he stretched flat out on the ground.

"What're you doin', comin' here?" the officer asked.

"Looking for you, sir. To take you to Howe, 3, 7. So's they can cross over to Seoul," Buddy answered.

A mortar shell fell close by; they jumped and bunched down lower.

"Where are they? They were supposed to be here. We're late, but Howe's later still," the warrant officer, Mr. Briggs, complained.

Buddy thought that Mr. Briggs was the oldest man he'd ever seen in uniform. In fact, he was one of the oldest men he'd ever met, and here he was in a war. He certainly didn't want to contradict Mr. Briggs.

"Well, sir, pardon me, but Howe Company's in position at Yongdong-Po, west of here several miles, and it's been there since yesterday."

"You don't say," the old gentleman retorted.

"Yes, sir. And I'm afraid there's NKA between you and them. We got hit on our right, our east flank, last night."

"I see. Well, son, what's the drill? We'd better go back and come up the main route, don't you think?"

"Yes, sir. At least we ought to move back a mile or so to level ground, before we cut west. Wouldn't you say so, Flip?"

"Yeah, Buddy. And, sir, we'd better move out. I got to get back to my unit."

"Let's move, then. The mortars have even stopped," old Mr. Briggs said and jumped up spryly.

Flip led the convoy in his dust-streaked jeep, the amtracks

close behind, followed by the slower amtanks. They proceeded south, toward the rear, and at a turn-off west, stopped so Flip could return to his unit. Waving good-bye to the friendly jeep driver, Buddy rode with Mr. Briggs in what was now the lead vehicle.

The bank of the river here was masked by high sand dunes and a profusion of weeds. Just before the road dipped between particularly high dunes, the column halted and the old warrant officer called an amtank forward. Fortunately, all that they saw in the draw were a few scattered North Korean soldiers' bodies. Probably the badly wounded, left to die, after last night's attack on Howe Company, Buddy thought to himself as they drove through the battle's waste.

It was still light when they cut the road behind Yellow Beach and drove into the Howe Company—Shore Party perimeter. Buddy climbed over the side of the amtrack and saluted Captain Hammond.

"I brought you the 'tracks,' sir!" he said, grinning widely.

"It took long enough. I had word from that light colonel at Ascon City an hour ago. But, no joke, good job!" the captain said in a mock serious voice.

"Aye-aye, sir."

"It'll be dark soon, mister," the captain said, addressing the warrant officer. "Why don't you feed your men?"

"Good idea, sir."

"And, Buddy, go eat your rations. There's a box we saved you in the C.P. And get some rest. You may have to work tonight."

"Aye-aye, Captain." Buddy disappeared into the C.P.'s shallow pit.

While Buddy was eating, there was another mortar barrage, which he ignored. The amtanks and tracks got excited and pulled out, driving back up the road, but returned when the shelling stopped. One amtrack was full of shrapnel holes on its left side, but suffered no serious damage. A couple of Shore Party men were slightly wounded and were carried to the rear for treatment.

As cool as the nights were in this mid-September period, the days, particularly the afternoons on the hot sandy banks of the river, were scorching. When men had to dig holes quickly under mortar attack and then cover themselves with hot sand, the end result was often severe. Heat exhaustion that day caused several medical evacuations.

Night came on. The captain called Buddy, the Top, Lieutenant Colliers and Mr. Briggs together, and they carefully crawled over the riverbank down a long, low beach uncovered by the outgoing tide. The Han here was near its mouth and responded to the same extreme tidal action as Inchon Harbor. Now that the tide was low, the junks were stranded on the dry beach. The group hurried up behind a small junk and began inspecting the opposite bank. The setting sun's rays illuminated the huge power plant and high bluff across from them. With field glasses they could see a large east-to-west viaduct over which rail cars could approach the electric plant. A road ran under this viaduct and up the bluffs into the city. This looked like a route the amtanks could take, leading Howe Company into the built-up area of the city of Seoul.

"But what's up that road?" the captain asked no one in particular. "We've got to know," he continued. "We've also got to know what forces are on that bank besides those mortars behind the plant and the rockets they run in there from time to time."

"Why not send a tank across?" Mr. Briggs asked.

"'Cause a rocket could take it out just like that!" the captain replied, snapping his fingers.

"Yeah, but it would be hard to hit, Skipper," the top soldier put in.

"You're right, but a tank would surely tip off whoever's

over there that we're going to cross in force. Then those rockets would have the whole column of tracks to fire at."

"Yep," Mr. Briggs agreed. "They'd have to hit somethin'."

"So?" Lieutenant Colliers asked.

"So," the captain said, "somebody has got to cross that big creek in a small boat or swim it, under cover of darkness."

"It's got to be tonight, and he'll have to reconnoiter the plant, that road, and go on up to the bluffs," the Top observed.

"Big job," Colliers replied.

"That's why we're going back and find the best swimmer among the men we can."

"No need to look, sir," Buddy said, looking over at the older men from under the bow of the fishing boat, where he was studying the river. "I reckon I'm the best swimmer in the Third Battalion. I'd be glad to go."

"I don't know, Buddy," the Top started to say.

"No, top," Hammond retorted. "Buddy, do you think you can swim that far? It's deep."

"Oh, yes, sir. I'm sure. I wouldn't be racing. Just take my time. No sweat, sir."

"Then let's get to the C.P. and plan this out. You ought to go about midnight. You need to get rested before that."

"Aye, sir, and eat something, too."

"You can have my canned fruit, kid, and my chocolate, too. It'll be cold in that water," the captain said, smiling at the excited youth.

"Do you want to pull a little raft with your gear or wear everything you need on your body?" Colliers asked Buddy some three hours later. The headquarters group sat in the C.P. hole.

"Well, Lieutenant, if it ain't too heavy, it's easier to have it on my body than trying to pull a raft along. What you want me to take?"

"You need a weapon. You need a light to make signals. You need a first-aid kit and maybe some chocolate bars for energy. You need at least that."

"Yes, sir. If the weapon's a knife."

"You want a knife? What about a firearm?" Hammond asked.

"Would it fire after I swim a mile in that black water, Captain?"

"I don't know. It depends on what weapon you took and how we wrapped it."

"I couldn't take nothing bigger than your pistol, sir, and that's awful heavy."

"You're right. But you need a weapon. Why go over there if some gook can kill or capture you as soon as you make the bank?"

"Yes, sir, there's sense in that."

"Then let's figure out how to wrap up that pistol and strap it on you."

"I think I know how, Captain," Mr. Briggs put in. "Let me call the amtrack platoon sergeant." And moving to the other side of the C.P., he cupped his hands and softly called, "Archer, hey, Archer."

"Yes, sir," a sleepy voice answered from the troop compartment of the vehicle parked by the C.P.

"Come on in the C.P., Arch. And bring one of them repair kits under the seat."

"Yes, sir," Archer replied. In a few moments, the lanky staff sergeant slipped a package wrapped in oily brown material over the edge of the hole, then rolled in himself. "Here's the tool kit, sir. What's broke?" he asked.

"Nothin'. I just want this here cosmoline-soaked paper or whatever the stuff is wrapped in. We want to wrap a side arm up waterproof," the old man answered.

"Well, Mister Briggs, you wrap your side arm in that stuff,

and you can carry it all year in a monsoon and it won't rust," the sergeant observed.

"That's not it, Arch," the warrant officer rejoined. "We got to wrap this .45 up so this boy can swim the river and still use it on the other side."

"If you'll hold up a shelter half and turn a flashlight on me, I'll do you a job," Archer said.

"Okay, Arch," the captain put in. "But hurry."

The top sergeant grabbed the shelter half-covering the radio and a box of C-rations, holding it over Arch's body. Arch took a GI flashlight from Lieutenant Colliers and held it in place between his field shoes. He opened the tool kit carefully and put the various items in his field jacket pockets. Then he held his hand out toward Buddy.

"Lemme see your piece, son."

"Here ya go," the youth said, surrendering his weapon, butt first to the sergeant.

Archer oiled the pistol thoroughly on the outside, re-placed the oiling kit in his leggings, and began to carefully fold the brown paper around the weapon. He folded it tightly to the lines of the weapon, then looked up saying, "Buddy, put your hand on this and hold the package tight." Buddy did.

Archer reached in a side trouser pocket and pulled out the stub of a candle. He lit this with a Zippo lighter fished from the same pocket. "Lemme hold it, kid," he said, and Buddy moved his hand.

Slowly, Archer sealed the whole package with wax from the candle. When he had a gob of it heavy enough to hold the package shut, he waxed all the edges of the paper. Finally, he pulled out some rubber bands from another jacket pocket and wrapped them around the weapon.

"That'll take some strain off that wax," he explained.

"See if that will fit your shoulder holster," the NCO instructed Buddy.

He took the lumpy package, "Just barely, but it will," he answered as he pushed the wax encased gun into its holster.

"Okay. There's your weapon, Buddy. Now let's see how you'll carry the other stuff. You got to go soon," Captain Hammond put in.

There was no real problem. Buddy stripped to his shorts and put on a sweatshirt the Top had in his pack. He wore a pistol belt with a Kabar knife attached. The waterproof .45 and shoulder holster went on his left breast. The flashlight, a two-celled, bent-head, G.I. job along with a metal-enclosed field dressing kit and a small bar of chocolate, was tightly wrapped in a rubber toilet articles bag, and the whole thing made more tight with additional rubber bands donated by Archer. This was tied to the back of the pistol belt.

"Not too bad," Buddy said, as he moved his body about with the gear on. "I think I can swim with it."

"Hold that shelter half-up around the kid," Colliers said, then played a flashlight on Buddy. "Looks good," he said. "Be careful," he added. Buddy suddenly realized that Colliers reminded him of a younger version of his Uncle Buster.

Buddy also noticed the multitude of shadows he cast, only for a moment, on the screen of the brown and green mottled tent cloth. It seemed as if he were many people in one body, all trying to get out. He wondered idly, as he finished dressing for his mission, which person would break free and swim the river tonight. As crazy as it was, he was happy, as happy as he was at eight or nine playing "soldier" with his brother, trying to find the younger boy who was hidden in the woods, ready to ambush him.

"Move out, Gordon," broke the boy's train of thought and he looked up to the captain, who continued, "You'll be a corporal if you pull this off." Then Hammond added, "But don't take any unnecessary chances," and patted the boy on the shoulder.

"Right, sir. I won't," Buddy answered, all of a sudden wondering what he had gotten himself into this time.

"If you find the whole area unoccupied, flash your light three times, stop, three times, stop, then three last times. Got that?"

"Yes, sir."

The captain noticed Buddy's attention wandering, so he repeated, "Nine times. Three groups of three."

"Got it, sir. Three groups of three," he said and thought to himself once again, three groups of three.

"If nobody's there, I'll mount up our people and we'll come across about 0400. But if the gooks are there, hold that light. Don't show it! You look the place over and swim back here. We may still cross over if they aren't in force or on the alert. Got that?"

"Yes, sir. I understand. Maybe we can get over in the darkness without too much trouble."

"You find out. We're counting on you."

"I'll do my best." A dull ache of emptiness started in Buddy's stomach. The reality of this escapade was just starting to register in his mind.

"Shove off!" the captain ordered, with a brisk slap on the boy's left arm.

"Yes, sir!"

Buddy crawled from the C.P. and walked silently to the river's edge. He stepped into the water. It was cold. His stomach flip-flopped. A cold watery finger crawled up his spine. He kept walking.

He heard the Top whispering to the men on guard to look out and be careful, as the company had a scout in the river. Buddy looked back over his shoulder from waist depth. He could see the dim shape of a helmeted figure on the bank, a carbine held at an angle, with the butt on its hip. He raised his hand in good-bye and quietly slipped down into the black water.

He began swimming silently. Something big and dark floated in front of him. As it drifted in closer, he silently tread water. A sickening, sweet smell also drifted across the water, as did an intermittent and faint whining, not unlike the air slowly being let out of a balloon. Then in the half-light of stars and a half-hidden moon, he saw the raft. Its planks were dull and grayed, heavy with water. Each, once a living, breathing person, now just one more bit of river debris. Buddy's stomach convulsed; he fought the urge to vomit his disgust. Instead he forced his face into the water, eyes open, and swam slowly, silently, purposefully around the raft and on toward the opposite shore, across the River Han.

8

Guessed at, but really unknown to Howe Company, the other two marine regiments were already across the Han, further to the east. The battle for the city of Seoul was in full swing, as the many fires and explosions across, to the company's right front, testified. No one at that point knew the exact disposition, the order of battle, of the North Korean army. All the field commanders knew was that something over one hundred thousand enemy soldiers were in that quarter of the battlefront. The hills and shantytowns west of the center of Seoul were still dark and, as yet, uninvaded. Were there large concentrations of enemy forces there? No one knew, but someone had to find out.

Buddy, as 1:00 A.M. neared, was about halfway across the Han. From the east, the first marine tank battalion was en route through the outskirts of the city toward the same power plant he aimed toward. Between these two marine elements, unknown to one another, lay Pistol Pete, the mobile Russian rocket launcher battery, and Foxhole Charlie, the heavy mortar company that had pinned Howe Company to the river's south bank.

Though no one knew it, there were also small units of North Korean infantry there. Though no major forces capable of stopping the assault of a marine battalion equipped with amphibious personnel carriers and tanks were present, the rockets and mortars could easily turn the river crossing into a bloodbath.

Buddy did not swim directly toward the power plant's smokestack. Many summers of swimming and fishing in just such a tidal river had taught him much. He swam west of the tall smokestacks, far to the right, knowing that the tide, now outgoing, would sweep him left, or east, toward the plant. He had to stop, look carefully, and correct the angle of his swim several times. Each time he saw explosions in the city fear gripped him. Swallowing the lump in his throat, he kept on going. Around 1:30 A.M., he reached the northern bank.

Letting his feet settle beneath him, Buddy paddled slowly until his toes touched the rough bottom. Then he walked in to the bank, watching the shadows behind it carefully.

"Thank goodness the marine corps emblem is about washed off this sweatshirt," he thought to himself. Needing the relief of humor, he continued the thought: "All I need is a gold globe and anchor flashing in the moonlight, shouting to all, 'The marines have landed!'"

The tired boy stumbled on through the knee-deep water, now moving more rapidly near the shore. When he reached a narrow strip of sand still above the water, he fell to his knees. Taking off the pistol belt, he unwrapped the flashlight and hung it on his belt. He put the belt back on. With some difficulty, he unsnapped the shoulder holster. The brown package was heavy, and Buddy noticed his left shoulder was sore.

"Damn, I'll need the knife," he whispered under his breath. The low sound of his own voice soothing, he continued, "This bastard sure is waterproof."

He took his heavy Kabar and cut through the wax, unwrapping the stiff paper, then wiped sand off his hand by running it through his hair before taking up the pistol. He wiped his left hand on his sweatshirt and worked the weapon's slide as quietly as possible. With a round in the chamber, he checked the safety and put the oily pistol back in his holster. His knife back in its sheath, Buddy knelt quietly for a few minutes. Struggling with anxiety and fear, and, most of all, the need to throw up, his left hand went to the small wooden doll suspended from his ID chain. Touching the smooth, wet charm he saw Koito, delicate, fragile and yet determined. She had called it Kuan-Yin, the Compassionate One. The one who vowed to save all living beings. He prayed that she was right.

Buddy stood up slowly, pushing himself upright with his right hand. His body was cold and his shoulders and thighs were stiff and beginning to knot from the long cold swim. He did, however, find that his vision was improving as he watched the bank line from the corner of his eye.

The ground rose up from the river and formed a high, flat area that stretched left to the power plant, which was fully dark, and, in front of him, widened into a darkened triangle, whose point lay against the high railroad viaduct. Buddy decided to check the plant first.

He hadn't gone barefoot for a long time, and the small rocks on the bank hurt his feet, but by stepping lightly and briskly he soon reached ground that was more comfortable to walk on. As he neared the buildings, he stopped to draw his pistol, for the black shapes sent a shiver up his already cold back. A silly thought entered his mind as he moved in among the silent black buildings: he thought how much he'd hate being shot with his pants off. He tried to hold humorous thoughts in his mind for fear was causing his heart to race and his body to chill.

Buddy believed that any weapons set up here were not likely to be within the huge concrete buildings but dug in behind or along the sheltering sides of the plant. Guards might well be stationed in the plant itself, since the windows on the second floor were as high as the top of a hill, giving good observation positions.

Always keep to high ground, Buddy thought. That's the first rule of land warfare. Approaching the shadowy bulk of the building, he climbed an outside brick stairway. His bladder felt painfully full and he thought he might be leaking but he forced himself on. The stairway entered a long storage area that stood open, dark and silent. Buddy crossed this room and came to another stair that led higher. Looking up this stair was futile since it was darker here than outside, he could tell it was ascending by feel rather than sight.

After a long moment, he reached a metal platform at the second floor level. Looking through an open window, he caught movement out the corner of his eye in front of the main plant building. A little moonlight, only a ghostly grayish glow, illuminated the moving shape and a darker object some fifty yards away. Buddy stole back downstairs, through the storage area, and around to the plant's front, facing the river. Creeping, pistol in hand, around the corner, a foot or two at a time, he soon made out a gun pit, probably a heavy mortar dug in under the shelter of the west wall. A sentry stood still for a minute, then walked stiffly right, stopped, turned and walked back toward the gun pit.

Imitating a baby crawling backward across a rug, Buddy moved to the rear and around the building before he stood up to stretch. He wiped his eyes, forgetting he still held the pistol, and gave himself a dig in the corner of his left eye with the weapon's blunt front sight. He came close to cursing and dropping the weapon. Biting his lip he held onto it and began shaking. His stomach was turning over slowly like a miniature cement mixer. It took a moment to get himself under control.

The pain over his eye and his anger at himself drove him on. He found as he slowly crept along the perimeter of the plant more gun pits. In thirty minutes he had found four. There were about twenty-five soldiers, with four very large caliber mortars dug in around the plant. These were the weapons that had banged away at his company for the best part of two days, and could, from what Buddy could see, very likely destroy or badly damage the amtracks when the company crossed the river. He knew that he had to swim back to the captain as quickly as possible. But first, he had to see what lay up that darkened road.

Up to now, Buddy had really done nothing but make a rather long swim and sneak around in the dark. Though he was cold, and his sweatshirt and pants were wet, he was not too tired. He hoped he could stay that way. His stomach felt cramped now, constricted around a cold, hard lump, but he still maintained control over the fear. A vein throbbed in the right side of his neck. He tried with all his might to ignore it. However, no act of will could stop his racing pulse, the overabundance of adrenaline.

It was now 0300. Buddy had spent a good deal of time on his equipment and scouting the power plant. He planned to look quickly up the road toward the higher ground, then swim back to Yellow Beach. There was no need, and no way, to signal by flashlight, since the blocking force of North

Koreans was in the company's line of assault. The captain would need that information before the company tried to cross the river.

Sticking to the shadows, Buddy moved up the road. He was careful to be silent, for the sentries at the power plant could certainly hear any loud noises from here. He saw nothing until he came to the viaduct. Beyond it lay vague shapes, which closer inspection resolved into a line of huge T-34's, Russian-made tanks. The sleeping sounds of many men came from the hillside beyond them, sobs, snores and an occasional cough. The wind and the myriad night sounds of the riverbank had masked them until now. Buddy had seen enough. He was also badly frightened by the realization that he was standing nearly naked and alone among so many enemy soldiers.

He hurried back to the riverbank, planning to wade out to deep water and swim over to the company immediately. But as he reached the flat ground near the river, a weapon bolt snicked, somewhere to his left, and an Oriental voice challenged him. Buddy stopped, literally standing on one foot. Frozen in place, he waited for the flash of a light to fall on him. No light came. Instead, as he eased forward, the G.I. flashlight on his belt came loose, falling with a startling loud clatter and rolled over the river rocks. The alerted sentry instantly fired a round in Buddy's direction.

"Crap!" Buddy screamed as he ran toward the water. A second rifle shot cracked and river stones splintered at his feet. He threw himself down, scraping both knees badly. He fired his pistol three times toward the unseen sentry, moving all the time toward the water until he lunged forward from the bank into knee-deep water. Before he could reach water deep enough to swim in several lights shined on him and the air resounded with rifle fire. Leaping like an enormous white fish into the shallows with a great splash, he felt a sharp sting on his lower right leg. Grunting, his mind filled with terror, he hit the water swimming and began to move away from the bank. The lights found him again, and an automatic weapon opened fire. The water behind him leaped in the air in geysers. He tried to dive, but the water was only four feet deep. He churned on, trying to get as deep as possible until a heavy blow caught him on the rear of the calf muscle of his already injured leg.

Buddy involuntarily rolled over in the water, grabbing for his leg. He quickly felt a hole above his ankle and another, a larger one, in his calf. Surprisingly, he could still move his leg, although it was numb from the knee down. The lights were now hitting the water some fifteen yards behind him, and only an occasional shot came any closer to him than that. He could hear the Koreans shouting on the bank as the wind blew toward him.

Gingerly moving his right leg, Buddy began to swim toward the opposite bank. Scared and cold, he moved as fast as he could. He was about halfway across when the mortar batteries opened up, throwing huge geysers of water in the air, right in the middle of the narrowed river, but fifty yards to his left. The cold knot under his navel seemed to grow. He felt a baseball-sized lump try to ascend his throat. He couldn't breathe. For the first time, Buddy seriously thought he might die. Somehow, he had never considered that to be a possibility before. The terrible knowledge that death was for everyone, including him, was suddenly as real and concrete as the pain in his bleeding leg. Involuntarily, he felt for the small doll around his neck.

The mortars were joined by the rockets parked near the tank column. The batteries walked fire across the whole river and up the opposite bank to the entrenched marine positions. None of the shells fell any closer than fifty yards from him but the explosions made terrific shock waves in the water, which knocked him over and over several times. Buddy recovered automatically after each blow, but soon developed a headache that affected his sight. His vision dimmed, the range narrowed down to a gray spiral, a tunnel that ended in blank whiteness.

As it became more and more difficult to see the bank where his company lay, his panic grew but events were happening too quickly for his fear and fatigue to paralyze him. He seemed to swim with unconscious intent. He was set on automatic pilot. There was no chance to think. Arms and legs merely churned on.

Although there were streaks of red dawn in the sky, he now was almost blind. His jerky strokes and kicks were taking him closer to the marine lines. Though he could still see well enough to make out an occasional flash on Yellow Beach when a rocket exploded, he couldn't hear the sound. Since the wind was at his back and his ears were ringing from the shock of the water explosions, Buddy was effectively deaf. His right ear gave him dull, steady pain.

After a time of steady pulling, he neared the shallows slightly to the right of the company's position. Near the bank his legs and stomach began to cramp in earnest. His toes curled and splayed painfully. Rolling into a ball to massage his legs, Buddy felt the .45 riding in the shoulder holster. He couldn't remember putting the weapon away, yet there it was. He floated for a time; the pain was creeping up his right leg from the ankle to the thigh, and his left leg thigh muscle was locked into a fist-sized lump. His head throbbed and he could only hear a buzzing silence. Buddy bobbed, curled tightly into a fetal position, lost to pain, spent and miserable.

Suddenly, something slapped the water in front of him. A rifle shot. Several more rounds hit the shallows, sending thin fountains skyward. Buddy moved his head. The fire was from the marine lines. "My God, my own people are trying to kill me," he thought. He knew he couldn't hear the rifle reports or any verbal challenges. He silently mouthed the words, "Mother" and "Koito." He hoped he could still talk and opened his mouth and bellowed, "It's me! Buddy. Buddy Gordon! Stop firing, you idiots!"

Three more rounds hit the water to his right front.

"I'm a marine! Hold your fire!" In his mind, Buddy could see his bleeding body, ripped by bullets, floating out to sea with the many mutilated Korean bodies, one more senseless murder to advance no cause.

Another round hit right in front of him. He couldn't hear the swoosh of huge water spouts caused by rockets hitting the river behind him. Though he was limited as to what he could see and hear, his anxiety did great things for his cramp. It dissolved, and he swam closer to the bank.

"Just let me out of this one," he prayed to God, "I don't want to die."

"Captain Hammond! Lieutenant Colliers! It's Buddy!" he screamed as loud as he could. No more rounds hit within his field of vision. He paddled forward, dimly seeing the muddy bank, with skinny weeds sticking up here and there, outlined vaguely against a gray-tinged, blue-black sky. His ears truly hurt now, and he felt pressure behind his eyes.

His feet touched bottom. He tried to stand but his right leg, still numb, wouldn't hold his weight. He hopped forward on his left leg. A huge wave of water came from nowhere, knocking him end for end into the shallows by the bank. A rocket had exploded behind him. Buddy blacked out for several seconds. A frantic voice in his mind screamed, "Help me, God! Help me, Jesus! Mother! Help me, Kuan Yin! Koito!"

Shaking his head, he slowly regained consciousness, becoming aware of his surroundings. He crawled to the weed-grown bank, caught at a sharp-spined plant, which pulled away under his weight. He rolled over in the shallow water, still shaking his head. He opened his eyes, and dimly saw two marines wading into the shallows, coming to pull him up. Their mouths were moving, but he couldn't hear their words and he slipped into unconsciousness as the grinning men grabbed him. They lifted his body under the arms and knees and stumbled up the bank toward the command post.

Water drained from Buddy's body, vomit leaked from his blue-lipped mouth. His head rolled loosely, and the man carrying his legs felt his right hand sticky with blood.

He was carried to the C.P. hole, wrapped in blankets by the Top and revived by slaps on the face by Captain Hammond.

The day was definitely breaking, light was strong even at the bottom of the hole. Hammond said, "Buddy?" and offered him a cup of coffee.

Buddy watched his lips move but heard no sound. He held up his left hand and said, "I can't hear you."

Just then, a corpsman came stumbling over the lip of the pit and sat down next to the boy. The captain motioned Buddy to stick out his wounded leg. He did and the corpsman began to examine the wounds. Buddy glanced down at his leg, afraid for a moment that he might be maimed for life. Then he turned to Hammond.

"Captain, I'm deaf. But listen. There are four batteries of mortars dug in around the walls of the power plant. One to a side. About twenty-five men there. Nobody was in the buildings. There are sentries at the riverbank, right where I crossed. I missed them going in, since the tide carried me downstream toward the plant. They saw me coming back. I guess they shot me. Don't know how many. Three, four, maybe six." The captain's mouth moved. Buddy frowned and choked out, "Don't stop me, I can't hear yet.

"Your big worry was right," he continued. "The gooks are there, up that road. Many, many. I could make out a column of tanks, I'd say seven, big jobs, but I can't be sure. At least seven. And the hillside back there is crawling with men. Many.

"They saw me. The sentries shot me. The mortars fired, too. I reckon the rockets, also, 'cause I saw explosions on the bank. So there's a rocket battery there, too." Buddy stopped for a moment and thought, trying to bring everything he'd seen back into view. Then he added, "That's everything, sir."

The captain grasped Buddy's hand and shook it. The medical corpsman looked up, annoyed, and asked Hammond to ease the boy on his side. The captain put his canteen cup down and did so.

Hospitalman Third-class Lawrence was a salty character who knew his business. As tough as any marine, he was also a fair medical corpsman. He told the captain, Colliers, Briggs and the Top that Buddy was damned lucky. The kid was hit twice. Once by a rifle round that struck above the ankle and passed through the flesh without breaking bone. The second wound was undoubtedly made by a burp-gun round that had struck the water and been slowed down before it hit his calf. This round had wadded up and smacked into the muscle for less than a quarter-inch, making a large hole, but also not breaking the bone. Both projectiles missed arteries. A few inches in other directions, either would have made Buddy's swim back impossible. If an artery had been cut, he would have bled to death in the water. As it was the injuries were not serious. If cared for properly they would heal quickly.

"Water is just like armor, you know," Lawrence told them. "It really slows slugs down."

Buddy leaned back, wallowing vigorously; his hearing was beginning to return. He looked at the corpsman and asked, "Doc, gimme some APC, please? My head hurts."

Lawrence gave him the APC as well as several injections. He also fastened an evac tag to Buddy's left wrist. Before the company mounted up to go across the Han, Buddy was on his way to the field hospital at Ascom City.

9

The hospital jeep arrived in the courtyard of a Presbyterian girl's school, now a field hospital. A small tent near the entrance to the three-sided square served as the triage station. A heavy-set hospital corpsman looked at Buddy's wound tag, glanced under the blanket at his leg and told two orderlies where to take him. Buddy found himself on a cot in a large, crowded room, literally filled with cots, spaced an inch or two apart, except for foot-wide aisles every few cots. The men in the C.P. had left him dressed in his still-damp sweatshirt and shorts, wearing a .45 in a shoulder holster. They had removed the pistol belt, and had put his tan field jacket on him to keep him warm. The field jacket hid Buddy's weapon.

The day before, the first sergeant had given Buddy one of his hand grenades and the boy had put it in the right-hand pocket of his jacket. Buddy, lying on the cot, had nothing to do with his hands. Fidgeting about, he thrust his hand in the pocket and found the grenade. He had already become so used to carrying weapons that it didn't seem strange to have a bomb in his pocket. He really hadn't noticed its weight there. Squirming about, for his leg was hurting, he pulled the grenade out and examined the pin. It was okay. A marine next to him noticed it and thought nothing of it, but did mention that the wounded were supposed to drop all armament at triage.

Innocently, Buddy called out to the next corpsman who entered, "Hey, where shall I put this grenade?" holding it up for the man to see. The sailor turned white and rushed out. He was back soon, with an officer who chewed Buddy out thoroughly for dangerous behavior. A walking wounded marine, with his left arm in a sling, was detailed to take the grenade and carry it out of the hospital. The officer left, threatening court-martial.

The wounded marine, named Brock, was back in a few minutes.

"What'd you do with the grenade?" a man with a shoulder wound asked.

"Saw a six-by of doggies going by, tossed it up to them. Hit the deck like hell," he scoffed.

"Lucky it weren't a six-by of gyrenes. They'd a sent it back for certain, opened!" another flat on his back joked and winced as his elevated leg started to bounce up and down.

Eventually, Buddy did get treatment. His wounds were dressed and he was started on penicillin. This was accomplished while he was wide awake and still dressed in his swimming clothes. He was fed and washed, put into medical corps pajamas, and his pistol was taken away by another upset corpsman. This time, however, there was no visit or lecture from the commanding officer, and no threat of court-martial, just a look of disbelief. Buddy did demand that the pistol be kept for him in the hospital's administrative office since it was the personal property of Captain Hammond. The corpsman assured him that it would be safeguarded and went out of the tent muttering something about jarheads.

Buddy worried all day and most of the night about that gun. He knew that anything let out of sight was gone for sure. The next day, the worry ended. Captain Hammond came to the hospital with a flesh wound in the upper right arm. As soon as he was treated, he came to the enlisted ward and looked for Buddy.

"How ya doin', kid?" he asked.

"Fine, Captain! How about you?" he answered.

"Okay, not bad at all."

"You ought to go to the office and get your pistol before someone walks off with it," Buddy exclaimed.

"All right. I'll go get it soon. I appreciate your concern, but I'm more concerned about you than I am that gun."

"Oh, I'm okay, Captain. I wish you could find out how long they're gonna keep me here."

"I'll see what I can find out, Buddy. I want to tell you, you're going to get a Silver Star for this, at least I'm gonna put in for it," the captain said patting the boy's arm.

"Wow, that's really great, Captain, but I don't think I really did all that much. I mean I thought you had to do something really important to get something like that," the boy said in utter amazement.

"Of course, you deserve it. And, furthermore, you're going to get a pistol of your own when you get back—this one here," and he slapped his leather holster. "I want to get that one I loaned you and clean it up. You know, it was my father's side arm in World War I, and I carried it in Saipan and Okinawa in World War II."

"I know. That's great. I'm proud to carry a weapon like that! Thanks for letting me use it."

"You lived up to it, kid. Well, I'll be back. I'll go look for that piece."

"Yes, sir. See you later."

When the captain left, Buddy fell asleep. He dreamed no dreams and awoke only when an orderly shook him and offered evening chow.

After chow, a greasy pork stew and dried, diced potatoes, Buddy was visited by Hammond again. This time, the major he briefly met in Ascom City was with him. The older man was Major Williams, the battalion executive officer. Williams had come to check on Hammond and, on hearing of Buddy's mission, came to visit the boy, too.

"There's no doubt you'll get a promotion and a decoration out of this, son," he began. "I'll see that the paperwork is sent on to the First Marine Division, Rear, in Japan. You'll need at least a month to get over these wounds, so you'll be going to Japan, too."

"You mean I've got to leave the company, sir?" Buddy asked.

"Just for a while. You'll be sent back to us. There isn't much wrong with you," the major answered. "Isn't that right, Fred?"

"Sure," the captain replied. "We'll be glad to have you back."

"Thanks, sir," the boy put in. "Would you tell me what happened at the river? How'd you get hit?"

"Not much to tell," Hammond began. "We loaded up and moved out before all the fog could burn off. Right after you left, in fact.

"It was clear the mortars were pretty inaccurate. The

rockets worried us, and the tanks, but a communications team came up by jeep around the time the medics left, and we had word of the marine tanks east of our landing place. That evened the odds some."

"How'd the crossing go?" the boy asked.

"It went well. We moved over as fast as those wallowing 'pigs' would go. We were shelled, but only suffered some holes in the amtracks and a few shrapnel wounds like this one in my arm.

"Those armored pigs took out the gun pits on the bank and suppressed the mortars 'til our fire teams waxed the gunners. We pushed up the road and found the tanks, seven of 'em, just like you said, still in position. A bazooka team blew up the one nearest us, blocking the road. Only one or two tried to move at all. We eventually knocked them all out, mainly by shattering the treads. The crews tried to escape and were killed or captured."

"Why didn't they fight?" Buddy asked in surprise.

"Because they were out of gas," Hammond answered with a big grin on his face.

"Outta gas?" The boy was dumbfounded.

"Yep, outta gas. Just like the marine tanks. They couldn't come up with us for hours because they were waiting on a convoy of DUKWs, those death-trap 'ducks,' to come over and refuel them and bring them ammunition.

"We'd have us one devil of a big tank battle to talk about if those armor people could keep their gas tanks full!" The captain said with a sarcastic laugh.

"Fantastic!" Buddy exclaimed.

"It sure is, boy. Now, get some sleep. You'll be on med evac in the morning. Enjoy Japan."

"Thanks, Captain. Take care," the boy said and continued, "Good-bye, Major. I'll be back soon."

The next day Buddy's trip to Japan started with a helicopter ride to Dogpatch One, an air force field in the south of Korea. A cargo plane, equipped with stretchers and a nurse (the first American woman the injured men had seen in months), flew the sick and wounded on to Pusan, the large port city on the southern coast facing Japan. An ambulance drove him breakneck to the docks, where he was carried aboard the hospital ship, U.S.S. *Haven*. He found himself below decks in a big, clean ward, full of tiers of bunks. The guy next to him was an army soldier, badly wounded in the chest, a brawny boy with an outgoing disposition. Buddy enjoyed the man's company. A huge body cast, with a brace protruding to hold the fellow's right arm up, made him look like a man in a white diving suit. Injured as he was, the young fellow was genuinely happy to be on the hospital ship.

Many of the men were in bad shape, but most were cheerful. The exceptions were those who were badly burned and suffered when they moved, or the silent ones with all four limbs in traction and their whole bodies in casts. The blind were stoic, most of the time. Buddy sat on the edge of one blind marine's bunk his second night on the ship and held the man's hand while he cried about his condition. Buddy had been walking past the young marine's cot when he heard a muffled gasp. Concerned that the man might be in trouble, he stopped to ask. With his head turned away from Buddy, the marine shook his head no and didn't say anything. Buddy saw the young man's shoulders shudder and realized he was crying. He seemed no older than Buddy himself. Not sure what to do, if anything, Buddy asked if he could sit down for a minute. His leg was hurting and he needed to rest it. The boy said, "Sure. Go ahead," but still did not look up at Buddy.

"I don't mean to bother," Buddy started, stumbling over the right words to say.

"It's no bother, I guess," the young soldier said, turning to face Buddy.

It was then that he could see that the bandages covered both eyes as well as most of the rest of his head. "Are you in pain? Can I get the nurse for you?" Buddy asked.

"No. I just gotta try to figure things out," the young man said. "I'm blind, and they say it's gonna be permanent. Forever." And with the word "forever" he began to sob. The words began to pour out, all the fears, all the lost dreams. The young man sobbed that he wished he'd been killed. "It would'a been better for everyone concerned."

Buddy, still a total of seventeen years old, sat looking at his hands. He wanted to cry, too, for the young man, but knew that he couldn't. Then he thought of being in the water and not wanting to die and he told the young man about it and Buddy said, "You know what I did, I prayed. I asked God not to let me die. And he didn't. Maybe, if you ask him for help, he'll do it. I only remember one prayer my Grandmother made me learn, you wanna say it?"

The young marine tilted his head for a moment as though trying to see Buddy through the bandages and the dead eyes. He nodded yes, and he and Buddy, holding hands, prayed the only prayer Buddy could think of, the Lord's Prayer, which had been drilled deep into his brain by Grandmother Gordon and catechism class; and, for a second, he was glad.

In the morning, the man stopped mourning and showed little grief thereafter. The blinded men bothered Buddy the most. He could imagine being blind as the worst burden to bear. Being helpless made Buddy anxious, and blindness, at first, seemed to him the most helpless of all states. He still remembered being stunned by the explosions in the river, not being able to see or hear, even though it was only for a short time. The boy was unaware of just how much of his hearing was gone. Only the aggravation of others who tried to talk softly in his presence, and got no response, made him gradually aware that he heard very little with his right ear. He began to develop a habit of cocking his head so as to hear on the left side, ignoring the problem, afraid to mention it to doctors since they might remove him from active service.

The third morning on the *Haven*, a group of doctors announced that all the men there were to be evacuated to Japan that day. Few of these soldiers and marines would be healed in under three weeks, and they were of no help to the war effort. Since many were army personnel, air force planes would carry them all to the Eighty-fifth Station Hospital in Fukuoka, in southern Japan. Marines would be sent to the naval hospital at Yokusaka, near Tokyo, after examination at Sasebo. Some men would be certified for further evacuation to the "Z.I.," the Zone of the Interior, better known as home.

A lot of cheering went up after that speech.

Buddy disliked being treated as if he were helpless. He had gotten up to go to the head and to visit other patients, but the corpsmen made him stay on a litter while he was transferred to the air force field, put on a hospital plane and strapped onto a stretcher.

The flight was uneventful, except for the screaming of the badly burned men. It was dark when they landed and the orderlies loaded the men into rickety, cracker-box army ambulances and drove them to a large, modern-looking hospital. The huge brick structure made Buddy feel as though he were back in the States. It faced a broad, tree-lined avenue that might be found in any American city. At first glance it seemed peaceful and clean. Silence covered the area. Buddy went to sleep as soon as he was put into a bed on the orthopedic ward.

The next day was confusing. He was told he could go to chow in a wheelchair and did so. He and the other young patients raced through the long hospital corridors as fast as they could spin the wheels. After breakfast, the first meal he'd enjoyed in weeks, the nurses told him to go to the clothing room and draw uniforms. Buddy thought this strange, but did as they said. When he reached the clothing office, he was surprised to be given an army duffel bag full of army equipment. At least he got one olive-drab dress uniform, shoes, shirt, and all, which at first aroused his sense of irony, then insulted him. He made it plain he was a marine, but the supply sergeant told him to take it anyway.

Talking to the nurses, Buddy discovered that his patient records listed him as being in the army. He demanded that he be sent to the navy hospital. The nurses said they'd look into it, but nothing was done for two days.

Buddy might have stayed in the army had it not been for the head nurse, who began to think he was suffering from combat fatigue. In all events, the next morning an army orderly came for Buddy and wheeled him to see Dr. Maxwell. "Private, what seems to be the problem?" the middle-aged major asked, looking up from the stack of papers on his otherwise neat desk.

Buddy, having no idea who this man was, asked, "What do you mean, sir?"

"Well, Martin—may I call you that?" he asked, looking directly at the boy, and continued, "I understand that you don't like being in the army anymore. Is there any special reason why?"

Buddy shook his head in disbelief and spoke directly. "Yes, sir. I'd say there's real good reason, sir. I'm not in the army. I never was. I'm in the marines, sir."

"Well, now how can that be? Our records show you're in an army outfit."

"I can't help that, sir. They've made a mistake on the records. I'm in Howe Company, under Captain Hammond's command, sir. I got tags to prove it, sir," and the boy held out his ID disks.

Five minutes later Major Maxwell had everything straightened out. He sat back in his chair and said, "Well, son, that's one of the easiest problems I've had to solve lately. You still have fifty-five minutes of my time coming to you, let's talk."

For the next hour Buddy and the doctor just talked. The major noted on his patient file, "Very intelligent, but very naive."

Buddy moved to Yokusaka by air the next day. This meant a flight to Kadena Air Base near Tokyo and a long ambulance ride across Tokyo and Yokohama to the smaller naval base city. The naval hospital turned out to be an attractive place, built as a Japanese naval hospital during World War II and taken over by the Americans in 1945. In 1950, it was large, made up of many low, white buildings, shady and pleasant. Marines, soldiers, and navy men of all the Allied countries were treated here. The fighting in Korea, which had already produced so many arm and leg wounds, caused the establishment of ward after ward for orthopedic patients. Buddy went to Ward W.

Beyond good food and rest, little treatment was necessary. Buddy received a course of penicillin and an occasional change of dressings. His major care involved physical therapy. Daily he went to the P.T. room for message, and as the wounds healed, for hydrotherapy and exercise. After two weeks, he was lifting graduated amounts of weights that fit over a special metal shoe. This exercise was necessary to restore the calf and other muscles that atrophied after the injury and the extended period of forced nonuse. The P.T. was enjoyable, but Buddy grew restless and wanted to rejoin his unit. Three weeks after arriving at Yokusaka he asked the head surgeon when he could return to duty.

"Well, your outfit finished the job at Seoul, even went all

the way to the thirty-eighth parallel. Captured one hundred thousand prisoners and was pulled back to Inchon," the stocky medical corps commander said.

"I understand they're boarding ships to go elsewhere soon. Maybe we can get you there in time to go with them. Would you like that?"

"Yes, sir. There's nothing much wrong with me."

"Okay. I'll see if it's possible. You might be discharged and catch a ride over to your division with a load of replacements. They fly out of Tachakawa Air Base, which is near the marine casualty company base at Otsu."

"I'd appreciate that, sir."

"I can find out for sure in the morning. A bunch of marine brass is visiting the hospital at 0900."

"Thanks, Commander."

"Don't mention it. Most people don't want to leave the hospital. We appreciate those who do."

Buddy wasn't released from the hospital until after lunch, causing him to arrive at Otsu at dark. The delay resulted from the visit of several high-ranking marine officers to Yokusaka, who came to hand out promotions and award.

At 1000 hours, PFC Gordon was standing at attention at the foot of his bed, still in bathrobe and pajamas, when a marine brigadier general handed him a warrant promoting him to corporal. The general then asked for a box from an accompanying major and pinned the Silver Star, "For gallantry," on his faded blue robe. He then pinned on the Purple Heart. This one said "For Military Merit." Buddy wondered if it was truly meritorious to get shot.

Buddy had both the warrant and the medals in the new seabag the marine clothing issue office had given him in Yokusaka. He also had several hundred dollars of occupation script in back pay and a batch of letters from his parents, grandparents, Mike, and even one from the Library Club of the River's Junior High School of Charleston, which had finally caught up with him before he left the hospital. The girls of the school club promised to send him a package of goodies if he would send them his correct address. It seems the marines released a story on him to the newspaper; he was a hero of sorts, the only student they knew from the junior high school who was at war and injured and with medals and all. They wanted to do their part to help, so the letter said. Buddy answered that one right away. Goodies from the Library Club was better than no goodies at all. Buddy shook his head. If anyone back home wondered what happened to him, well, they knew now.

IV

To the Mountain

10

"Blasted Zippo!" Buddy exclaimed, shifting his slung rifle slightly. He looked around for any response to his unprofessional behavior; smoking on watch was an offense against standing orders. As the light of hidden sun leaked across the horizon, running in streaks like a broken egg yolk across a plate of faded blue-gray, he pulled on the cigarette; at the same time he also grasped a strand of the barbed wire above his head and pulled his body up, giving his numbed right leg a rest.

Buddy had been released from hospital and sent to Camp Otsu, near Lake Biwaku under the shadow of Mount Fuji, with its snow crowned cone. Otsu was the site of the marine casual company, and staging area for replacements for the division's units in Korea. As with all released hospital patients, he was given a period of light duty as a recovery period before going back into action. After a few days doing nothing, Buddy was glad to volunteer to stand guard at the First Amphibious Tank Battalion's base at West Camp, in Kobe.

Camp Otsu was a genuine war prize of World War II, a former Imperial marine base taken over in 1945. Used only for transients or "casual" personnel, the concrete barracks and separate, Japanese-style toilets and bathhouses were little changed, except for the installation of western style "crappers" and showers. The barracks were cold, furnished only with crowded bunks. The food made all the sick and injured actually yearn for hospital chow again.

Traveling by fast train across the mountains and through the lovely cities of Honshu: Kofu, Iido, Ogaki, Hikone, and Kyoto, Buddy and several other volunteers laughed and joked all the way to the inland sea. The "rear," or baggage train, of the First Marine Division was based at Kobe, the personal gear of its thousands of troops stored in long warehouses on the docks that jutted out everywhere. Guarding these possessions was part of the duty of the guard company based at West Camp.

Buddy was not only bored, he was capable of guile. He knew that Kobe was near Osaka, Koito's home city. Indeed, he had learned from a hospital corpsman on Ward W that Kobe and Osaka were part of a great urban sprawl along the coast, joined together by an inter-urban train system. A letter to Koito, sent in care of Mashuko, the old cook, was mailed at Otsu before Buddy caught the train. He asked her to come to the West Camp and ask the main gate guard to send him word of her arrival as soon as she could safely come.

Upon arrival, the men ate cold sandwiches and went to

bed in the clean, neat Quonset huts erected for the occupation forces. The next day, Buddy and his casual company friends were delighted to find that the chow at West Camp was good. They attended an orientation lecture, were told that the rest of the day was their own, and that liberty passes could be picked up at the main guard shack by the main gate. Beginning tomorrow, they would stand guard, four hours on, hour hours off, for twenty-four hours of liberty if they wanted it, and if they found girlfriends in town, as most "green machines" did, they would want it. Buddy thought it sounded like heaven.

He stopped simply thinking he had died and gone to heaven and knew it as a fact at 1300 hours, when an amtrack corporal knocked at the door of Quonset hut number four and asked of there was a Buddy Gordon there. Buddy stopped preparing to sew a button on his green Ike jacket and identified himself.

"Well, Stud," the tall redhead said, laughing, "there's a Nipponese musume, excuse me, I mean young lady, dressed fit to kill down at the main gate asking for you. The sergeant of the guard didn't like it much but she apparently has a military dependent ID so he asked me to get you down there ASAP."

"Thanks, man!" Buddy cried, shuffling into the dress green jacket in spite of its missing button. "Thank you!" he shouted again, pushing past the amused marine, walking as quickly as his weakened leg would allow.

"Thank you," he said to himself, "Thank you, God, who runs the world!"

Koito was overjoyed to see the boy she'd known for so short a time. She was too shy, too reserved, to show her feelings standing in the afternoon sun outside the guard shack.

"Koito!" Buddy cried, with no such shyness.

"Buddy!" she replied warmly, saying, "This is a miracle! How did you get here?"

"That's a long story," Buddy responded. "Can we go somewhere? I'll tell you the whole thing!"

"Of course, there's a candy store, an American restaurant, nearby. Can we go there?"

"Sure! Just let me draw my liberty card."

Buddy hustled into the office where he was met with wide grins and quite a few lascivious comments by the sergeant and several corporals sitting around at or on several battered wooden desks.

"Whoowee," one man observed. "You must be hot 'cause most of us have to go look for our women!"

Buddy knew none of them meant any harm, so he smiled back and asked, "Could I draw my liberty card?"

"Yep, it's been in that there box since 0800," the sergeant replied.

"Then I'll take it and go," the boy responded. Shifting through the small laminated squares marked "Liberty Card," Buddy found one made out to Martin Charles Gordon, took it, gave a half-salute, and hurried out.

"Just be careful, lover," the sergeant called out after him in salutation.

At the candy store, Koito broke through her shyness and covered the boy with kisses. "You're getting lipstick on my shirt and field scarf," he said, "but I couldn't care less!"

After they had ordered steaks from the amazingly cheap menu, they sat together whispering. Their plans for Buddy's brief stay in Kobe were laid. Koito, who had few demands on her time during the day, would meet Buddy every day that he had liberty, beginning the day after tomorrow. She would show him Kobe and Osaka. They would shop, eat out and go to movies. They would be together.

That night, walking Koito to her train, Buddy would not

have been surprised if the raucous Japanese pop music blaring from every bar and store was not suddenly transformed into celestial harmonies, blown by trumpets in counterpoint to angel's wings. No hero himself, somehow he had slipped unnoticed into Valhalla; no saint, some mistake of St. Peter had opened The Gates to the Golden Streets. Buddy vowed to walk them all before the inevitable day when he would be thrown out of Paradise.

The emerging light made the half-mile perimeter fence stand out against the shadows of the still sleeping city. Kobe was a mass of broad streets, peopled by dingy two- and three-story buildings, but near West Camp, the home base of the First Amphibious Tank Battalion, First Marine Division, the lots were still rubble-strewn from the bombings less than six years before. Behind Buddy stood row on row of metal Quonset huts and cinder block "heads" or wash houses left over from Japanese military use. One sentry patrolled each side of the perfect square that was the camp. Buddy saw no one, usually, unless the guards at either end of his post tarried to pass the time at the corners of the camp.

What seemed to be a heap of rags moved beyond the storm fence. Buddy stopped, threw down his cigarette butt and yelled, "Who goes there?"

From the distance he heard the sniggering voice from the pile of rags ask, "Boom—Boom?"

The young man blushed deep red as the pile of rags moved closer, revealing an old woman half-crawling and half-duck-walking. Again she half-laughed and half-cried, "Boom-Boom?"

Violently, Buddy struck out at the fence, yelling, "No! *Etawa*! Move out!" The old crone laughed and moved a foot or two closer. "Haul ass!" the boy shouted, menacingly pointing his rifle at her. As suddenly as she had appeared she disappeared back into the shadows of the rubble beyond the wire.

He looked back down to the ground at this feet and bent forward to retrieve the smoldering cigarette with a shaking hand. The idea of the old woman and her question appalled and disquieted the boy more than the solicitations of any of the streetwalkers met on late-night wanderings. He took a last drag from the cigarette butt and tried to calm himself. He looked at his watch, 0333. At 0800 an all-day liberty began, up to the midnight curfew. He smiled at the idea. To have a day like any other normal human being. Koito was going to meet him at Moringa's Candy Store on the Ginza by 0930. He suddenly pinched his smoke and straightened his gear. A chill passed over him as he thought of Warrant Officer Davis, the oldest, meanest man he'd ever met. Davis seemed older than his grandfather yet here he was fighting his third, if not his fifth or sixth, war, and scaring the pants off eighteen-year-old, six-foot-tall, 200-pound athletes, some of them already neurotic from their first campaign and bearing the marks of their first wounds.

The thought of WO Davis got Buddy into motion walking from one end of the base's eastern fence to the other, some half-mile from corner to corner. WO Davis did not need insignia of rank or fancy uniforms. His age, his gruff, weathered face and manner, the clearly marked badge of rank of his bald head—all brought a fear-filled obedience from any enlisted marine in his presence. Buddy was not frightened but he was deeply concerned about any contact with Davis. The old mustang had crawled all over him at inspection the first day he had arrived at camp. Buddy's right boondocker was not properly laced and tied. Before he could explain Davis began his tirade. It was not so much that he thought Buddy was a slob, it was just the WO Davis believed that there was only one way to do everything and that was the marine way. Whether it was shaving or lacing boots, it had to be done the marine way. Finally, it was explained that Corporal Gordon was lacing and tying his boot in a nonmilitary manner due to the wounds from which he was recovering. Corporal Gordon was ordered to remove the boot to expose the vivid red gash across his ankle. WO Davis stared at the wound and, finally, said, "Huh!" and moved on down the line to the next guard in the inspection party. It had not been necessary for Buddy to pull up the leg of his trousers to reveal the huge hunk of flesh missing from the calf. For the moment, Davis had been satisfied.

In the chilly dawn Buddy shivered more from the memory of that brief tirade rather than from the wind that bounced harmlessly off his thick, green blanket coat. The last tour of the old guard was almost over. Corporal McKeown would be here with his relief soon. Buddy began to picture the soft, small, powdery, sweet-smelling Koito, for whose company he had broken a dozen rules and risked court-martial. He smiled to himself at the image of the tiny girl walking under his arm. He was amazed when they walked past the store windows and he glimpsed the amazing differences between them. He was lean, six foot, four inches, with a light brown crew cut. She was five feet at most, with long, glossy black hair. He was fair; she was not "yellow" but a lovely light beige. He was a child of poverty; she was of privilege. He, occidental; she, oriental, though better-educated in English and more familiar with higher American culture than Buddy. Yet, none of this mattered. Aside from her distinct femininity, her gentleness and beauty, it was her utter, unconditional love she held for him that tied him to her. From the beginning she was totally given over to him, and in return, he to her. If slightly damaged male adolescence was attractive to her, then the scarred boy was hers. No barbed wire, no duty, no regulation would keep him from her. Yet, today, legally, his time was hers. An animal joy rippled over him as the corporal of the guard, McKeown, and his relief, Johnson, rounded a Quonset hut and loosely marched toward him.

"Halt! Who goes there?" Buddy ceremoniously called out.

"Corporal of the guard. Relief of the watch," McKeown replied.

"Advance, corporal of the guard," Buddy responded, thinking of the illegal cigarette butts in his coat pocket as he presented arms.

A man with a slowly mending broken arm, whose name Buddy could never remember, lay stretched out, in full gear, on the bunk next to Buddy's when Buddy entered the Quonset barracks of casual company. The marine had that look found only on the countenances of the severely injured, old convicts, and the survivors of campaigns that had lasted a few weeks too long.

"Beat?" Buddy inquired.

"Yeah." The blondish, sun-wrinkled face turned toward him while answering. "But you look happy, kid."

"Yep. I'm meeting my girlfriend in a little while."

"Pretty neat. Got your own moose already?"

"No. Koito ain't no moose. She's no whore. And I've known her since last year, before I got sent to Inchon," Buddy replied testily.

"All right!" the man replied. "I think I'll sack out 'til midday chow. Good night."

"Sure," the boy called back over his shoulder as he moved toward his locker.

Inside the metal upright box stood a nonregulation Japanese doll, next to his barracks hat on the small top shelf. It echoed the equally forbidden small wooden doll tied to his service tags, perpetually worn about his neck. In fact, that doll and his service tags were all the personal gear he'd brought out of Korea, that and the memory of Koito. He had finally arrived at the naval hospital and settled in when a Red Cross volunteer, some officer's pretty, middle-aged wife, wrote to Buddy's mother for him, but balked at the idea of writing to a Japanese girl. No one wanted to, or could, believe that one of the acne-marked teen-agers could have a genuine relationship with a normal girl over here. A poor girl would have been another matter; they were sold into prostitution, everyone understood. Buddy bristled at the thought. His romance, his relationship with Koito, was no different than anyone else's here, or at home, except for the vast social gap between his family and hers. Angrily he had asked for paper, pen and envelope and wrote to her himself. An ambulatory patient had mailed it for him.

Buddy brushed the small talisman as he stripped down and was calmed. He took up his towel and toilet articles and walked naked through the open air down the duckboards to the common showers, a hundred yards away. The Japanese civilians walking the street outside the north fence paid no attention. In the head several marines were threatening to turn in one man, Crews, who was painfully urinating into the troughlike urinal.

"Man, you gotta dose. You gotta go to sick bay," they were saying as Buddy walked in.

"I got a strain, that's all," Crews hotly retorted.

"No, you ain't," one man said. "You got the clap. Turn in or we'll tell Mr. Davis."

"You shithead!" Crews cried, real tears starting at the real pain.

"No, we're not! We're your friends, damn it! Now, you're goin' to sick bay or else," another marine put in.

"You want maybe it should fall off during Tromp and Stomp? See Brown at the dispensary. He's a good man. Three shots, that's all, won't even be on your record, man," a third marine pleaded. "You'll be okay then. Okay?"

"What the hell, okay. It's gotta be better than this." Crews finally relented; a slick sheen covered his grimacing face.

"Crews, you put your dick in places you wouldn't stick your bayonet," Buddy observed.

"Who's talkin' to you, shitface?" Crews said with disgust, leaving for sick bay.

Buddy asked Lon Peters to hold on to his new wallet while he showered. Unlike a regular company, where men knew each other and generally respected one another's property, casual companies were made up of strangers, many of whom would steal the tattoos off your arm if they could figure out how. Peters stuck the billfold in his pants pocket and walked toward the barracks, while Buddy got in the shower.

Fifteen minutes later he was dressing in his best greens. He had a half-hour before meeting Koito. He finally felt as though the night watch was really over. He checked his uniform in the full-length mirror near the door. As he turned to leave the barracks he noticed the blond man still sleeping. Buddy shook his head when he noticed the man still wore a side arm, even in his sleep, even when out of danger.

Gunnery Sergeant Walls sat behind a folding desk, an armed forces paperback in front of him but staring into space. The red welt of a bullet gouge ran from his right eye through his ear.

"Can I get my pass, Gunny?" Buddy asked.

"Sure, here ya go," Walls replied, taking a laminated square from a cigar box and adding, "Have some coffee? You didn't go to chow, did ya?"

"No. Thanks," Buddy responded, "I could use some." He sat on a bunk and drank the oily coffee.

"Think you'll ever swim again?" Walls asked, referring to the action that had put Buddy in the hospital.

The boy felt a coldness well up inside. "Yeah, I think so. I'm not afraid of the water, never was, guess I couldn't be," he observed.

"That's not it. I was there, remember?" Walls looked sharply with newly focused eyes at the younger man. "We all watched you swim that half-mile, then saw the water boil up from all those rounds. You're lucky you made it."

"Yeah," Buddy replied in a flat voice, not really wanting to go over it again.

"We were cussin' you for drawin' all that fire," Walls started.

"Yeah, I'm sorry," the boy responded in a sarcastic tone that belied his real regret.

"Forget it," Walls said, standing up and stretching. "We'll be back there soon enough. Better get goin' now, kid."

"Buddy stood up and saluted, smiling, "Outta here, Gunny."

With an evil leer, Walls saluted back and winked, saying, "Have a good time!"

"I'll work on it," Buddy said as he strode out the door.

Buddy showed his liberty card to Wilson at the gate, stepped around the road barrier and turned left toward downtown Kobe.

A Japanese policeman stood on a white box directing traffic. He carried only a club. The occupation rules forbade the arming of Japanese. The developing military organization was called a police force. Something like calling the marine corps the navy's police force, Buddy thought sarcastically. Buddy spotted a bus, ran for it and got on without paying. He rode for ten minutes through streets that reflected little of the bomb damage of 1945. School children and teen-aged girls pointed at his lanky height and giggled. The bus turned left, then right into Motomachi Ginzano. Within a block he reached the candy store, which was actually a small restaurant.

The chill that Wall's conversation had induced in him faded into the background when, through the glass, he saw

Koito sitting at a booth in the restaurant. Maringa's Candy Store was a small room with American-style booths, painted a light blue and filled with light from the glass windows that filled the top half of the wall facing the street. The restaurant was clean and the bulky white American china, ringed with dark blue, reminded Buddy of the greasy spoon he and Mike used to frequent for their four A.M. "lunch." Knives and forks topped every table, not chop sticks. American music, schmaltzy and crooning, echoed from wall to wall. Maringa's was a bit of 1950's Kansas City although there were no bobby socks, pink shirts, ponytails or sideburns on any of the customers.

Entering, she saw him and jumped up to embrace him. "*Anatawa watashi aisemust*, I love you," she whispered.

"I love you, too," Buddy said out loud.

Koito's broad forehead, topped with a mass of blue black hair, invited a kiss. She smelled slightly of a delicate flower-scented cream and powder. Her voice was light and she seemed to purr when he brushed his lips across her eyebrows before sitting down.

A month earlier, Koito had received a letter from the navy hospital. She caught the fast train from Osaka on the same day. Buddy looked down the aisle from his cranked-up bed, one of the dozens backed against the walls of the huge gallery that was Ward W. There Koito stood, small and vulnerable, looking in at the ward through the gap between the nursing station and the entry to the head. A nurse looked at her curiously. Koito displayed a pass signed by the head of military government for the area. Raising her eyebrows, the short, heavyset nursing lieutenant allowed her to enter. Koito walked quickly behind the nurse to Buddy's bed, midway down the ward and beside the window. Tears in her eyes, she bowed. Buddy reached up to embrace and kiss her. She smelled like Christmas and Easter and birthdays all rolled into one.

Astounded by her presence, all Buddy could say was, "How?" and "Why?"

Koito smiled shyly and reached into her purse and pulled out a small package. "For you," she replied softly.

Buddy carefully unwrapped the brightly colored paper from the contents. He held a small silver belt buckle and tie clasp with his name engraved on the fronts, and on the back "Koito." For the rest of the day they sat saying little, holding hands, looking out the window on to a small garden.

Buddy had never realized a garden could be so beautiful, so full of peace and solace.

After that Koito traveled from Osaka to Yokosuka by train every week. Buddy was a sponge soaking up her company.

"I love you," Koito said softly as Buddy slid into the booth.

"I love you, too," Buddy replied.

Looking into her eyes, he remembered the river with the raft of human bodies who once, when alive and smiling, must have had eyes as beautiful and gentle.

"Why do you look so sad?" she asked reaching for his hand. "We have all day together."

"Yeah." He forced himself back to the present. "What'll we do? The park? Zoo? A movie? One, two or all?" he said, starting to smile as he watched her delicate face contort under the burden of decision.

"Yes, yes, yes, hai!" she laughed back at him.

At that moment, and for the rest of the day, Buddy was a normal seventeen-year-old boy, and Koito was a normal seventeen-year-old girl. They could have been anywhere in the world, rather than a few hours away from violence and death.

At last it was time for Koito to take her train back home. They rushed to the train platform where in the shadows they hugged and kissed by the elevated walls. They missed the first train, then the second. Moving to a bench in the darkness, they continued petting. Near midnight Buddy finally came to his senses.

"Will you be able to get a train this late?" he asked Koito.

"Hai, yes, there is one at midnight that will get me home in the morning," she replied.

"Good, let's go up on the platform so you won't miss it."

"No, you must go. The curfew comes very soon. You must be back on post," she said, taking his face in her hands.

"I won't go until you're on that train," Buddy shot back. "And that's the end of it. I'll get back okay."

He would allow no argument. When Koito boarded the train, Buddy was already ten minutes late. No one was now supposed to be in the streets but the MPs. Theoretically, it dawned on him, he could be shot. In the Korean districts of the city a person could very easily be stabbed. After curfew no one entered these areas but Koreans and MPs with loaded weapons. Buddy had to travel very near to one of these off-limit areas to reach the West Camp.

In thirty minutes he was on the roof of a shanty beside the east fence of West Camp. More than Buddy's reconnaissance experience made the journey on foot easy for him. As a boy, his brother, Chester, ran away from their dirt farm everyday, it was Buddy's job to fetch him home. Chester was a master by the age of six at hiding in the dense North Carolina forests. It was Buddy's duty, as elder brother, to go and find the wily master of concealment. If he made noise in the dry, brown leaves or brittle branches of the thickly placed trees and brush, then Chester would move away, deeper into the woods. The kid could have given lessons to the Indian scouts of old, grubbing out shallow holes in the humus of the forest floor, then burying himself in them beneath limbs and dried leaves. Yet Buddy found him often as not; he had learned to be as silent, as stealthy as their father's ancestors.

Buddy stretched way out from the shanty roof and grasped the outer strand of barbed wire of the "Y" at the top of the high fence and swung out landing with both feet next to his hands. He caught his right pants leg in the barbed wire as he scrambled over, and let himself drop to the other side. "Uff," he exclaimed as he looked up into the startled face of a guard.

"What the hell?" Collins cried.

"Don't shoot, it's me, Buddy!"

"You asshole!" Collins snorted. "What're you tryin' to do, get your ass shot or somethin'? Get outta here, 'fore we both get into trouble!"

"Thanks, Collins. I owe you!" Buddy whispered as he turned to run for the barracks.

"You bet your stupid ass you do!" Collins barked back, shaking his head at the stupidity of the kid.

Buddy thanked God that Davis wasn't around and slipped into his barracks. He fell asleep fingering the little wooden doll that rested on his chest. In his dreams he felt the dreaded impact of the bullet in his calf and the water filling his mouth as it opened in an involuntary scream of shock and pain. Awakened by the sensation of drowning, he bolted upright to get air in his lungs again. He was troubled, and after smoking a cigarette, he turned over and fell asleep again. Once more he dreamed. This time he stood by, nauseous and paralyzed, while the corpsman unslung his toy carbine and, as if underwater, raised it to his shoulder in slow motion and put a round through Koito, who lay motionless, covered by empty, dirty sandbags on the hard, brown Korean soil.

Awakened by a stabbing pain in his chest, Buddy lay restless for ten minutes, then got up, dressed and walked to the guard shack where he sat drinking coffee with the sleepy corporal of the guard until time for morning chow.

• • •

Buddy had the twelve-to-four watch that day. After breakfast he crawled into a bunk in the guard room and slept for three hours. Collins looked at him at chow, grinning, but nevertheless honoring the marine's "Code of the West," and remained silent. Buddy had already forgotten the fence escapade but he couldn't forget the dreams. He slept in the guard room not only because of duty but more for the sense of companionship he found there. The guard shack had as much grab-ass and joking as a school playground and as much gossip and idle talk as the ghetto kitchens and small-town bars of Charleston. The sound of weapons slapping sides and rough voices sharing obscenities was comforting to Buddy, as comforting as his boondockers touching the body of the man sharing a fighting hole when with his mind half-asleep he knew the other was there, alert against danger. He woke refreshed.

The daylight watch went down easy. Buddy and a Japanese policeman walked the length of the huge dock, inspecting the open warehouse that spanned its length and most of its width, from time to time. Once more, two together made life half as hard. The Japanese kept an eye out while Buddy smoked, then the marine repeated the favor. Around 1500 the policeman made tea in a police coop in the warehouse. Buddy drank his cup walking post, sharing PX cigarettes with the smiling, good-natured man. He found it hard to believe that only five and a half years before fellow marines had taken twenty-nine thousand casualties and left only two hundred alive out of twenty-seven thousand Japanese soldiers on Iwo Jima. Buddy, as he walked back and forth, up and down, the old, wooden, warehouse dock, shook his head at the puzzlement that was called politics and war.

Buddy read in the guard room after the watch. He returned to his book, an Agatha Christie mystery, after evening chow. It was so good he didn't go to sleep 'til almost 2200.

Awakened at 2330 for guard duty, he felt quite tired as the 2400 guard section assembled. Out on post after a bumpy truck ride, he amused his Japanese buddy by yawning, stretching and complaining.

"You very tired, man. Just walk for an hour or so. All policemen have nice break planned. We go," the older man said with a self-pleased tone, crossing his arms and smiling more to himself than to Buddy.

"Hey, we can't leave post!" Buddy exclaimed.

"No need," the cop replied. "Police meet right here on pier 12, in lunchroom you saw today. Here. In this warehouse."

Well, okay. Maybe I can make it," Buddy responded wistfully. "I'm beat, ya know. I've caught about five hours of Zs in the last two days," Buddy continued, yawning larger than ever.

"No problem," the cop said, smiling.

Around 0230 the policeman left Buddy and plunged into the shadowy warehouse, his flashlight casting a band of pale light on the boxes, bags and pallets of military gear stacked inside. Five minutes later Buddy saw the light approaching him from within as he passed an open door farther down the pier.

"All ready. Come on. Other policemen watch. Give word if officer come," the policeman's voice cheerfully whispered from the shadows of the enormous warehouse.

Somewhat troubled, but tired and hungry, Buddy followed the scruffy Japanese through the darkness that smelled of cosmoline and mold to a small, dimly lit room. Here, seated on the floor, were a half-dozen cops taking their ease. Bowls of rice and tea sat everywhere. A bottle of Suntory, a cheap, Japanese whiskey, covered with colored rice paper that made it look like a giant firecracker, also sat there. Straw mats and wooden neck rests lined one side of the room; one cop snored lightly on a soiled mat. Rubber shoes and night sticks lay piled beside him.

"Hungry? Tired?" a burly police corporal asked. "Need a drink?" he added, nodding toward the firecracker bottle.

Buddy knew this man had fought at Okinawa yet was one of the friendliest cops around. "I'm really sleepy. A cup of tea would be good," he replied as he sat down, cradling his M-1 across his knees. A younger cop handed him a cup of tea from the charcoal braiser as well as a small bowl of cold noodles coated with spices and oil. The noodles were delicious and the tea warmed him. He yawned. The older cop handed him a small smooth cup without handles and poured a little Suntory into the bottom. Buddy took a small sip and grimaced. The cheap liquor burned all the way down, at first gagging him, then filling him with a golden warmth. Buddy smiled across the teacups, cold noodles, and festive liquor bottle at his new friends.

"More?" someone asked.

""No. I just want to lie down a minute. Is anyone watching my post?"

"Hai," a policeman by the door answered and continued, "no worry. Rest eyes."

Buddy rested his eyes until 0330, waking to the crash of his equipment being kicked and a blinding white light being shown on his face. When the beam moved and his pupils adjusted themselves to the dim light of the police coop, Buddy saw WO Davis, his broad, dim figure in dress greens, holding a huge flashlight.

"Oh, my God!" he whispered to himself, more as a prayer than a curse.

"What the hell is going on here?" Davis demanded. "Why are you off post? You know desertion on watch is a death penalty offense?"

Even in the dim light, Davis's face was dark red with anger. The warrant officer kicked Buddy's helmet over, "Get up! Get your gear on! Get back to the post!"

"Yes, sir, Mr. Davis, sir!" the boy blurted out.

The Japanese police scattered; in thirty seconds, no one, not even the sleeping man was there. Cups and the liquor bottle rolled on the floor. The teapot had tipped and a large, warm puddle marked the center of the coop.

Afraid that Davis would kick him all the way out to the edge of the wide pier, Buddy ran through the darkened warehouse, bumping into boxes with every other step. Shaken more by discovery than bruises, he reached the open door. Slowing, he slung his piece and began to walk post in measured steps. Davis's flashlight shined through another door shortly after, the beam followed by the old man himself. Buddy stopped smartly and saluted. He didn't dare report Post Number 12 all secure. Davis glared at him.

"After you're relieved, you come to my office," he declared with a deep growl.

"Yes, sir!" Buddy responded, feeling the searing pain of heartburn that rose and fell with his every hyperventilated breath.

In twenty minutes, the relief truck arrived. Buddy was relieved by McKeown.

"Damn, man, what'd you do?" McKeown asked. "Davis said you was to report to him as soon as you get back."

"Oh, hell. I'm royally screwed," Buddy almost sobbed. "I'll tell ya later. That is if I get the chance." Buddy climbed into the six-by with a grunt.

Having once seen a movie about the French Revolution, Buddy thought of the condemned being carried by cart to the guillotine. All that was missing were the slobbering crowds.

When the guard section got back to base Buddy made straight for Davis's quarters. He was not in his office. Buddy waited, sweating, then finally decided to go to bed. He was awakened for chow after an hour and a half. He forced himself to eat, then returned to the guard room to wait. There was no sign of Davis all morning.

"Maybe he's sleeping in with some little moose," the new sergeant of the guard said. Buddy left for his quarters, took a shower, dressed as for an inspection, and went back to the guard room.

"What's with you? Ya love work?" asked a pimply-faced corporal who was holding down the desk.

"I'm waiting for WO Davis," Buddy told him.

"Well, he ain't around. Nobody's seen him all day," the corporal reported.

"I'll wait," Buddy mumbled, and pulled his paper back out of the waistband of his trousers. He lay back on a bunk and read through noon chow and into the afternoon. After 1500 hours a rather scared-looking PFC hurried into the guard shack and stared at Buddy.

"Man, that old warrant officer is looking for you. You better haul it over to his office."

"Yeah," was all Buddy could say, then, "Thanks."

"For nothing," the kid replied. "Good luck!"

Buddy was numb as he walked across the narrow roadway that cut the camp in two. Davis's office was in a small, white building of traditional nondescript military style. Once inside, he saw an open door on his left. A silver desk sign, with C.P. Davis and the striped bars of a commissioned warrant officer 4, was fastened over the top of the door frame. All the blood seemed to have left the boy's legs and congealed behind his eyes. Although he didn't know it, Buddy's blood pressure had spiked. He felt nauseous and lightheaded. Gongs pounded in his ears. He addressed the door, squaring his shoulders, and marched in, halting at a stiff attention. With all his will he tried to keep his nerves under control, but in spite of his efforts every muscle of his body was aquiver.

"Corporal Gordon reporting as ordered, sir!" he boomed

out. Buddy didn't salute since his cap was off.

"Dammit, Gordon, what the hell's going on, what's the matter with you?" the old officer began, without preamble. "Are you just a no-good or are you still working at it?"

Buddy was too paralyzed with shame, an emotion stronger in him than fear, to answer.

"Well, poophead, can't you talk?" Davis demanded.

"Yes, sir!" Buddy barked back.

"You could be shot, you know that, boy?" the officer asked in a flat voice.

"Yes, sir, I know that," the youth answered in a similar tone.

"More likely, you'll do hard time at Portsmouth Naval Prison," Davis observed, almost to himself.

"Yes, sir!" Buddy almost shouted as he began to seriously panic at the thought of prison.

"Don't get your bowels in an uproar," the old man shot back. "We don't spend all this time and money on people who are strong enough and dumb enough to do the jobs we have to do to throw them away. We try to keep them, you understand, boy?"

In that phrase "you understand," Buddy was reminded of his father. Why, he might have served with this old man! "Yes, sir. I think so, sir!" Buddy replied, mystified.

"You're too young to deep-six," the old man continued. "And you've already been tested. I know you got scars. I know walking that post is hard for you now." The tanned, lined face almost showed compassion.

"Yes, sir!" Buddy choked, feeling blistering, hot drops forming at the inner corners of his eyes.

"I'm going to give you this one pass—this one chance. But if you screw up again, I'll wash my hands of you. You're history, you understand?" Davis said all this in a moderate tone.

"Yes, sir! I understand, sir! I appreciate it, sir!" Buddy shot back, relief spreading rapidly though his limbs, bringing the tingle of renewed life.

"Then get your sorry ass out of here, and don't let me see you in here again," Davis snarled, back to his old self.

"Yes, sir!" the youth cried, turned sharply on his heels, and left.

Buddy walked out of the small frame building numb from the experience. He felt relief, but only intellectually. His feelings were still frozen. He was free of the danger of shame to his future. Free because beneath the profane, almost brutal exterior of the old man, there was a fatherly concern for the oversized boys under his command. Perhaps forty years ago some elder had given him a break, too. Perhaps he had sons of his own. Perhaps he had seen too many end up wrapped in bloody ponchos. Buddy realized that Davis was more than military, he was human. He began to see that he had done with WO Davis the very thing that he resented others doing to him. He had labeled him, limited him, without ever getting to know him. Buddy stood in the middle of the deserted roadway, in full uniform, suspended between the disgrace behind him and the continued duty of the guard shack before him, wondering about the people he thought he'd known.

11

The night's watch at Kobe ended soon after Buddy's encounter with Warrant Officer Davis. After his return from liberty, he was told by the chief hospital man at the base dispensary that his "light duty" was over. He was to report to Camp Otsu on Thursday in two days' time.

"What time will I go?" he asked.

"After noon chow," the chief replied.

"Good," thought Buddy. "I can tell Koito in the morning before I leave."

The next day was guard. The tours were uneventful. Buddy's nerves had settled from his close brush with prison and dishonor. His leg was now almost fully recovered, the limp and stiffness almost totally disappeared, and his strength was back to its normal, robust level. On his return to the guard shack, he was able to sleep a few hours before morning chow. Upon relief of the guard, he hurried to the barracks and packed his gear. Carrying it to the guard office, he asked if he could leave it there until he was ready to catch the bus for the train station, around 1300 hours. He wasted time talking with acquaintances around the shack until 1000 hours, then walked to the candy store to meet Koito.

The lovely young woman had just arrived and stood by a peddler's cart outside the restaurant. She knew something was different before he spoke. "What's wrong?" she asked in a soft, husky voice.

"My light duty is up. I've got to report back to Otsu," Buddy explained.

"Oh," she responded. "Oh" was one of her favorite expressions, yet this "oh" was tinged with despair. "It's not so far away," she observed, with forced cheerfulness.

"No, not so far," Buddy echoed and his voice began to break. "But I've got to be fair to you. Truth is, I won't be there long. Everyone who can walk is needed by the division. I was told that not only the recovered men but all people who could possibly be spared in Japan are being sent to Korea right away."

"Oh." Her "oh" this time, soft as a cotton ball, was nonetheless a cry of pain. "When?" she continued.

"*Ima*," he responded. "Now."

"What?" A note of hysteria began to break through into her voice.

"By 1300 hours, one o'clock."

"No! Oh, no, no," she cried, grabbing his arm, tears beginning to pour.

"I'm sorry. I don't want to go to Korea, or America or any

place else, ever again. I want to be here with you," the boy declared, drawing her tiny body into his long, strong arms.

"Oh," she sobbed into the coarse, green wool of his jacket.

"You know that, don't you?" he asked, rubbing his cheek against her silky black hair.

Her head buried in his chest, she nodded and mumbled, "Hai!"

Pushing her gently away, he stooped to look down into her eyes, saying, "I can't lie to you. You know the military and I know what it's like over there," and he stretched his arm out vaguely east. "You mustn't ruin your life worrying about me," he continued.

"Why?" she asked, looking puzzled. "Why say that?"

Buddy looked down at her tear-streaked face, also puzzled. "Because," he began, searching for words, "as much as I want to be with you, to never leave here, I want to be there, too." He stopped and shook his head, realizing that what he was saying sounded crazy and stupid, but he continued. "As much as I love you, I have to go. Not because of MPs and the brig or the naval prison, but because something in me doesn't want to miss what's happening there." He stopped, looked deeply into her eyes and said, "Please, please understand."

"I know," she said, stifling the tears, returning his steady look. "I know, and I'll wait for you, whether you want me to or not, and you'll wear my good luck charm," she said, rubbing the small wooden doll that lay beneath his shirt. "And you'll come back to me just as you did this time."

Drawing her back into his arms, he whispered into her hair, "If I have to break every law ever made, I will," and then he kissed her long and hard, until they were forced to break apart, gasping for air, and laughing at the chagrin of the Japanese who stared in obvious disapproval as they passed.

Buddy caught the train for Camp Otsu, the First Marine

Division's casual company, where replacements, recovered sick and wounded, and AWOLs were sent to await transport back to division. He met several men he knew there, including one from the amtrack battalion who tried to talk him into asking for an assignment to the "tracks." It seemed the amtracks had returned to Kobe, Japan for refitting and the men could go on liberty every other day.

Buddy requested reassignment to his old outfit, and a day after, returning to the cold, bare barracks at Otsu, after a night of frantic beer-guzzling in a nearby bar, he was on a rattling R4D marine transport, on his way back to Howe Company in central eastern Korea.

The plane flew blacked-out when it approached Korea, the crew even handling out the in-flight meals by the aid of flashlights. Buddy's hot meal of pork stew was greasy to begin with, but as the plane began to bump and grind its way through a mass of stormclouds the mess, aptly named, was almost too much to bear. When the aircraft suddenly dropped like a broken elevator and then as rapidly rose, Buddy grew faint and sick to his stomach. An older marine, in the web bucket next to him, grew alarmed, thinking that he might be having a relapse from his wounds. With great difficulty the boy finally got across to the concerned soldier that he'd been wounded in the leg, that he was merely airsick.

The R4D landed near Inchon, using a dry riverbed for a runway. When the cargo doors were opened, Buddy could see a vast tent city stretched out in every direction. The division had not yet out-loaded; he was in time to join his unit for the next campaign. Waiting to throw his gear in a truck detailed to carry the men to their companies, he was once again aware of the starkness and filth, the oppressive atmosphere and stink of Korea. He had not noticed this as much before, for the tension and speed of their advance had overshadowed everything else. Now, the contrast with the cleanliness and cultivation of Japan was obvious. "This is a really poor country," he said to himself, echoing the sentiments he had heard, but not comprehended, from others many times before.

He got on the truck and thirty minutes later threw his seabag down in front of Howe Company, 3, 7's C.P. The Top came, stooping over, out of the open door of the pyramidal tent, looked up at Buddy and scowled.

"Well, the wandering hero returns! Welcome back, combat marine. You got a death wish or somethin'?" he asked nastily.

"You're a grade-A bastard," Buddy thought, "but I guess I'm home." He shrugged his shoulders and smiled at the sergeant, saying, "Good to be home, top."

He saw the company clerk, a new man, signed himself in, and asked after the captain.

"Go down to the left three tents. That's where the skipper and the exec sleep," the clerk said.

Buddy followed the directions and slapped the tent flap, calling, "Captain Hammond, may I see you, sir?"

Buddy heard the rustle of paper and the shuffle of a chair and a familiar voice drawl out, "Hey, is that Buddy I hear out there?" Captain Hammond's face, lined with exhaustion, popped out through the tent flap. "Come on in here, boy. Lord, but it's good to see you." He pulled the young marine into the tent, saying, "Welcome back. Did they ever give you that medal?"

"Yes, sir. A promotion, too," the boy said proudly.

As Buddy's eyes adjusted to the dim light of the tent he saw Lieutenant Colliers lying on a cot to the right, reading a paperback with the aid of the flashlight he held in his left hand. The lieutenant looked up as he turned a page, saying, "Welcome back, kid. Congratulations!"

"Thanks, Lieutenant. It's good to be back."

"Ask Nieman in the first platoon for some corporal's

chevrons," the captain said. "He made buck sergeant, so he'll have to rip off all his double stripes. You may as well have them and sew them on."

"Yes, sir. What job do you want me to do now?"

"Well, we still need a runner and a radio man, for the SCR 536. We got a new communicator on the SCR 300, the big radio, but we need an all-around bodyguard, runner, scout, and patroller. You know anyone who could do that job?"

"I reckon I'd take a stab at it, sir."

"Okay, then, you move your gear in to the next tent, over here," Captain Hammond rapped the left wall of the tent, "with the radio man and the medic. You got any 782 gear or weapons?"

No, sir. I got a nice stateside seabag, but no field gear."

"Well, get some rest. You can draw gear later. Oh, you eaten yet?"

"No, sir. Not for a while."

"Then go on down this company street," Hammond pointed left. "You'll see a galley. Get some food. Tell them you just got in; they'll give you coffee and sandwiches. Then get some sleep. In the morning, we'll get you a pack and the whole bit." The captain stopped, then said, "Meanwhile, I promised you this."

Hammond took his pistol belt and holster from the deck under his cot and handed over his sidearm. "You wear that. You can draw a carbine, too. They got in some nice M-2s that are fully automatic, got thirty-round banana clips, though they're hard to get.

"But this is your issued weapon, sir."

"Oh, everything is expendable in combat. I've got my dad's .45, the one you used. It cleaned up real well. Maybe we can get you a shoulder holster sometime for that piece. Those tankers got 'em; they got thirty-round banana clips, too."

"Then maybe I ought to liberate us a holster and some

banana clips the next time we get near tanks," Buddy drawled slyly.

"I expect you're right, son," Hammond opined with a grin. "Go eat, Corporal. That's an order!"

"Yes, sir!"

"Night, Buddy!" Colliers called.

"Good night, sirs," Buddy said, stooping forward to leave the tent.

He stopped in the company street, right by the big lister bag, hung up on a tripod of logs, and buckled on the pistol belt.

The night air felt cool. He was exhilarated to be back. He felt more at home with the company than he had anywhere in many years. It was already too dark for shadows to fall as he walked to the mess tent.

The thick sandwiches of spam and the dark, hot coffee hit the spot. He walked back to the company C.P., got his seabag from a corner, told the clerk good night, and went to the tent next to the captain's. He lifted the tent flap and saw his bunk mates, a grizzled, hairy communications man he'd never met, and HM3 Lawrence, whom he knew and liked.

"Well, Lew, how you doin'?" he asked.

"By gosh, if it ain't Buddy, the Marine Corps' answer to the frogmen!" Lewis said, jumping up to slap his shoulder. "How's your leg? You need some pain pills?"

"Naw, I come to bunk with you guys, if that's all right."

"Sure. Come take this bunk on the rear wall. Meet John McNair, our communicator. He's a good dude."

"How you, McNair?"

"Tolible, tolible," the man answered in a Tennessee drawl. "I heard about you, kid. Glad to meet you at last."

"I'm glad to be here." Buddy walked to his cot. "I'm afraid I've got no blankets. Is it real cold out here at night?"

"Not too bad. Here, I've got a sleeping bag and a blanket.

You take the blanket," McNair replied.

"Thanks a lot."

"No sweat. You're a southern boy, too, ain't you?"

"Yep, born in North Carolina."

"That ain't far from my home. I'm from Bristol, on the Tennessee side."

"No kidding, I'm from near Ashville."

"No. Where?"

"From the Cherokee reservation."

Well, if that don't beat all. I'm right proud to know ya. Got a little tomahawk in me, too."

"You'll do," Buddy laughed.

"I told you he was a good man," Lawrence put in. "Only trouble is, he's a *big* Baptist, don't smoke or drink."

"That's not all bad," Buddy joked.

"No, you can live with McNair. He'll give you his smokes from the C-rations in the field and will pick up other stuff for you from the PX box at chow here in camp."

"I guess we can't complain about you, John McNair," Buddy said, lying down dressed and pulling the blanket over him.

"Just as long as you let me read a little Bible from time to time," the Tennesseean observed.

"Go ahead, I belong to the church myself, and Lew ain't an absolute heathen, either."

Lawrence laughed, and McNair flicked on a flashlight to read a dozen verses from St. Matthew.

As the flashlight clicked off, Buddy, now seventeen years, eight months old, and four months at war, dropped off to sleep the sleep of the invincible child.

The day after Buddy reported to Howe Company, he took his turn on guard. The company had drawn divisional guard duty, so he ended up walking a post on the perimeter of the camp. He passed the day easily, chatting with men he hadn't seen for a month.

When night fell, he went on post at 2000 hours. He and a friend walked up and down near the camp bakery, located in a huge tent. From time to time, the sweet, warm smell of freshly baking bread floated by. Around 2300, one of the bakers came out and invited them in, one at a time, for a taste.

"You go first, Buddy," the other marine said.

"Okay, I'll be back quick."

When Buddy entered the tent, he got a real surprise. The bakers not only had fresh bread but also Tiger liquor, a potent, unusually nasty, local brew. Buddy had a drink and three pieces of steaming hot bread, dripping with jam. Then he thanked the laughing group and went outside. He found his friend thirty yards away and reported the situation.

"Man, let me at it!" the guy said.

"Okay, go on, man, but be real fast," Buddy said, looking at his wristwatch. "It's 2320 and the guard will change at 2400."

The marine hurried off, whispering loudly back across his shoulder, "No problem, man."

Buddy felt a cold chill crawl up his spine and said to himself, "Famous last words."

Buddy's partner was only gone ten minutes when the relief, led by the sergeant of the guard, arrived early.

"Where's your partner?" the sergeant asked.

"He had a gripping pain and had to go to the head," Buddy explained.

"Okay," the sergeant said, "but he'd better get back soon."

The bedraggled marine walked up at that moment, and Buddy rushed to tell him that he'd just come from the head. The man said, "I sure did have a gut pain," and the two of them fell in with the guard and marched off.

Back in the guard tent, Buddy lay down on a pile of straw

in a corner. Just as he began falling to sleep, an officer came in. He addressed the group in a loud voice, "All you men from Howe Company! You're relieved. Go back to your company area. Division Reconnaissance Company is relieving you. We'll get your other men off post and send them to your area. Now move!"

Buddy and the others quickly walked to their area. Tents were already being struck and folded. Packs and weapons were piled up in the company street. Buddy saw the lieutenant and asked, "What goes, Mister Colliers?"

"We're moving out, Buddy. Get your gear out here and pile it by mine. Then help Lew and McNair strike your tent."

"Yes, sir."

For the next hour, instead of sleeping, the men of Howe Company struck tents and loaded their gear on trucks. Around 2:30 in the morning, 0230, they were trucked down to the docks. Off-loading, they put their gear in lighters and were carried out to a large troop transport, the APA 222, an attack troop ship. Around five o'clock, they found themselves in the troop compartments, trying to get an hour's sleep before breakfast call.

The next campaign had begun. No one knew what it was or where, but they were on their way.

12

The troop ship sailed out past the horizon, putting the coastline just out of sight. For twelve days the ship zigzagged up and down the coast, avoiding the naval mines that were becoming more and more prevalent. The big, round ugly balls of metal had short horns that if touched would be set off. The sailors and the marines were called to the rail on the third day to shoot at the mines. If they could hit one of the "horns" the mine would explode harmlessly. There was a lot of shooting but only about a half-dozen mines exploded. However, when one was hit, a huge fountain of water was sent spraying high up into the air along with the cheers, clapping and stomping of the bored men. More than once while Buddy was enjoying the pleasurable pastime of taking pot shots at the round bouncing balls, he idly thought that the enemy should have no trouble finding them, if they really wanted to, all they had to do was listen for all the commotion.

Buddy found that this sea voyage differed from the Pacific voyage over from the States. He had been too young, too green, to think about what lay ahead of him. Even the time he had just spent in the hospital was spent resting and recuperating, not thinking. This voyage gave him the chance to do just that, to think.

He was tested, at least once, and apparently not found wanting. Most of the men in his outfit accepted him. The captain, Lieutenant Colliers, Lawrence and McNair, in particular, seemed not only to like him, but to respect him as well. The swim in the Han, no big thing in itself, was more than rewarded. His decoration was the third highest a soldier could win in combat. His wounds, painfully real, were actually not much to complain about. He had two bluish-purple marks on his leg, one of them a groove in the flesh, but nothing disabling or disfiguring. He had money and a steady job. He felt somewhat matured, and not only accepted by the men in his unit but also by his family and friends back in the States.

When he had returned to the unit there was a pile of mail from stateside that astounded him. His mother and father each wrote a page or two for each of their combined letters. His mother worried about his health and told him not to take too many chances, to be careful, that she missed him and loved him; his father included in his pages a veteran's wisdom and advice on how to survive a war and the marine corps. He was inclined to a sense of humor that Buddy had not remembered. He also included his love and praise. These letters inevitably brought tears to Buddy's eyes. His little sister, who was growing up, was concerned about the danger, and wasn't he scared. Chester, his kid brother, the escape artist of the reservation, wanted all the gory details and wanted to know how many people he'd killed, but also wanted him to be careful because he wanted to hear all about everything when Buddy got home. Buddy's aunts were concerned that he was eating enough for a growing boy and that he had warm, dry accommodations.

He couldn't help but laugh at the ladies who had each married men who'd been to war but never understood that war is unavoidably messy and uncomfortable. That old, southern air of chivalry and belief that even war should be performed with an air of gentility and respectability still clung to them and even to the letters that now rested on his bunk. They perfumed the air, just as the magnolias perfumed the air about their small, dark, Charleston houses.

The letter that shocked and surprised him the most was the one he couldn't read. It was from his uncle, Buster, and was written in a decidedly drunken scrawl. He thought he might have seen the word "sharks" but wasn't sure. With a twinge of regret, he felt that this indecipherable message had to hold the answer to the questions that had haunted him since he was a boy. Why catch all those sharks, and why drop them on the front lawn? He would have to ask him when he got home.

His grandparents wrote, showing real concern and love, as did the members of their church. He also now had Koito. Perhaps Gloria was gone; Mike had written to say that he'd heard she'd been sent somewhere up north to go to school, but he had found in Koito someone who did not care if he was white, black or blue. And for the first time in his life, he did not care if he was white or red or both, he just was beginning to care that he was himself, the person all these other people seemed to care about. He didn't believe he was self-dramatizing, but he came to the conclusion that he must be doing what he was supposed to be doing.

Yet, the war troubled him, and the callous way the marines spoke of the bodies, which day by day became more numerous in the water. But in particular he could not help but think about the way the men had shot and killed wounded Koreans that morning after the night attack at the river, and be disturbed.

He remembered one Korean who infiltrated almost to the C.P. before being shot. The man lay all night without dying. When daylight came, one marine crawled to him and bandaged his arms and leg. Then, an hour later, a corpsman had looked at the enemy soldier, pulled his carbine off his shoulder, pointed it between his eyes, and shot the man out of hand.

Buddy had always been keenly aware of the threads of racial superiority that seemed to run through all Americans to one degree or another, but it was rampant here in the military. They spoke of "gooks," "slants," and "slopes." Somehow, they didn't think of the Orientals as fully human. He supposed it was easier to kill someone who was different in some way, for example, if people had slanted eyes and yellow skin. Yet again he felt a contradiction. He watched men who had lowered the "gooks" in their minds to the status of animals, to be treated kindly or cruelly or eliminated without moral compunction and yet show a deep sense of loss when certain other men, friends or highly respected men in the regiment, were killed. He also figured that it was easier to kill than to see one's own killed or wounded. Buddy knew that some men seemed to have no humanity at all, but he couldn't help but believe that most did. He recalled the tenderness with which he was treated after he was wounded. The discordant elements in the very men he respected, the men who accepted him, disturbed him greatly. As he stood on deck of the troop ship watching the bobbing mines and the floating bodies and the barely contained hysteria of the men around him, the only thing that Buddy knew for certain was that he would never kill anyone unless it was absolutely necessary. He knew he would never kill a prisoner, and promised himself he would do all he could to prevent others from doing so. Buddy was morally confused. He knew he wanted all the adventure he could find, but he had no desire to hurt anyone. As he approached his twelfth day of contemplation he was standing on deck, getting ready to go below to the mess when he thought to himself, "At least I know who I am, or at least I think I do. I guess I'm just Buddy Gordon." On that thought he turned and went below to the ship's store to search out ice cream.

On the twelfth day, the company was assembled on the aft deck before Captain Hammond. "Men," the captain began, "we will run in the utility boats toward Wonson Harbor in North Korea, then shift to amtracks from the LSUs at the large sandbar across the harbor mouth, and go in to land on Red Beach, just south of the city of Wonson. We will then drive through the city and turn north, moving toward the Chosan Reservoir. All three regiments of our division, plus supporting troops, will be involved. You will need the winter gear you were issued before we left Inchon, for it is cold ashore and will get a lot colder. More cold-weather gear will be issued later. Right now, draw rations and ammunition for the landing."

"Well, pin a rose on me! North Korea! We're going to turn around and invade those commies!" one sergeant cried out.

"Good show!" another said in a mock British accent.

"Go, Big Seven!" a whole squad roared, reacting like football players before the big game.

Many of the troops seemed delighted by the news. They were bored with the sameness and ease of shipboard life. They wanted action. Other, more experienced, marines were con-

cerned about the need to shift from landing boats to amtracks.
They knew that they would be sitting ducks for the artillery
and mortar fire. Watching and listening to the variety of
responses from his fellow marines, Buddy's own feelings
bounced up and down a similar spectrum as he tried to take
in what lay before them. With his own mixed emotions he
turned and went below to draw his C-rations and ammo.

The trip to the shallow water line and the enormous,
crescent-shaped sandbar inside Wanson Harbor was uneventful. There was a lot of slipping and cursing as the
company transferred to the amtracks, but no enemy fire.
Everyone but the veterans of World War II felt cheered. The
older men were still suspicious. Allowing the first wave to get
ashore, then opening up on the later waves of landing marines, had been a favorite tactic of the Japanese.

Buddy and the company wallowed ashore in the amtracks,
grinding up on the coarse sand of Red Beach without taking
fire. With hushed voices the squads tumbled out and ran for
the sand dunes behind the beach and set up an all-round
perimeter defense. All that day, the troops landed without a
single shot being fired. The officers called it a dry landing, or
administrative landing. Buddy was secretly happy, but also
left feeling a bit foolish. He and the others had been so
psyched up for the big encounter that he felt a bit let down as
did, it seemed, some of the others. He also felt grateful and by
the end of the day he, and many of his comrades, felt utterly
confused.

Though the landing had been militarily uneventful, it had
not occurred without the loss of life. There were mines in the
water and on the beach that the frogmen had not taken care
of. Three men who sat down to rest on a log half-buried in the
sand never knew what happened to them. The terrific explosion scooped out a huge crater. The three were buried

together in a hand grenade crate. This made the men trigger-happy and Buddy began to think that his own comrades were going to be more of a danger than the enemy hidden somewhere beyond the beach line.

As night fell and the men were in their holes, a fifty percent alert was called.

"Shoot anything that moves out there," one staff sergeant ordered.

During the night, the same staff NCO decided to check the men's alertness. Another marine saw him creeping through the dark and shot him through the heart. He made no sound, no cry, and it wasn't until morning that the platoon discovered what had happened. Buddy watched the grief-stricken men carry the bloody, inert body of Sergeant Stoneman down from the high sand dune, wrapped in a shelter half. He, as did many of the younger marines, felt a deep twinge of loss. The twenty-eight-year-old sergeant had been somewhat of a father-figure to the eighteen-year-olds and, especially, to the seventeen-year-old Buddy.

There was a discussion of who should get the blood-soaked pistol belt and the lightweight automatic carbine Stoneman had carried. Though many of the men expressed a desire to have the carbine, none could force themselves to take the blood-soaked carbine in their hands. Finally, Buddy said, "I'll take it," and gave his own carbine to a squad leader. He tried to clean the piece, but the bloodstains never really came off the weapon parts, or the cloth ammo pouch that was attached to the stock. Buddy kept his own thirty-round clips and didn't mind the state of the weapon. The sergeant's death had bothered him more than he could tell anyone, and he felt that as long as he carried the carbine, something of Stoneman would still be alive.

The second day, the battalion started out on foot to push deeper inland. They marched fast and long, encountering no resistance, covering about thirty miles before they stopped to sleep in an area that had been cleared by the South Korean army several days before. Each man carried full gear, plus one mortar shell. Buddy tied his round to his pack and labored along with the small radio as well. Since he and the men now carried winter sleeping bags which could be tightly rolled up, they took on the image of an endless line of old-world tinkers, in long procession, roaming the countryside carrying everything they owned on their backs.

After a fitful sleep on a stony plateau that faced an upturning road that wound into the North Korean Mountains, the column headed north and west. Some of the men already wore the alpaca-lined parkas, but Buddy was not one of them. He still wore his green, wool dress overcoat which he was beginning to realize lacked the needed warmth. As Buddy and his group passed a perimeter line set up by the Eleventh Marines, the artillery regiment, they noticed that all of these men had the new cold-weather gear and looked enviously fit, alert and more comfortable that they should have been. Buddy prayed that before the really cold weather set in, they'd all get the promised new gear.

One of the artillery men was detached to accompany Captain Hammond as a forward observer. Mitchell was an older man, with the flushed face of an alcoholic, as well as scored and lined by the years in the Merchant Marines before, while on a drunken binge, he had enlisted in the corps. He was to act as a forward observer and direct the fire of 105-mm howitzers.

McNair and Buddy looked up from their conversation as the breathless fellow fell into step with them saying, "Hey, you birds, don't walk so fast!" He continued in his thick New York accent, "I ain't use'ta this. I'm used to riding."

"Don't look at me," McNair replied. "I'm not setting the pace. The top soldier is."

"Okay, okay," Mitchell responded, smiling.

Over the next few days Buddy, Lawrence and McNair got to know Mitchell and liked him well enough, in spite of his strange New York accent and peculiar New York ways. Buddy especially found him to be friendly and kind. On a number of occasions, he offered to carry additional equipment when Buddy or McNair were asked to carry additional rifles and such. Though he carried his own cumbersome radio, he often volunteered to carry Buddy's.

Though they all seemed to like each other, in a few days Mitchell began to march with the heavy weapons platoon, after striking up a conversation with Roberts, a buck sergeant from Texas. The two lifers each had too many years experience to feel they had to wet-nurse a bunch of children. They also found that they also shared a common love for powerful Japanese whiskey. It seemed to those that knew them that it was inevitable that they would became close friends and put up their shelter halves together.

Buddy had been told by many a veteran sergeant not to make close friends. The odds were too good that you'd lose them, permanently. However, Buddy, like most of the men in the company, did not pay attention to the advice. As he walked up that mountain road, about the only thing he had to keep him warm was the good, joking, childish conversation with his friends McNair, Lawrence, and Conover. Their words and laughter did what his thin wool overcoat could not.

At Koto-ri, the first mountain village the company came to, part of the First Regiment was detailed to stop and establish a base, to protect the division's line of communications and maintain a force in reserve. The Seventh bivouacked for the night. After eating their rations, the men from the several squads of Howe Company spread out to find diversion for the evening. Buddy and McNair were not faced with that challenge—their entertainment was to be guard duty. A number of the others found a deserted building with a table and several overturned benches inside. This they quickly righted and settled in for an evening of a friendly game of poker. Buddy noticed a number of the same men gathering at the dilapidated building to win whatever they could for the same reasons they'd used on board the ship on the Pacific crossing. Buddy still found it illogical to gamble. So he didn't mind pulling duty.

McNair, on the other hand, was ambivalent about gambling but he hated the cold and voiced his feeling eloquently as they passed the weapons platoon, where Roberts was lying next to a .30-caliber machine gun. "Wooee, it's cold!"

"And you with all that long hair all over your ugly body?" Roberts called out as he clapped his hands in the cold night air.

"You're right jealous of me manly body hair, is all!" McNair snorted.

"I wish I had it," Roberts said, "then I could throw these smelly long johns away!"

"I'll take your smelly long johns," a passing marine cried out from behind them.

"It's so cold it'd freeze the brass off a bald monkey!" Conover put in as he walked up.

"Yep, them're my balls that just rolled downhill and smashed into ice cubes," Fig Newton announced from his tent doorway in a high, thin voice, causing a general roar from inside the crowded tent.

Buddy and McNair moved away from the C.P. tents and headed back toward town, retracing their steps past Roberts and the battalion weapons company. Ol' Mitchell, the former sailor who got so drunk one day that he enlisted in the corps, now stood morosely by a light machine gun. Roberts stood with him.

"Well, look at those slow mommas," Roberts said good-naturedly.

"Some of us ladies don't ride in trucks," McNair retorted.

"You're right, as always," the Texan answered with a comic salute.

"You boys sure look colder'n hell," Mitchell put in. "Especially, the kid. Where's your durn parka, boy?" he asked, speaking to Buddy directly.

"I didn't get one," Buddy answered. "There weren't enough to go round, and I was out on a run when the supply truck dropped off our company's share."

"Well, hell! That barracks coat is the best-looking item the service ever issued, boy, but it sure ain't fit for Siberia!"

"It'll do," Buddy replied. "Cap'n says I'll get one when the next supply truck comes up."

"No 'do' to it," the older marine went on. "You're out there running around and it's 25 below now and division predicts it'll fall to 45 below before long."

Neither McNair nor Buddy liked the sound of that news.

"Here," the wrinkled-faced Mitchell exclaimed, while he pulled off his parka. "Take mine and give me that spiffy barracks coat."

"I can't take your gear!" Buddy protested.

"Hell, son, you're goin' up that road tomorrow. I'm stayin' here. I got blankets. We can build a fire. Don't be foolish, take the coat!"

Buddy laid down his carbine, unbuckled his pistol belt and unbuttoned the greatcoat, giving it to Mitchell. He took the down-filled parka and put it on, too moved to say anything but a mumbled thanks.

Buddy and McNair turned and recommenced to walk guard duty. As they moved closer to town, a small group of mud huts that stretched for several hundred yards along the mountain road, they heard a shot, then yelling. The shot and commotion came from the abandoned building where the men were playing cards. A private ran out of the building yelling madly for a medic.

McNair grabbed the boy as he scrambled past them and screamed, "What the hell is going on? What's that fire?"

The boy, pale and wide-eyed, repeated, "Medic, we need a medic. Been an accident. One maybe dead, one wounded. Bad."

"I'll go see," Buddy said to McNair. "Better let him get a medic."

Buddy pushed his way through the crowd that had gathered by the door. Several men were near the table kneeling by three other men. "What happened here?" Buddy yelled out to anybody. The man next to him, a middle-aged private said that one of the BAR men had been cleaning his rifle and pointed toward one of the men kneeling beside a man lying motionless on the floor.

Buddy walked over to the group. He recognized the lifeless man who was still holding his cards as Jean Paul Luc, Lucky for short. The BAR man knelt beside him holding his rifle in one hand and shaking the dead man's shoulder with his other. "Come on, Lucky," he was saying, "this ain't funny, you bastard, now get up!" Tears were running down the grown man's cheeks, as he shook his dead friend's shoulder.

"Shepherd, what happened?" Buddy asked the sobbing man, but got no answer. He touched his arm to raise him from the floor but Shepherd merely shook it off and continued to try to wake the dead.

Buddy looked up to see the brass enter along with Lawrence, the medic. He moved back from the scene as the captain came toward him.

"What happened here, Buddy?" Captain Hammond asked the boy.

"I'm not sure, sir," he answered. "I heard one shot while on rounds, sir. Came in here and saw this," and he pointed to the group on the floor. There was only one shot, sir, but three men are hurt. One dead for sure, Lucky, sir. Shepherd did it, I guess, but he doesn't make sense. Keeps tryin' to get Lucky to wake up."

"Fine, Buddy. We'll take over. Return to your post."

"Yes, sir." The boy took one more look around at the mess and returned to McNair.

McNair was standing at post looking up and down the road, swatting himself trying to keep warm, when Buddy rejoined him.

"What the hell happened in there?" McNair demanded.

"Shit, man, I don't know. Lucky's dead. Lyin' there flat out on the floor, still holdin' his cards, and Shepherd—you know, the BAR man—bendin' over him actin' crazy. Two others are wounded. I don't know. There was only one shot, wasn't there?" Buddy asked McNair.

"Yeah, only one I heard," McNair agreed.

The next morning, the company started out again, still marching north by west. The main subject of conversation was the accident of the previous night. Buddy and McNair had cornered Lawrence after he had returned from patching up the two wounded men.

"Well?" Buddy and McNair both asked simultaneously as Lawrence reentered their tent.

"Jesus, guys. It's really weird," Lawrence said as he climbed into his sleeping bag.

"How's the guys?" Buddy asked.

"Oh, Matthews and Johnson just have flesh wounds. They won't even get to go back down the mountain. Lucky's dead, but you already knew that," Lawrence added as he pulled the zipper of his bag up close to his head. "Shepherd's just plain looney-tone-time now," he concluded.

"But how'd it happen? Shepherd couldn't a done it on purpose?" Buddy asked.

"Naw, it was a friggin' accident. Those bastards came all the way over here to get shot by accident," Lawrence observed in disgust. "Seems Shepherd decided to take the opportunity to be inside the warm building and the lantern light to clean his Browning. I guess there was a round in the chamber but he didn't know it. Was just sittin' there talkin' to Lucky and the gun went off. That damn bullet hit Lucky square, passed through him, hit Johnson, grazing his shoulder, ricocheted off something and hit Matthews in the leg. Freaky," Lawrence said, turning his back to the guys to go to sleep.

"But what about Shepherd? What'll they do?" Buddy persisted.

"They're sending him back down the line in the morning," the medic said, yawning. "I'm a medic, not a lawyer. I don't know what's gonna happen with him. All I know is, he was in bad shape when I last saw him. Go to sleep," Lawrence said, pulling his bag up around his head.

Buddy and Howe Company marched for the next day and a half to Hagaru-ri, the next village. Here, too, sections of the First Regiment dropped off to establish a fire base. Elements of the Eleventh Marines' 105-mm howitzers also set up here. Buddy's battalion moved on, marching into the growing cold toward the huge hydroelectric development at the Chosan Reservoir. In another day, they reached a tiny cluster of grayish mud huts that had opened areas under their packed mud floors, designed for charcoal fires that could heat the whole house. These houses were built for the Siberian winter that was beginning to strike the area. Already snow was falling, although it stuck only in patches. The wind was sharp, and the men were glad to get into their down-filled sleeping bags at night.

The company was ordered to stop for the night at a barren spot in the road called Yudam-ni. Though no one was quite sure about the date, after a semi-serious argument it was generally agreed by all that it must be November 24, 1950. The next day, air force cargo planes flew low overhead, dropping supplies. Some of the canisters burst open on impact, spewing boxes in every direction across the hillsides. Many of these packages brought uproarious laughter from the men. Odd PX items like chewing gum, shaving lotion, and hundreds upon hundreds of packages of Charms hard candies.

"What do they think? We're gonna feed the gooks candy?" Lawrence demanded.

"No, we're gonna shave 'em," was the good-natured reply.

V

March to the Sea

13

Buddy's company was on the main service route, the mountain road that was the sole land link to the sea beyond Koto-ri. Beyond them the frozen reservoir lay on their left, the mountains that ran to the Yalu River and the Soviet border to their right. Beyond the reservoir the Yalu formed the boundary with Communist China. To this point the hills and mountains were eerily still, yet menacing, like a child's bedroom in the dark where monsters hide in the closet or under the bed.

The only supplies the men enjoyed were what was brought with them, piled in the backs of the battered, green six-by's of the First Motor Transport Battalion. Since they had exhausted the dreadful pork and gravy and multipurpose ham served by their field kitchens, C-rations sufficed for every meal. A runner appeared from behind clad in an old green wool barracks coat and carrying a short M-1 carbine in one large fist. "Thanksgivin's comin'," he shouted. "And division's gonna air-drop us hot turkey and all the trimmin's." A deep, heartfelt cheer rose from the file of resting men. "And PX supplies!" the messenger added. "Candy, gum, tobacco, snuff, toothpaste and all that crap!" Another cheer.

"Maybe I can find me a pipe and tobacco," the man next to Buddy said.

"Maybe I kin get me some Brown's Mule," another cried, laughingly.

"You reckon there'd be a beer in there somewhere?" another asked with a smile.

"Why, hell no," another answered. "Don't you know you're too young to drink it?"

"Old enough to die but not old to vote!" someone else shouted.

"Old enough to bleed but not old enough to smoke!" a falsetto voice observed.

"Ain't no one old enough to drink. It ain't good for you," came a mocking voice.

"But, gyrenes, there is turkey. That I know for sure," the newcomer announced. "Beyond that, you'll have to take your chances."

Thanksgiving and Christmas, Buddy soon learned, were high holidays in the U.S. armed forces. Stateside, the men were being given leave to be with their families, overseas or aboard ship, traditional dinners were being served, and turkey was considered traditional. Even in the combat zones, the military was going to great lengths to serve these holiday feasts, air-dropping the food in the large canisters to the front line positions if necessary. Where Buddy was, it was necessary.

Thanksgiving morning dawned gray and cloudy but not completely overcast. Several C-130 transport planes suddenly popped over a mountain range, gliding lower and lower as they followed the winding road to their drop zone. The captain detailed a squad to lay out colored panels and to pop a canister of smoke to mark the company's delivery site. Once lined up, the planes unloaded large containers that dropped down through the cold, mountain air, only slightly retarded by their parachutes.

So it was that as the men weeded through the canisters of boxes of candy, drug store notions, and miscellaneous goods that the PX hadn't been able to sell for the last twenty years, the men found packages of real turkey, potatoes, cranberry sauce, stuffing fixings, canned vegetables and canned fruit. The squad recovered the containers that could be found, picked up their signal panels and started back to the company.

The top sergeant organized the meal. Mess cooks were detailed to distribute the Thanksgiving dinner and at noon each man's mess kit was filled with white meat, brown meat, gravy, potatoes, peas, cranberry sauce, rolls, cake and coffee. Like hoboes in a freight yard visited by a Salvation Army truck, marines lay on the cold ground, cushioned by panchos and sleeping bags, or sat back to back and ate their fill.

Buddy, who really had little opinion on turkey, ate as he had never eaten before. As a child he'd never seen turkey. Chicken was the epitome of holiday food until he had moved to his grandparents'. Mrs. Gordon did occasionally serve a turkey, and, like chicken, it was acceptable but just plain food to Buddy, whose preference ran toward seafood and roast beef. The few times he had eaten turkey in the marine corps were unexceptional experiences. But today, he and McNair sat facing each other shoveling in the grub as fast as they could get the food to their mouths. Occasionally one or the other would glance off into the distance, anxious about the silence. They were almost as far up the road as they could go. They were almost to China. Not even rumors reached them, let alone the news of the action that their fellow marines were seeing in other parts of the country.

For roughly three weeks, as near as Buddy could figure, they had been on the march. From the beginning, from that perfect landing, they had been expecting major encounters with the enemy, but they had not materialized. Perhaps MacArthur was not concerned about China, but Captain Hammond was, and so were many of the others as they continued their march toward that exotic, unknown world.

When they had finished their Thanksgiving dinner, all of the men began to carefully pack their mess kits, empty ration cans, even old gallon food cans tossed away by the field kitchens, with leftovers, especially turkey and turkey bones. "This'll make good soup tonight, if we can build a fire," one man said.

"And it'll keep in this cold," another added.

For the next two days the men of the First Marine Division marched farther inland, closing in on the Chinese border. The time passed uneventfully. More C-rations and ammo were air-dropped. Over the men and the frozen countryside, a quiet expectation hovered in the freezing air. Though Buddy and the men laughed and joked and talked a little about Christmas, it was always in hushed tones. All the while, waiting quietly in the blind mountain ravines, inside the Korean mud-wall shanties, and on the reverse slopes of the craggy hills, tens of thousands of veteran soldiers of the Chinese communist forces bided their time.

On November 26th, the men settled in for the night at Yudam-ni. They set about putting up their tiny pup tents as best they could. The ground was frozen solid and the tents were nearly impossible to anchor down. Most were just propped up and held in place by packs and other gear laid against the sides. Any protection against the icy wind was welcome.

Buddy drew guard duty for two hours, then was relieved by McNair. The guard shifts were shortened because of the cold. Buddy was lucky to share a six-man tent that had been jeeped up to the village for use as a C.P. Several other larger tents had been set up, and stoves made of oil drums were started in them to serve as warming tents, to give the troops a little relief from the cold.

The C.P. was filled with straw and not too cold. The captain, Lieutenant Colliers, Lieutenant Newton, Lawrence and Buddy lay on the deck trying to get some sleep while the officers nervously talked.

"We're too close to that border," the lieutenant was saying. "There's no need for us to be out here unless they're expecting something," he continued, raising to listen to the wind that was beating the sides of the tent.

"I got to admit," the captain said, "this has got me worried. If those Chinese do get involved, we're in for some serious times."

"Wouldn't somebody tell us somethin'?" Buddy raised up on his elbow to ask.

Fig Newton, who was visiting, chuckled at Buddy's question, "Boy, the people in the know don't tell us dog meat what's really goin' on. They're afraid we might tell the enemy, I guess." He shook his head wearily. "Whatever it is they're thinkin', they usually let us find out on our own what's really going on."

The captain, lieutenant and Lawrence all shook their heads in agreement.

"Whatever the situation, we're gonna have to proceed,"

Captain Hammond began, "as though the Chinese are involved or getting involved. We're gonna have to watch our tail."

Fig stood, pulled his parka hood up over his head and said, agreeing, "You got that right!" and then turned to leave the tent, saying, "I gotta get back to my men."

As he left, McNair returned from walking guard and collapsed into a shivering bundle on a pile of straw near Buddy.

"Want some coffee?" Buddy started to ask when the radio sounded.

McNair groaned and rolled over to face the radio that sat near his bed of straw.

"Shit!" he said as he translated the coded message. "Sir, we're on a fifty percent alert," he added as he handed the message to Hammond.

"Well, I guess the Chinese aren't really thrilled by our presence," the captain said as he read the message. "Buddy, get it together! You're gonna have to get these new orders over to the First and Second Platoons, as well as Heavy Weapons. You got that, boy?"

"Yes, sir," Buddy responded as he pulled his parka close about this body. He took one sip of hot coffee and left the tent.

The wind beat against his body and lashed his face with ice particles as he made his way to the First Platoon and then the Second Platoon with the new order. As he neared Heavy Weapons he saw the forward observer, Mitchell, with Roberts, the Texan, in charge of the machine-gun section. After he'd asked for the headquarters tent he suggested that Mitchell might want to get over to the captain's tent, since he might need to contact the artillery. Buddy knew that the captain did not know that Mitchell had lagged behind with the Heavy Weapons platoon.

"I'll come over in a minute, okay?" Mitchell replied.

"Yeah, sure," Buddy responded and hurried back to the warmth of the C.P. and the relative comfort of his straw bed.

About one in the morning, Buddy jumped up from his sleep, awakened by a terrific clamor. "What the hell?" he screamed as a heavy mortar barrage hit the company.

"Out of the tent!" Hammonds yelled as the mortars were followed by the deeper roar of heavy guns and the nerve-shattering swoosh of the Russian rockets.

The troops swarmed out of the tents and hit the deck around the hamlet. Suddenly, heavy machine-gun fire poured into the marine position. Hammond and the lieutenants were screaming out commands over the din when in the near distance a bugle was blown. Startled heads raised everywhere. "What's that?" Colliers asked no one in particular. Then the single bugle was accompanied by a multitude of shrill, piercing whistles. Buddy felt goose flesh rise at the sound. It reminded him the bosun's whistle on board ship only multiplied a thousand times. With the whining of the bugle and piercing whistles, the Chinese attacked.

The sleeping monster that had been hiding patiently in the dark recesses of the mountains struck the First Marine Division all along the MSR, rising from the mist of the icy night to slam against the leading two regiments in an attempt to cut each unit away from the next.

The long-feared intervention of Communist China in the Korean police action had begun. And with it, a new war in effect had begun. The lack of resistance by the North Koreans had, unknown to the marines, signaled the defeat of the first string and initiated the second. The second string, however, much stronger than the first, had decisively entered the game.

The Chinese seemed to come from nowhere and everywhere. They swarmed over the top of the ridge beyond the village and came pouring in. Buddy and the marines, momentarily overwhelmed by the flood of enemy soldiers, were struck with a terrific barrage of rifle and automatic fire, hand grenades and mortar rounds.

"Where's Mitchell?" Hammond yelled. "We gotta get the artillery in here."

"I saw him back at Heavy Weapons, earlier, sir," Buddy responded. "He said he'd get back here immediately. I don't know where he's at now."

"Dammit! What's he doing back there! He's supposed to be up here with us," Hammond yelled. Buddy had never seen the man like this. If Mitchell didn't have a real good excuse up his sleeve, he was dead meat for sure, Buddy thought. "You want me to go find him, sir?" Buddy asked.

"No. Hey, McNair, you got your radio working?"

"Yes, sir."

"Then get Artillery, now!" Hammond barked.

"Yes, sir, I'll try."

"Dammit, man, don't try, just do it!"

Captain Hammond got through to Artillery on McNair's radio and called in fire, as well as requesting close air support by the First Marine Air Wing, at first light. Until dawn, there was nothing the planes could do. The mortar men started firing white phosphorus shells that sent sparks flying when they hit the frozen ground. Marines on the line switched to the "Willie Peters," white phosphorus grenades, themselves.

Soon the battle yells of the ChiComs were turning to screams of pain. Hundreds were killed or wounded in front of the marine positions. Yet, some made it all the way into the tent area. These bulky forms were engaged with bayonets, pistols and entrenching tools. Shovels hit heads and flew through the air like battle axes. The attackers were killed, wounded and captured, and the remaining waves of troops, out there in the darkness, drew back. Their attempt to cut each unit off from each other had failed. But they did successfully cut the whole division off from either escape to, or aid from, the sea. The First Marine Division was alone and surrounded.

Buddy was not sure how long the attack had lasted but it was over an hour, a long time for any assault to continue. After the infantry pulled back, the Chinese mortars continued to fall for another half-hour or so. However, by 0300, the quiet had returned and a count of dead and wounded began. Hammond, still furious at Mitchell, sent Buddy to find him as well as check on the condition of the other units. When he got to the Heavy Weapons unit he went to the unit officer and asked for Mitchell or Roberts. The officer cocked his head over toward a heavily mortared area. Buddy excused himself and went over to the destroyed tents. Inside one lay what remained of Roberts and Mitchell. An unbroken bottle of Tiger Brand liquor lay on the floor nearby, its fiery contents melting the frozen earth. Buddy stood staring at his friends, now frozen splinters of flesh, bone and canvas. He began to shake and pulled the warm parka tighter around his body as he looked at the remains of the man who had taken it off and given it to him. In death he still wore the thin, green, wool overcoat that had been Buddy's. It didn't seem fair, he thought as the platoon sergeant walked up and touched him on the shoulder.

"We don't have to say anything about this," he said, pointing to the bottle. "They're dead, and nothing said now will hurt or help them."

"Okay," Buddy mumbled as he turned and walked away.

When Buddy returned to the debris that marked the C.P., he found the captain, the exec and the Top, along with McNair, gathered together trying to get reorganized. All were okay. Lawrence was out treating the wounded. The captain was using McNair's radio.

"Yes, sir," he was saying as Buddy walked up, "we'll move

to link up with the rest of the battalion at first light. Can you have air cover in here by then?"…"Okay, thank you, sir." Then he turned to Buddy and spoke in a strong but strained voice. "Okay, Buddy, give me the casualty list and get out to the platoon commanders. Tell 'em to be ready to leave just before dawn. We're moving back down the road to link up with George and Item companies. Tell them George Company was nearly overrun by the enemy. We've got to mass our forces."

With a "Yes, sir, Captain," Buddy ran off, first to find Fig Newton, and then to spread the word to the other officers and noncoms.

When he reached Fig's platoon area, he found the young officer seated on the frozen ground, nervously moving his arms and legs, unable to be still.

"What the deuce was that?" Newton asked Buddy with a nervous laugh. "What hit us?"

"I don't know, sir. I think it was the Chinese."

"I dee-double think it was chinks, Buddy. There's millions of them not a hundred miles from here. What was old 'Dugout Doug' thinkin' of? That mangy ol' medal chaser!"

"I don't know, Fig, it seemed like a coal truck hit us. We got twenty-two dead and thirty-seven wounded. MacArthur will have to get a rifle and come help us out if it gets worse."

"Run on around the line, Buddy. It'll be a cold day indeed when that doggie helps a marine," Fig said bitterly.

"Aye, sir," Buddy answered, a shiver running through his body.

At dawn, the company moved back down the mountain road. Several six-bys had come up to the hamlet and were being used to transport the dead and wounded. Legs and boots of the dead men stuck out the back of the canvas-sided trucks bouncing stiffly up and down in a ghastly frozen salute as they passed the retreating soldiers.

In order to reach the staging point with George and Item Companies, a deep gorge had to be crossed, by way of what looked to Buddy like an ancient, narrow, wooden bridge. As the column, led by one lone heavy tank and a bulldozer, followed by trucks, approached this gorge, the Chinese, lying in wait, attacked on their left flank.

Fortunately, there were squads of marines patrolling out on the ridges on either side of the road, so warning was given. The men took cover, the tank blasted away at the ridge to the left, and the patrol on that side attacked the enemy. As the squads along the road built up their fire power and began to achieve fire superiority, the Chinese fell back. The ridge was dotted with motionless bodies, clad in padded, mustard brown uniforms, wearing caps with ear flaps that reminded Buddy of the aviator hats he'd worn as a child. These "flying caps," even with their red metal stars on the front flaps, still seemed childlike.

Despite this small victory, the bridge was blocked. A field ambulance, riddled with bullet holes, lay on its side on the marine's end of the bridge. The bulldozer approached to push it away. A sniper killed the driver, and the machine swerved into the left bank. More sniper fire rained down, joined by heavy mortar rounds. Then Fig Newton ran to the tank, knelt behind it, and took out the communications phone on the vehicle's rear panel. "Push both of them into the river," he ordered. The tank rumbled forward and pushed at the heavy equipment. The dozer wouldn't move. The tank jockeyed about and pushed again. This time the dozer shifted. Soon the tank toppled both the ambulance and the dozer into the gorge and led the way across the bridge in a lordly manner. The ancient span groaned and creaked under the weight of the men and vehicles.

Late that evening, Buddy and Howe Company joined her

sister companies and prepared to move on to the fire base at Hagaru-ri. Neither he nor the others realized that the battle of the Chosan Reservoir, later to be called the "March to the Sea," was well underway. However, no one had a sense of history as they watched the number of the dead and wounded mount.

As units and companies began to trickle in during the early morning hours and communications were reestablished with the other divisions and groups at the other fronts, the real horror of the massive attack began to be revealed. Whole units had disintegrated. One artillery column was simply overrun and disappeared. By the thousands, army soldiers were captured. Once the regiment assembled, Buddy found that George Company had been decimated.

George Company fought to the point of death but did not die. Item Company, half-frozen and badly bruised, merged with the others. These columns, cold and battered, converged with one another and pointing their weapons, from pistols to howitzers, at every point on the compass, soldiered on.

Buddy was amazed at the massed force that the parts of three marine regiments and their combined arms made. He was awed by how formidable a fighting unit, even with their losses, they had become. The defensive perimeter that they set up at Hagaru-ri started at the edge of the village and, like a circling wagon train under Plains Indian attack, curved around the main body of men, all guns pointed straight forward. Not only rifles, carbines, pistols, and BARs, but heavy and light machine guns and the field guns and howitzers of the Eleventh Marines faced the reported seven Chinese divisions and elements of three others opposing them. Like Fig Newton, sitting on the frozen ground, Buddy stared out from the perimeter and in the freezing cold felt the perspiration of fear at the thought of the vast number of invisible enemy just beyond the line.

Buddy and the rest of the division found that the Chinese

did not lack fighting spirit. Unlike the North Koreans, who often melted away or surrendered when faced with strong opposition, the Chinese attacked, again and again, and then attacked again. As he lay in his shallow hole, scooped out of the snow-covered ground, he came to respect the Chinese in ways he never did the Koreans.

Night after night, he witnessed a human wave crash onto their line and then ebb back into the darkness. At first it seemed mindless, without rhyme or reason, but as time passed it became apparent even to Buddy that these people knew what they were about. Each time they crashed upon the beach of the division's line they kept that mass of marines in check. The First Marine Division did not seem to be going anywhere.

When these massed formations rose up and crashed on to the lines, sometimes units counted in the hundreds of men, the field guns of the Eleventh Marines were depressed as far as they would go and fired point blank, with instantaneous fuses. These shells, often white phosphorus, cut swaths through the Chinese ranks and turned the perimeter from darkness to a light brighter than that of the wintry days.

When such human waves were turned back, the marines joked, "How many hordes in a Chinese platoon?" The First Division respected the Chinese but they were not afraid of them.

Food became a problem. The roads were cut, the division surrounded. Only air drops could bring in supplies or fly the wounded out. Air drops, like the close air support of the marine fighter-bombers, required good flying weather. Full-fledged winter had set in. Air commanders could not always give the help they wished to give.

Over the first few days, small fires burned in the crude stoves made of large ration cans, fueled with diesel that burned slowly, heating snow water into which was tossed turkey scraps, turkey bones and whatever else had been hoarded from Thanksgiving dinner or found in their haver-sacks. The result was turkey soup, the only food available. Buddy had his share since two men from his squad had been among the far-seeing, and he was deeply grateful. But his attitude changed toward turkey soup as the days passed. The only thing they had to add to the cans of soup each day was more snow to melt down for broth. The bones had remained the only ingredient. They had been gnawed over at least once and boiled over and over since. When it was his turn to go into the warming tent, leaving the frozen firing line, Buddy would begin to feel sick at his stomach from the smell of boiling bones. He silently promised himself that he would never eat turkey again.

As early December wore on even the turkey soup ran out, while the overcast skies kept both Marine Air Wing and U.S. Air Force transports from air-dropping food.

"You can't fly if you can't see," an air controller reasonably replied when Captain Hammond complained. Not even growl-ing stomachs could contest that logic.

Of course, there's never a complete shortage of anything when there are several hundred men about, some of whom are more capable of taking care of themselves than others. Buddy was always amazed to see the things they would pull out of their packs or pockets, in the middle of nowhere. Mail bags full of Christmas gifts had arrived with an air drop right after Thanksgiving, and most of those packages contained food. As the long, slow march to the sea started the men reluctantly began to discard presents of little use: hairbrushes, books, clothing except for socks and scarves, but not food. In the dark, snow-clouded days, meals were made among friends of pepperoni, Vienna sausages, malted milk balls, hard candies, canned fruit and frozen cake. One group got fairly high on some bottles of shaving lotion cut with melted snow. Buddy threw away his gifts, strewing the frozen ground with gaily colored paper, but holding tightly to the cans of sausages he found in one small box sent by the students in the Library Club at Charleston High School. He shared them with McNair and Conover. John offered crackers. Poor Conover had gotten nothing.

However, soon the Christmas gifts gave out, and Buddy, who was four months from his eighteenth birthday, though by all standards of warfare he was a man, in reality was still a growing boy. And growing boys need food. During lulls in fighting, Buddy, as did others, took up wandering aimlessly around camp picking up old cans looking for something to eat. One day, he picked up an open can still half-full of frozen ham and lima beans and ate it happily. The awful Charms candy that had been air-dropped earlier and had been stuck down in the bottoms of the men's pockets and forgotten were now taken out and eaten. One man remarked about those orange and red squares, "Hunger makes anything taste good."

Another responded, "You can eat my shorts then, if you want."

The whole section broke up in laughter. The poor guy turned bright red and said nothing more.

Eventually, even the Charms were gone and the cans empty and Buddy found himself seated at meal time with a dozen men of the First Platoon. A young sergeant, as though announcing a magical act, waved his hands and pulled a can of corned beef hash from a parka pocket. "Voila!" he exclaimed. "Everybody eats. This is a magic can and we'll all have supper from it."

Everyone was so tired and hungry they were willing to believe him. Opening the can carefully, working the little P-38 can opener with cold, stiff fingers, the youth prepared the meal. He stuck a metal mess-gear spoon in it and took a spoonful in his mouth. He chewed contentedly, stuck the spoon back in the hash and offered it to the fellow on his right. "Take some," he said, "but leave some for the next man and pass it on."

The marine took one spoonful and passed it on, and so did the next and the next and the next. Just as it was about to reach Buddy a new fellow came up, dropped down and asked "Food?" in a happy voice.

Conover said, "It ain't your food, bud."

The new man looked hurt but the youthful sergeant looked sternly at Conover and pronounced, "Take some and leave some. Pass it on. Anybody who comes will get food." The marine holding the can looked startled, took his share and passed it to Buddy. He took a delicious spoonful, placed the spoon in the near empty can and passed it to the newcomer.

"Anybody, even if he's Chinese, will get fed if he shows up," the boyish NCO intoned, lightheaded from hunger and cold, and continued, "whoever comes, gets supper."

There was still a scrap in that magical can, that sacramental can, when the stranger took his share and handed it round to the sergeant again.

It was afternoon, Buddy wasn't sure of the day, when they received radio orders: the column was to abandon Hargaru-ri and start out toward Koto-ri. The division had taken on a definite formation. First came the heavy equipment, road graders and bulldozers, then jeeps, trucks and tractors pulling artillery pieces. Trucks pulled water and gasoline trailers. An occasional crackerbox ambulance broke the pattern. The wounded and dead rode, and, while everyone else walked, from time to time men would hang on the doors of trucks or sit on the hoods of jeeps. Buddy hung on the passenger door of a six-by in which Lawrence was riding.

A few men rode on the tanks, which was a very bad idea, since the tanks drew enemy fire first and thereby posed another, more subtle, health hazard. A few marines, he knew one of them, found that riding on the rear deck of a tank was warm. The huge engine sent warm air up through its ventilation system that felt wonderful in 35 below zero weather. But, like all good things, there was a catch. A man's feet began to sweat inside the rubberized cold weather boots and heavy socks after being warmed by the tank's engine. Then, when he got off, the perspiration froze on his feet and, in a short time, that man had frostbite. Buddy's friend, a tall country boy from South Carolina, was crippled. Later, his toes were amputated in Japan.

Most of the men knew that getting warm wasn't worth the risk.

The road and surrounding countryside was bleak in the gray winter light. The hills were dirty, gray-black, not completely covered by the snowfall. Snow fell almost every day but not in great amounts. There was actually more of it along the road than scattered over the rugged mountainsides. It was too cold to really snow except in the warmest part of the day. Then, there were often fierce blizzards that blacked out visibility.

The men walked along, now, covered with grime. Their faces, which usually had only stubble beards, now looked as if full-grown beards were planned. Even Buddy sprouted hairs on his chin and the sides of his cheeks, but still no mustache. Grease and soot, from the fires built whenever possible, covered all their exposed skin. Buddy wasn't aware that a green pea from one of his ration meals was frozen to the right side of his mouth until McNair pointed it out. He tugged at it, then left it alone. It would have taken the skin with it, if he'd pulled it off. He decided to wait for the spring thaw.

The company reached a crossroad and stopped to rest and eat whatever rations the men had left. Lawrence moved around, handing out APCs to people with fevers. Many of the men had severe colds, and some were developing pneumonia. One corporal was breathing hard and had a terrible pain in his chest and side. "Pleurisy," Lawrence said. "The guy could die." He had this man put in the front seat of a truck and gave him a shot of antibiotics. When the column moved, Lawrence rode with the sick man, the passenger door open, with Lawrence's yellow leggings and field shoes hanging out.

Just as the truck began to move, shots rang out. Buddy, Colliers, Hammond and McNair were marching together, walking by the right side of Lawrence's truck door.

"Crap!" Buddy heard the corpsman yell.

"What's wrong?" he called out to Lawrence.

"I'm hit in the blasted leg, Buddy," the medic answered in a disgusted voice.

"Well, sit still. You got the medical kit. Fix it, you quack," Buddy answered, not knowing what else to say. He was badly shaken by his friend's wound. He was the man who fixed everyone else. Now he was hurt and here Buddy and everyone else were lying flat on their stomachs with their faces in the frozen dirt, unable to help him when he needed it the most.

Newton's platoon was firing to the left front and the squads behind Buddy were taking on the enemy to the right front with heavy firing. In a few moments, the snipers were cleared, and the men got up and started walking again.

"Kin' I go with Lawrence, Captain?" Buddy asked.

"Sure, Buddy. Tell him we'll get him out on a chopper at Koto-ri," Hammond replied.

"Yes, sir."

Buddy ran up to the truck and grabbed the door, throwing one foot on the door frame and pulling up. The cab was crowded with the driver, the sick corporal, who looked unconscious, and Lawrence. He sat with his right leg pulled up in both hands, a bayonet scabbard held tightly to the outside of his shin.

"How bad?" Buddy asked.

"Not too bad," Lawrence said carefully, as if it hurt to talk. "It's a rifle round through the front of the shin; my shinbone's broken. That's why I'm holding it like this."

"What can I do?" Buddy asked, looking concerned.

"Nothin' 'til we stop," Lawrence said in a soft voice.

"You bleedin'?"

"Not much," Lawrence answered. "You can pack the wound with a field dressing and splint me when we stop. Don't worry. It's not all that bad, and it's a million-dollar wound. I'm for Japan, man!"

"Congratulations! Captain told me to tell you that!" Buddy cried, and jumped off the truck, relieved that his pal wasn't more seriously hurt.

"You'll be dancing in a month," he yelled at Lawrence. The medic smiled, his face white when he did, and didn't reply. "You deserve taxi service now," the boy shouted at the slow-moving truck. "You can go home now and ruin other people's health," the boy continued, fighting the panic that was building at the thought of his friend's pain.

A roadblock and a firefight several hundred yards in front of Howe Company stopped the truck only a few minutes later. McNair and Buddy got Lawrence down and dressed his wound. They had to cut his right legging off and slit his trouser leg to do it. All they had for a better splint was the man's carbine, which Buddy carefully unloaded before they strapped the injured leg to its stock with McNair's web belt and a length of clothesline Lawrence carried in his medical bag.

"I don't want you to reach down and scratch and blow yourself away," Buddy told him.

"Thanks a heap, Injun," the medic answered. He was beginning to look very white in the face. Shock was beginning to set in, and the men were careful when they lifted him back onto the truck seat.

A terrific explosion marked the destruction of the road-block, and the column jolted forward again.

That evening, the men halted for a rest right on the road. There was no way to pitch tents and no food to cook. Some candy and whatever odds and ends people had in pockets and packs were all there was to eat. Buddy rummaged in what was left of his pack, which was now composed of his sleeping bag, rolled up and tied with a tent rope. He had a few articles in a toiletry bag stuck in the toe of his sack. All he had saved was a hair brush, his two medals, with his corporal's warrant folded inside the Silver Star case, his wallet and, to his surprise, a can of meat patties. Pulling out this tin, Buddy and McNair made dinner.

A few yards away Fig Newton's men were having a great time griping and making fun of some strangers who had joined the column. These men were a platoon of British marine Commandos who were attached to the Fifth Marines. First, some other marines went over to talk with them as they tried to melt some snow for water. One of the Americans saw the Brits put something in the juice can they were using as a pot, and thought it was cocoa. The Brit told him they were making tea, and moreover, they didn't have any cocoa. That struck the Americans as funny, so they were sitting around crying out, "Blimey, even the bloomin' queen ain't got no cocoa."

The British tiredly laughed with them, repeating, "Even the bloomin' queen..." over and over again.

"Hey, Fig Newton, we ain't got no cocoa," somebody shouted from down the road.

"I ain't got none, neither," another voice added with a realistic sob.

"Man," Newton yelled, "cocoa—I ain't got no momma! I

ain't got no papa! I ain't got no seabag! *Habe no*! I ain't got no bleeding cocoa, neither!"

Loud roars of laughter ran up and down the road. In discovering they had no cocoa, they forgot they had no food.

Buddy slept under the truck in which Lawrence still sat. McNair woke him around 0500. It had snowed during the night and was still snowing in the morning. There would be no planes in to evacuate the wounded until the weather cleared. A C-130 transport droned overhead, but the pilot was unable to see the signal panels laid out, and dropped a load of food and ammunition in Chinese-controlled territory.

Lawrence, now wrapped in a sleeping bag, had been moved to the back of the truck, along with several other wounded men. The column moved forward, its motion so slow that it was measured in yards rather than miles. The division was still not to the last, unnamed hamlet along the reservoir road.

A couple of squads of Chinese infantry, as cold and miserable as the marines, attacked Buddy's part of the column near two wrecked mud huts. A sharp, almost blind, firefight erupted. Several of the marines and Chinese were hit and the rest of the enemy retreated except for two men who were flushed out of a ruined mud hut. They lay belly down on the ground, heads straining up toward their captors, looking frightened but resigned, arms outstretched in an angled "V" behind them.

"Don't shoot them!" Buddy cried. But no one had any wish to harm them. The tired marines roughly pulled the Chinese to their feet, frisked them, and then made them march in the column, in front of a guard. An old master sergeant, who had served in China, said that the youngest fellow was a kind of ensign, or sublieutenant, the first live officer they had captured.

In the afternoon, the sky cleared. The column halted near a frozen field. Steam rose from several spots along its edge. These marked the sites of honey pots, or dung holes. Air signal panels were laid out and an evacuation plane was called in. Soon Lawrence and a number of other wounded were ready to board. Buddy helped Lawrence through the door of the battered transport.

"The noise of the props will scare the dickens out of you," he told the medic. "You'll think they're shooting at you, but it will probably just be the motor noise."

The marine pilot waved Buddy out of the door. Clean-shaven, in a neat leather jacket, he looked unreal and out of place.

"Hang loose," Lawrence said. "Take 'er easy."

"See you, Lawrence," Buddy said, shaking his hand. "Now, get your arm inside that sleeping bag."

"So long," the wounded medic said.

"So long," Buddy replied as he ran to the side of the field and crouched down covering his face with his arms. The plane moved forward, then turned around and raced full throttle across the field and rose into the air. It was too frozen for there to be any dust, however, and only a thin slip of snow whirled about. Buddy watched the plane disappear behind the cloud cover and felt more and more lonely as the sound of the plane's engines became fainter and fainter. As he stood there on the edge of the empty field he turned and looked at his companions. They were a thin, filthy lot. He suddenly tried to remember when he had last taken a bath, when he had last worn clean clothes. He shook his head and returned with the other marines to the road, to continue their march.

The column had rested long enough waiting for the evacuation. Though evening was coming on, Buddy and the men moved forward, shuffling their tired, cold feet, trying not to think about food or warmth, or anything but their objective. They knew they were drawing closer to the American defense perimeter around Hungnam, Hamhung and Wonsan, but they also knew that the Chinese forces were getting stronger and that the winter was becoming more frigid, more icy. They knew, each and every one of them, without ever being told, that it was imperative that they reach the sea as soon as possible.

14

For several days the company had been in route march formation, fighting only when attacked, or when its combat patrols, scouring the snow-covered hills that flanked the road, ran into enemy concentrations. Now the captain's radio crackled with warnings and orders.

"It's regimental H.Q., Captain," McNair said quietly. "The word is that a large formation of Chinese troops is moving in on the column to reinforce the smaller blocking units that are barring the way to Hamhung-Hungnam."

"It looks like a set-piece battle," Hammond told Lieutenant Newton.

233

"In this sub-zero weather?" Newton asked incredulously.

"Yes, here and now," the Virginian answered.

"Buddy, you're gonna have to get out there and spread the word," the captain told the boy.

"Yes, sir. What's the word?" the boy asked as he watched his breath cloud and freeze in the air before him.

"Get to the other companies, tell them to move to the left of the road and to set up defensive positions on higher ground," the captain said and then turned toward Fig Newton. "Fig, the equipment, the wounded, the cannon cockers and service units can't leave the road. The line outfits will have to stand and fight. I want the rest to form a circle, you know, the ol' wagon train defense, around the road." Looking over at the lieutenant, he continued, "I want you to have a couple of runners help Buddy with this. We haven't got much time."

Howe Company set up along the high series of ridges that almost paralleled the road. Positions were scooped and scraped out of the frozen ground, though barely a few inches deep. Rocks were broken loose from their frozen positions and placed around machine guns and mortars. Men settled in behind their packs, using them as shields from the icy wind as much as anything. Though still afternoon, it was so dark and cold that the marines could barely see the Chinese moving over the next range of ridges, just as the Chinese could only dimly see them. No one shot at them. They shot at no one. It seemed to Buddy that a momentary truce had been called. Half-frozen, the men, both marines and Chinese, appeared to have no interest in fighting.

Behind the ridge, several oil drums were rolled up and makeshift stoves built. Men stood around the roaring flames of the diesel oil fires, warming their hands. Outposts reported the Chinese were also building bonfires on the reverse slope of their ridge, since greasy smoke was rising from and hanging over their positions.

A grizzled tech sergeant looked around the miserable group that surrounded the oil drum with Newton, Buddy, McNair and Colliers. "Is everybody happy?" the sergeant screeched, looking around the circle with an evil leer. Buddy was dumbfounded, at first, then began to grin. So did most of the others. "Come on, ladies," the sergeant cried out at the top of his lungs. "Sound off! Let's hear it! Is everybody happy?"

"Man, yes!" someone yelled back.

"I'm ready to re-up!" a deep voice put in.

With that most of the men started laughing. "For sure!" another agreed.

"Marines are number one!" a man said in a fake Oriental accent.

"But they ain't got no cocoa," another young fellow said in falsetto.

"Bloomin' right!" Newton cried. "Even the queen ain't got no cocoa!" Everyone broke up.

"You mean even the bloomin' queen ain't got no cocoa?" Buddy asked and laughed as if he were drunk. Suddenly he stopped. Amid the roar of the fire and the men's shared laughter, he realized that he truly was happy. In the most dangerous place he could imagine, hungry, cold and filthy, he felt the adrenaline pumping, the natural high that athletes know, and he was happy. Yet, it was more than the adrenaline rush. He wasn't hurting badly. He'd eat when there was something to eat. He wasn't exhausted. There was nothing important that he really wanted. A feeling welled up and he caught his breath, realizing that there was really no other place he wanted to be. Even the smooth wooden doll that still rested snugly against his chest, reminding him of Koito, did not tempt him. He was content. The rumpled shadow thrown away from his body by the leaping flames, though it wavered, was a single, solid whole. He felt part of something larger than himself, larger even than the war. He felt part of a human fellowship, even with those men on the hidden slope of the opposing ridge. "Life's hard," he muttered to himself, "anywhere, for everyone. People are tough: just making it is enough."

Then he turned to McNair and asked the tired, dirty man, "You're happy, aren't you?"

"I have discovered how to be content, in abundance or in want," the Tennessean replied, quoting the Bible much more than half-seriously.

"That's what I mean," Buddy said, and walked away to find the captain.

The fire shooting up from the oil drum cast a red light over the men's dirty faces and the oddly inappropriate mottled, jungle-green helmet covers. Buddy was cold and ached all over but a feeling of peace rose and spread through him and like a boy on a walk through the woods he whistled into the icy wind.

The battle began at sundown. An opening mortar barrage broke the frozen truce, scattering the burning oil cans like mud splattered along the roadside by a rushing bus. The marine artillery answered, and the darkened hills flashed with fire. Then, almost unheard in the wind that blew toward them, the ChiCom bugles and whistles sounded. The dimly moving mass of shapes was huge, like the crowd at a football stadium moving toward the entrance to the stands. Literally thousands of enemy soldiers pushed forward across the ridge toward them, coming silently but swiftly straight into the high explosives and steel ranged against them. Buddy watched as the Chinese took the brave man's walk in the darkness, which, lit by white phosphorus fires, was now even more starkly illuminated by the rising moon.

The attack was equal in its intensity and duration to its size. Chinese formations came on again and again, even though the slaughter among them, as they sought to move uphill against the massed automatic weapons fire, was immense. Buddy and the headquarters group served as line infantry. There were few tactics now to coordinate. Events had melted into the thin puddle of endurance, of aggressive hanging on, of being able to kill and kill and kill again. McNair and Buddy had carried a wooden case of hand grenades up to the ridge, as had so many others. Behind a big rock that served as the C.P., ten boxes of grenades were placed. A stray mortar shell would have sent everyone nearby straight to eternity with no announcement.

Buddy's arm grew tired as the night wore on. The four men threw all the grenades in ten cases at the enemy. They steadily rolled them downhill into the milling masses of Chinese, who, caught up in the shock of explosions that came with the speed of machine-gun fire, turned from a hostile horde into a panic-stricken mob.

That night Buddy was forced to the realization that killing on such a large scale was exhausting, hard work. It was also self-defeating, for the heaped-up bodies of the enemy now blocked the fields of fire and the machine gunners found themselves shooting the same dead enemy soldiers over and over again. The effect, nonetheless, was to stop this desperate attempt to destroy the marines, and Buddy was relieved to see defeat and destruction on the other foot, as the milling ChiCom troops began to disengage and retreat. He could hear the Chinese NCOs shouting out commands as the whistles, this time, sounded for a general withdrawal.

An order crackled over the radio. "Attack. Destroy the enemy." The time was perfect for the complete defeat of these blocking forces and to clear the way for junction with forces at the coast to the east. Captain Hammond sent Buddy to inform Newton, the other platoon leader, Lieutenant Hill, and "Guns," with Heavy Weapons.

Buddy slithered on his belly, hard to do wearing the bulky parka, and approached Newton's position.

"Anybody got any cocoa?" Buddy called.

"One of them chinks probably does," a marine yelled back.

"Where's the Fig?"

"Just keep coming, he's about twenty yards on down the ridge."

"Thanks."

Buddy found Lieutenant Newton and passed the order to prepare to attack. The time was set for 0330, the signal, a red flare. Three such flares would be set off, so no one could miss the jump-off.

He moved on around the rear of the hill so he could run, and quickly reached Lieutenant Hill with the same information, adding, "These guys are moving out, and we're goin' to help 'em move a little faster."

"And get a lot deader," Hill responded. "Sounds good." The tall, dark-complexioned officer wiped his eyes and blew his nose. His wind-burned face was streaked with oil. He stood bareheaded, with an off-handed indifference to danger. He eyes were so inflamed by smoke that he appeared to be ready to cry.

Firing from the entire marine line died away except for an occasional shot of opportunity when a target, illuminated by a mortar blast, presented itself. Mortars still worked up and down the reverse slopes of the Chinese-held ridges. As 0330 approached, Buddy had returned from his rounds to the platoons with his messages to find Captain Hammond and Lieutenant Colliers in consultation about ordinance distribution.

"It's a madhouse out there, sir," Colliers was saying.

"Everyone is in a mad scramble bringing more ammunition and grenades up from the trucks parked on the road. I'm afraid we're going to use up everything we have, sir. Even with the resupply flights we had the other day, when the wounded were evacuated, this attack could run our ammo stocks all the way down."

"I can understand your concern, Lieutenant, but we don't have a lot of choices. That ammo isn't going to do us any good in the trucks. We have to break through those lines. The ammo's there," Captain Hammond said, pointing off toward the road and then continuing, "We haven't had much opportunity to destroy the enemy since this whole campaign started. Now we have the chance. We better take it, Lieutenant, before we lose it. You understand?" The captain looked at the young officer and then continued without waiting for a response.

"Have the C-rations that were dropped in yesterday sent up to the ridge and distributed," the captain ordered.

"Yes, sir. Anything else?" Colliers asked, waiting to be dismissed.

"Yeah, better distribute them one for every three men. Let's try to make the food last as long as possible. With this weather, it may be a while before we get any more," the captain added as he nodded toward the door as a way of dismissal.

An hour later the rations had been dispersed. The men with cold, numb fingers were trying to open cans with their tiny P-38s; most chose to abandon the ineffective can openers and used their bayonet or knife. Buddy opted to use his knife. Once the can was open he sat and greedily ate. He wasn't sure what it was, but it tasted, he thought, like cold, greasy hamburger patties and also a lot like soap. Wiping his greasy gloves on his parka, Buddy checked his carbine, trying to do it by feel. He stuffed grenades into his parka pockets and fastened his helmet strap, a tough job, since he was also wearing an old-fashioned fur hat under it. Opening his holster, he took out his pistol and shoved it between his pistol belt and parka. He even checked his carbine bayonet, although he felt a bit foolish doing so. The command "Fix bayonets" always reminded him of a John Wayne movie. He was as ready to slaughter as he would ever be, he guessed. He was certain that he was very ready for it to be over.

"Let's move out, fast!" the top sergeant cried. "Move downhill and into them. Keep together. Use your bayonets when you get close." Then he cried, dramatically, "Fix bayonets! Follow me! You want to live forever?" Buddy could not help but think at that moment as they took their first steps down the hill that the Top must have seen every awful war movie shown on the marine bases, too.

Fitting personal action to words stolen from "Iron Mike," the marine who actually said those famous words in World War I, the Top scrambled down the ridge, followed by the first platoon. Buddy, the captain, Colliers and McNair ran stiffly after them, followed by the second platoon. In the darkness and thin, cold air, burdened with so many layers of clothing and the weight of his weapons, Buddy felt as if he were swimming under water again, in the chill of the Han. Even without the weight he carried, he would not have been able to run easily. The ridge was steep and slippery with a thin layer of snow over another layer of small pebbles and stones that rolled easily and threw a man down even easier. Buddy chugged along, carbine held out in front with one hand and the other holding the pistol in place. He wondered if he really should fix his bayonet, but there was no time to stop and do it, so he forgot that.

Ahead, the top soldier and the leading squad of the first platoon had reached the panicked rear guard of the withdrawing Chinese. Shots rang out, singly and distinctly, as marines shot these luckless enemy troops. Buddy thought it was odd to hear the snap! bam! crack! of the individual shots so distinctly, since automatic weapons and massed rifle firing obscured the sound of the single shots in most firefights. Somehow, the bam! crack! sounds were more frightening to Buddy than the hysterical roar of a larger skirmish.

As the bulk of the company came up against the retreating enemy, the noise of gunfire increased, punctuated by shouts from platoon and squad leaders and angry cries from individual marines. The Chinese, if they yelled at all, Buddy could not hear. Dimly, lit by muzzle blasts from small arms, dusty snow rose up from the melee in front of him. The shapes of men spun and fell, leaped up, ran, grasped chests and stomachs, cantered dizzily and heavily dropped to the sloped ground.

He raced forward, once he had reached level ground, keeping close to the captain and McNair. Buddy was determined to stick close by Hammond and protect the older man. The thought of the nearness of his own friends was comforting. He had taken too many risks alone, before now, not to be glad of human company as he closed in on the enemy.

At this instant he could see nothing but the bulky, coated backs of fellow marines, who shuffled forward quickly, looking like huge animals from the rear. Hammond jibbed left, like an overweight football player, and Buddy and McNair followed him, or rather, ran parallel to him. Colliers split straight ahead now, shouting, "Newton, follow me. Hill, what's happening?" For answer, there was a burst of carbine fire and the noise of many rifles. Hill's platoon had rammed into the main body of the rear guard.

Buddy, McNair, and Hammond ran puffing into the left flank of this close-in, now hand-to-hand encounter. Pale light was breaking over the draw where the Chinese, frightened and confused, were trying to flee, yet were now prevented from doing so and were forced to turn to beat off their pursuers. As a hand grenade went off in their midst and a crescendo of gunfire erupted, Buddy saw for a moment the image of men clubbing rabbits or rattlesnakes to death. The bulky forms, both Chinese and American, were clutching long wooden-stocked rifles and short submachine guns, and bodies were falling everywhere, piling up on one another.

Buddy let rip with a short burst of his carbine, striking two soldiers just as he witnessed his first bayoneting. A huge marine ran the dull, flat blade of his M-1 into the belly of an enemy who had turned to shoot him. In a grotesque synchronization, the two wounded Chinese fell backward as the stabbed man moved forward, doubled over, and the marine kicked him in the body with his left shoepac, yanking out the bayonet. Buddy felt ill but ran on.

The noise of killing filled the draw. Men's screams were muted and distorted by the physical pounding of a hundred firing weapons. Only the coughing snort of burp guns, fired for a long second before the Chinese gunners were killed, had their own, peculiar sound. The enemy company was trapped against the wall of the draw, a ridge too steep to climb, and was squeezed to death in the increasing light by the mounting fire of the Americans. Suddenly, the fight was over. Survivors threw up empty hands and screamed for permission to surrender.

"Cease fire! Cease fire!" officers and noncoms shrieked for many minutes before their authority took effect. Howe Company had destroyed its opponent, but on either side, other marine companies fired on, as company after company of Chinese soldiers were killed or captured.

"Radio regiment. Ask if we should withdraw to the column and bring in these prisoners," Captain Hammond ordered McNair. The radio man was slumped on the ground, dealing with his SCR 300, giving the report to the Seventh Marines C.P. when, suddenly, his head jerked up and he called, "Captain, this is for you!"

Hammond grabbed the phonelike unit and spoke into it. He shook his head positively as he listened. "Buddy! Get ready to run around to the platoons," he yelled.

"Yes, sir!" the boy answered, loping over to the radio.

"We've got to climb that ridge in front of us and set up again. The Chinese are turning to counterattack. Charlie Fifth is ahead of us on the left, on that high ground, and they can see them assembling. Go tell top, Hill and Fig and get them started up. I'll stay here with a squad to guard the prisoners."

"Yes, sir!"

"Buddy."

"Sir?"

"Buddy, come back to me and report; then I want you to run back and get Guns and Heavy Weapons up here, too."

"Yes, sir!"

Buddy could fly again. He felt exhilarated, glad to be free to roam the arena of action. He found Hill and Newton together and gave the captain's order, then ran on to find the Top, who was organizing a guard for another group of prisoners. The Top was carrying a Chinese burp gun and had two Russian pistols stuck in his belt. Buddy repeated the new orders and suggested that he take the prisoners and their guards back to the captain. The Top agreed, calling a staff sergeant over to relay the order.

"Kid, you're goin' lose that .45, like that," Top told Buddy, pointing to the heavy pistol in his belt. Buddy flushed and transferred it to his holster.

"You need your own personal pistol, Buddy," Top went on, smiling at the boy for the first time ever. "Hey, Collins, bring me some of them Red sidearms," he yelled.

A short guy came over, wearing four Russian pistols stuck in an M-1 cartridge belt.

"Give this here marine a pistol, will you, Chuck?" Top

asked.

"He's earned one. Hell, yes, take two, Buddy. We got plenty and goin' get more," Chuck said, smiling. And the man cheerfully gave the runner two brand-new Russian automatics.

"Thanks, man," Buddy responded, too surprised to say more.

"Forget it. That's for the river gig. I saw that," the short marine said and walked off.

Before going back, Buddy unzipped his parka and stuck the Russian arms in the rear pockets of his waterproof, olive green pants. Zipped up, he called to the staff sergeant and led the guard and prisoners back to the captain. He felt like a one-man army with all those weapons, and a bit burdened down.

By the time Buddy returned, leading the guard and prisoners, the draw was suffused with a cold, gray light. Hammond and McNair were at the radio again. When the captain at last handed the phone back to the Tennesseean, he turned to Buddy saying, "Guns has got the message, but I still want you to go back and guide them here and then on up to the ridge. We need a third platoon and, with our losses, we don't have it, so we need Gun's men to cover that ridgeline as much as we need Heavy Weapons. The mortars will stay here with me; you'll take the .30-calibers on up to Newton and Hill."

"Yes, sir. I'm on my way."

"Want a candy bar or a smoke, kid? You've been running more than the rest of us," the captain said.

"Chocolate sounds good."

"Here," McNair said, and held out a small ration bar of chocolate.

"Thanks," he said, wondering how to unwrap it as the other man waved him off.

Buddy took off and made the return climb of the ridge

quickly.

"Halt! Who goes?" A challenge greeted him as he approached the Weapons platoon.

"It's Buddy," he called. "Buddy," he shouted even louder when he heard the loud, heavy snick of a .50-caliber machine-gun's bolt, as its breech was closed and readied for firing.

"Durn!" a voice said above him. "I thought I had me a gook. Come on in, gyrene."

"How'd you like that .50-caliber shoved up your left nostril?" the boy retorted, scrambling over the ridge, holding out a hand for an assist. A greasy glove grasped his two-fingered mitten and pulled him on up.

"What's up, Mr. Runner?" a deep southern voice asked. Platoon Sergeant Gurney Toliver, known to everyone as "Guns," knew some change in orders was represented by Buddy's presence.

"You got to move your guns, Guns," Buddy answered. "The captain needs your whole platoon up on that ridge we just occupied," he continued.

"Okay," Guns replied. "I reckon we better break them weapons down and get on the road."

"I'll stay and lead you back, Sergeant."

"Good. Give me a hand and carry the radio?" the southerner asked.

"Sure," Buddy replied, his heart pounding from all the running he'd done.

The mortar crews and machine gunners knocked their weapons down quickly. More trouble came from loading everyone up with extra mortar shells than from anything else. After some cursing and grunting, the heavy weapons men got moving and began to carefully descend the ridge. After several men fell and slid down the slope, the whole crew reached the draw, sliding on their backsides, throwing wild arcs of dirty snow through the air. As they crossed over to where the captain had set up his C.P., Chinese mortar rounds started falling.

"Here's Guns, Captain," Buddy reported as he and the platoon pounded up to the C.P.

"Okay," Hammond replied, sounding very southern in his tiredness. "Guns, get your machine gunners up the ridge to hold that line. Put your mortars in support in this general area," and he swept his hand around the rocky, snow-streaked draw. "If you think your men can find it, the runner can take a break."

"Yes, sir," Guns said. "Mortars, start to set up in this sector. You gunners! Get them thirties and that fifty up the ridge. Ask the platoon leaders where they want 'em!"

The overburdened platoon shuffled off to set up. Buddy sat down beside McNair.

"Tired?" McNair asked.

Buddy nodded and said, "That chocolate helped me out. I finally got the wrapping off up on the road."

"They should be hitting us soon," Lieutenant Colliers observed quietly.

"Yes, they should," Captain Hammond replied. "Buddy, you better go on up to the ridge with Guns, anyway. Just take it easy. Take the handie-talkie and keep in touch with us."

"Yes, sir." Buddy got the small radio from the captain, who was carrying both sets on his shoulders. He and Guns climbed the steep ridge. When they neared the top, they were challenged and then allowed to crawl up into improvised bunkers made from stones rolled together.

"What's happenin'?" Guns asked Lieutenant Newton.

"They're massing to attack, on the reverse slope of that opposite ridge line," Newton replied, nodding his head forward.

"Then I'll call down some mortars on the suckers!" the sergeant exclaimed.

"Do it, man!" Fig cried, raising his hands to the sky and pulling a face at the sergeant.

Guns took the handie-talkie and reached his mortar section leader. Giving careful directions as to the distance in yards from the marine position, he ordered them to fire a few rounds to get the range, then let go with a barrage.

The mortar shells were dropped in the mortar tubes, making a dull explosive sound and sent hurtling up and over the marines, falling behind the opposite ridge.

"I can't tell if you're hitting anybody, but you got them rounds in the right neighborhood," Guns drawled into the radio set. "Keep it up!" using his field glasses again he murmured, "We could use some 4.2 tubes, but they're on the road."

The mortar attack pushed the Chinese timetable; the bugles and whistles soon were shrieking on the enemy ridges. First, tiny figures wee seen moving cautiously; then, as they drew nearer and grew larger, the ChiCom troops hit a steady downhill stride. They fanned out in a pyramidal shape with the broad bottom facing forward, making a simultaneous attack all along the marine line.

"Let them come to the middle of the draw, then hit 'em!" Newton told his men.

The charging formations reached the invisible line, and automatically the marine machine guns, BARs, M-1s and carbines opened up. The effect was one of a butterfly flying through a window fan. Chinese soldiers fell everywhere, screaming unheard cries with open mouths visible to the executioners above them. Most of the first wave was stopped a few feet from the center of the draw. A few got over it and huddled at the base of the ridge, firing upward at their tormentors.

"That'll show 'em!" Newton yelled.

"They need cocoa, Newt!" someone cried.

Then the second wave of attackers broke over the crest of the ridge.

The marine mortars were still falling, their range decreased by Gun's directions. When he laid the radio set down, Buddy used it to inform the captain of the situation.

"Tell Fig to watch out for those people at the foot of your ridge, Buddy," the captain ordered.

He relayed the message to Newton.

"Okay," the lieutenant replied. "We'll try to clean them out after we stop this next charge. Guns, you go to that mound of rocks just up the way and check out this next wave. Take the radio, but get back here fast. You got it?"

Guns nodded and headed farther on up the ridge.

There was no time. Some of the first wave had crawled up the slope under cover of the second wave's attack. These daring Chinese now took Newton's position under fire from the left. Buddy and Newton leaped forward and turned their carbines on this attack. Buddy saw eight ChiCom soldiers crawling toward them, firing burp guns. He shot one, then two, then three of these attackers. Several near misses by automatic fire made him stumble toward the shelter of a large rock. He didn't make it. A Chinese burp gunner sprayed the area, hitting Buddy in his previously injured leg. One round of the short burst tore off his right kneecap, slamming him to the ground. His pants leg quickly soaked in blood and shock drove him close to unconsciousness. Buddy rolled over painfully, facing the enemy soldiers now closing in on him. He fired the carbine on full automatic and knocked down his assailant and two more figures behind him. Newton, Buddy noted, was sprawled face down on the ground. Grief for Fig Newton filled his mind, but the two remaining attackers were almost to the ridgeline. Buddy fired a single shot, dropping the first Chinese. He slowly squeezed off a second shot, hitting the last enemy soldier in the face. Then he collapsed into half-consciousness, his body losing strength but his thoughts, deep within, racing out of control.

Buddy was really hurt and not just in body. His mind screamed out, "What? What is happening to me?" and "This can't be happening!" The seventeen-year-old boy who had always tried so hard to cover his emotions, now found himself overwhelmed by them. As he rolled about on the frozen ground surrounded by the freezing bodies of nine dead men, he was saved from complete madness by his semi-consciousness. Fear, guilt, and grief boiled toward the surface of the boy's mind as thoughts of "How could this happen to me? I should have prevented this!" And "How could I have let this happen?" Anger at himself, at everyone, burst through for a moment; then, blessedly, he fainted. The shadows of the cold, gray world darted around him, impotent demons. They were no longer a threat to the boy.

15

When Buddy resurfaced into full consciousness, there was a noisy firefight going on in the ravine below him. Daylight came, and he cautiously lifted his head to reconnoiter the situation. The forward slope was littered with Chinese dead, and the Top, with marine dead and wounded. He could hear some of the badly hurt groaning. He felt like groaning himself when he moved his mangled leg but, instead, gritted his foul-tasting teeth. His nose, stuffed up, could still detect the brassy, nauseous smell of dried blood.

One surprise hit him. Newton's body was gone. The eight Chinese lay scattered in a zigzag line starting a few feet from his own body and running on down the slope for fifty or sixty yards. The fighting in the draw was confused. Seen from above, men were running around and around. Maybe it was hand-to-hand combat. Whatever it was, it was apparent to Buddy that the Chinese had not only been held off, but were now being chased away, shot down by plunging fire as they retreated. It was last night all over again.

Regardless of what was happening down there, Buddy knew he was no help to anyone, including himself, up here and decided to try to return to the C.P. He began to half-crawl, half-drag himself toward his friends. This was more difficult than he'd expected. Not only was his right leg ripped open, but splinters of bone and bullet fragments were lodged in the left leg as well. He dragged himself along, pulling his useless legs behind him like a sled. If the route had not been downhill he would not have made it. By rolling the last fifteen or twenty yards, his mangled knee and leg slapping the ground over and over again, his scream of mindless pain announcing his approach, he neared the edge of the C.P.

"My God, Buddy," Captain Hammond shouted when he saw the boy flopping over and over, coming down the ridge. "Get him!" he cried to a mortar crew, who stood there gaping. Several men dropped their weapons and ran up the slope, grabbed Buddy, and rolled him on to a shelter half.

"We ain't got no corpsman, sir," one man reported. "The other medic got killed, and Lawrence's been evacuated."

"I know," Hammond said. "Take Buddy on down to the road and get a doc from another unit to treat him. The boy's losing a lot of blood. He's going into shock. Cover him up good. Get him down there, you hear!"

"Yes, sir!" a corporal answered and began to lift the boy with the other three marines.

"Take it easy, Buddy. I'll see you down the road. You'll be okay. You been shot before," the captain said with a forced grin, then coughing hoarsely.

"Right, Cap'n," Buddy answered weakly, as he looked up into the face of his leader and friend. Hammond looked tired and sick. Clearly, Buddy thought with regret, he was coming down with pneumonia.

As the litter bearers started out across the draw Buddy limply waved a hand and let it fall as he slipped back into the land of shadows, away from the world of ice and cold. The men had a hard time carrying the heavy youth across the uneven ground, littered with rock and dead Chinese.

"This kid's heavy," one remarked, puffing white vapor, his breath leaving a hoarfrost on his scraggly beard.

"Shut up and walk faster," the other responded.

They reached the uphill slope and got up and over, cursing and sliding. Buddy moved in and out of consciousness throughout the trip. After half an hour, the party reached the road.

All was confusion. Mortar rounds had fallen on the column and men were working hard and fast to straighten the disorder out. The vehicles were supposed to move shortly, all the units were expected to gather in the Hamhung perimeter.

"Better look at this boy before he bleeds to death, Doc," one of the Howe Company marines told the gray-faced hospitalman first class he found in an artillery unit.

"Okay, lay him down. I'll see what I can do," the middle-aged corpsman replied tiredly.

"Wow!" he exclaimed as he looked at Buddy's leg. "He had a pretty good surgeon on that gun that did this! Took the kneecap right off, some of the bone, too."

"He's lost a lot of blood," a man put in.

"Not as much as he could have," the corpsman answered. "He's lucky it's colder than hell here. We'll fix that best we can. You know this stuff freezes," he continued, pointing to a bottle of clear fluid, "out in the wind. We'll put him in a covered truck and try to warm up the plasma. Otherwise, he'll have to make it without a transfusion, or not make it," the weary medic concluded.

Buddy knew none of this. He had sunk completely into the land of shadow. He was at the top of one of the high North Carolina mountains again. He could see the prayer circle around a dim, glowing fire. As he drew nearer to the fire he saw his boyhood friends sitting cross-legged; comfortably seated beside them was Koito, her legs crossed, elbows propped on knees, her small chin resting delicately in her hands. She smiled into the fire. The old man, Longleaf, walked out from the woods toward the circle. When he had stepped inside, he turned to the boy and said, "What is the matter, my son?"

"I have seen war, and my heart is sick," the boy replied.

"Buddy of the Night, there has always been war. You are not afraid, are you?" the elder asked gently.

"No, Grandfather, I am not afraid. But I am filled with disgust."

"What disturbs you, Son?"

Buddy arose and circled the fire, looking down on the bowed, meditating heads of his peers and across the coals into the bright eyes of the old man, the Conductor of Visions. He began to pace, to prance, then to dance in a limping fashion, and chant,

> I am sick at heart
> over human cruelty.
> Can I not be a man
> without being cruel?

"Why, my son? Why these feelings? Tell us all," the grandfatherly figure commanded. From her place in the circle, Koito looked pained but suddenly nodded and smiled, coaxing her lover on.

The shadows of the pines beyond the fire circle shifted; even in the pale moonlight's glow the shadows were noticeable.

Buddy watched his shadow, double now, eerily phosphorescent, glimmering like a luminous rock in a dark cave. One portion was thrown out to his left, toward the Cherokee clan seated by the fire, and one portion projected to the right, running down the mountain, pointing south, toward the coastal cities and the world-encompassing seas. As the double shadow glowed, flickered and danced, it seemed also to undulate, to move, even to pull his body off balance, in both directions at once. So deep was this feeling of tugging that he almost lost balance, and felt a sharp pain in his knees, a dizziness in his head.

Buddy did not know where he was, in the Highlands or the Tidewater or the Piedmont or North Korea. It seemed he was by a great river. He could hear the river moving, and on it his voice came back to him in the singsong chant of a Cherokee ceremony with a hypnotic rise and fall,

> *I am sick at heart*
> *over human cruelty.*
> *Do we have to kill*
> *to prove we are brave?*

Buddy knew where he was then—Korea. He recognized the seated figures of his comrades in Howe Company as they stared into the fire. He saw the gaunt figure of McNair, with his usually kind eyes flashing. Buddy sang once again, both to his elders and to his comrades in the field.

> *On the sands before Yong Dong Po*
> *where we watched sixteen-inch shells*
> *pass over us,*
> *where we burrowed deep to escape*

Russian rockets
where mortars fell
like meteors,
we hid behind beached sampans,

Down there, on Yellow Beach,
where I made my swim
and bleeding,
brothers pulled me in

Down there, across from Seoul
where friends died
as corsairs lanced
and rockets screamed

Forgive me,
fleeing feeling,
I did what I did.

Buddy stopped. The faces in the circle grew faint. His weirdly shining shadows evaporated. Suddenly, the darkness of the green mountains faded and he was alone, suspended in a void where there was no light, no dark, no hot, no cold, no sound, no taste, no touch. Then a sudden shifting once again, and the cold, thin light of the Asian hillside emerged.

"Well, he's coming out of it," the corpsman remarked to the other wounded marines who shared the back of the truck with Buddy. "He just opened his eyes."

"The kid'd be better off asleep and out of it," a master sergeant with a head wound replied.

"Ain't that the truth," agreed a sallow-faced corporal with bandaged hands.

"What's happenin'?" Buddy asked, his mind in a daze.

"Nothin', kid, you're okay. We'll be moving out soon," the corpsman answered. "The line companies are coming back to the column, but it's slow moving. That sunlight that woke you up was pretty pale, and short lived. It's snowing again. Just lie still and keep warm." The corpsman turned on his knees to another patient.

"I must'a been dreaming," the boy muttered absently.

"Good for you, kid. Try to get back to it," the master sergeant said with a brown-toothed grin. He touched the bandages around his head.

"Life is a dream," another man put in. "That's what they said when I was stationed in Cuba. '*La vida est la suena.*'"

"Then let's never wake up," the fatigued corpsman remarked, as he crawled out of the truck to check the sick and wounded in the trucks behind them.

Buddy drifted back into a half-faint, half-sleep. Vaguely aware of the initiating circle, life had become a split-screen picture show. He was aware of the dreamlike state that led him to Koito and the ritual of the Circle. Buddy saw, in fast forward, his predictive vision, that he would see every part of the world and carry the struggle of two races, two cultures within him, but he also saw, as it were, an invisible hand guide him from the ship through the park in Kobe to the very spot where Koito waited for him. He could not have expressed verbally what he suddenly knew, in his spirit, that Wakan, the Great Spirit that every Cherokee knew pervades the world, and Jehovah, the Father God of the Scots, Irish and Germans, were one and the same. The twin visions merged, as his beliefs merged, the rapidly passing islands and seas converged upon an oriental ginza, his Indian vision culminating in a soaring hawk, his predestined steps pass the leprous decay of the old woman and across the curving bridge leading to a heart-stopping portrait of the lovely Koito, who turned into a hawk. And the two great soaring birds swept away and up, spiraled higher and higher and disappeared. He slept.

Buddy woke from a light sleep as the column neared the

end of its two-week, fifty-six-mile fight in another direction. He was cold and stiff. Pain was no longer localized in his knee, but ran from the calf of his right leg up into his hip and lower back and down the other leg as far as the knee. He was barely able to move, but when he did, found that some of his discomfort came from sleeping on the two Russian pistols in his back pockets. Pain made him dizzy, and dizziness made him forget his hunger, although he was aware that he was thirsty. Sitting up, he asked for water and was responded to at once by a friendly marine near the rear of the truck. "There's a can up here, I'll pour you a drink in this here clean ration can," the fellow told him.

"Many thanks," Buddy replied.

The marine handed the boy the half-can remnant of an old C-ration. Buddy noted that the man's face was covered with a brown field dressing with only one eye uncovered. The nose was a blob under the gauze. Sipping from the can, Buddy gagged, and involuntarily spat fluid out over himself.

"Good God! That's white gas!" he cried.

"White gas! I thought it was water!" the other man sheepishly shot back.

"Well, damn, it's gas! Boy, that really dried out my mouth!"

"Screw it! I'm a sorry bastard. But, see, I can't smell anything. My nose is all busted," the marine explained.

"Forget it. You meant well," Buddy said, feeling his tongue beginning to stick to the roof of his mouth, and lay back down.

Just then the truck ground to a shuddering halt. "We can see the perimeter at Hamhung," an officer told the wounded men from outside the rear of the truck. "We're almost home!"

"Let's hear it for 'almost home!'" the master sergeant boomed out.

"You bet!" another marine put in.

"Let's hear it for getting warm," Buddy whispered in agreement.

"And getting rid of these damned lice and crabs," called another, loudly scratching under a parka-clad arm.

"And for seeing girlfriends again," Buddy whispered again.

"Oh, yeah!" several men answered in unison.

The column of filthy trucks and jeeps parked near the Hungnam docks, an area dirty in peace and now a debris-strewn garbage dump in war. "We'll be here for the night," the driver, Chet, told the men in Buddy's truck. "Anybody who can walk is welcome to get out."

There were a number of pyramidal tents set up at odd angles along a street that ended in a long dock. A Shore Party officer came by telling the walking wounded to go to the tents on the far right end and get chow for themselves and bring some back to the others, if they could. Several men left Buddy's truck with Chet and returned later with sandwiches. Buddy wolfed his down, finding the freshly baked bread, from a nearby ship, the most delicious thing he had ever eaten and proceeded to tell everyone that it was so. It was so good, he said, that it even made the canned lunch meat taste like steak. The friendly driver laughed at the boy and offered him coffee from his canteen cup.

"There's a church service about to start in that middle tent," a man with his arm in a sling observed. "Anyone want to go?"

"I'd go, but I can't make it," Buddy answered.

"You want to go?" the driver asked.

"Well, yeah. I'd be glad to," the youth replied.

"Well, let's all of us go, that want to," Chet suggested. "I know Anderson who drives the truck behind us would go. I'll ask him and maybe the two of us could carry you on your stretcher. It's not far."

He jumped down from his seat on the tailgate and walked to the truck parked behind them. In a moment he returned with Anderson. "Sure, we can go," Chet announced.

"Well, heck, I'll go, too," the fellow with the sling put in. "I'll even carry one handle in my good hand."

The two motor transport men carefully slipped Buddy's stretcher to the tailgate and lifted it down. The wounded man took one handle at Buddy's head and Anderson, the other, while Chet took both handles at the foot. They slipped and stumbled a bit but were soon at the tent. It's front flap was thrown back and a yellow-orange glow filled the interior. Stooping down, Chet and Anderson began to enter and stopped, facing nine or ten marines seated in straw around the sides of the tent. Someone had spread a bale of straw, bright and shiny in the lantern light, evenly over the frozen ground. From his litter Buddy thought he could smell the warm, clean scent of the manger.

A skinny, middle-aged navy chaplain was seated cross-legged in the middle. His three friends placed Buddy's stretcher along the left wall, where it sank into the softness, soon the warmth, of the straw. The chaplain, who had traveled the same road by land and the cruise by sea as they, began to speak in a tired voice. "Soon it will be the birthday of the Prince of Peace. We will celebrate it this year in the midst of war. It would be ridiculous for us to be here if we had started this bloodshed, or even desired it. But none of us did, and, if I'm not mistaken, few of us had ever heard of this place before we were told to come here. Our profession is that of arms. We do what we are told and what we are told to do is to repel the war makers, to force them to stop for the sake of those who live here and for the safety of our own country. That can't be wrong.

"But there is more that keeps our meeting here from being simply absurd. We are poor men, who live on the ground.

Everything we own is on our backs. He was a poor man, too. He was born in straw, like the straw we sit in and find so luxurious after the snow and frozen earth. Many of our friends have died here, and he, too, was killed by soldiers who knew not what they did. He shared with his friends," and here he produced a communion set, opened it, spread crisp, white wafers on the patton and filled a small chalice with red wine, "what he had, as we daily share what little we have with one another."

And reciting the Words of Institution of the Lord's Supper over the bread and the wine, the minister passed the plate of wafers, saying, "This is the Body of Christ, take and eat but leave some for the next man and pass it on," and the cup, too, saying, "The Blood of Christ, shed for your sin, take and drink and pass it on." The skeptical faces of the young and the grimmer faces of the older men relaxed and seemed to soften as they took their share, and, without a hint of mockery, as reverent as the Pope, repeated, "Take and eat and pass it on."

Buddy took the tasteless wafer, light as air, and felt it dissolve in his mouth, following it quickly with the sip of wine, passing each element to Chet, who took them with an equal seriousness. And as the plate and cup passed from him, Buddy saw the drab, cold tent transfigured, filled with light. The faces of his tablemates seemed now to shine, their eyes, so clearly etched by rings of black exhaustion, appeared jewel-like, refracting a brilliance that came from nowhere but filled everything, outlining even the tiny hairs of an eyebrow, the tight white blemish of a scar. Buddy felt light, weightless, as if his prone, unmanageable body were rising, defying gravity, although his consciousness was unclouded. A deep, warm feeling pervaded his whole body; even his feet were warm. He saw, in that moment, his first glimpse since boyhood of the world behind the world. As through a crack in time the manger scene appeared: Mary, Joseph, Jesus, wise men, shepherds, donkey, camel, sheep, superimposed upon the materially dense form of the tent's interior and his green-clad companions. The baby Jesus, wrapped in white rags in a box of straw, lay at the chaplain's knees, in, with, under and over the materiality of the communion kit. His ears burned and his eyes teared and he thought his voice called, "Hosanna!" over and over although in reality he, and all the others, were silent. He was filled to overflowing with joy and contentment. Only after several seconds did he begin to refit himself into his body, to feel the hard earth beneath the straw and find the great light diminished by the yellowish illumination of the gasoline lantern. It was night. "Christ the Lord is born," the chaplain intoned.

"Christ is born," the circled men replied, fresh, silent tears washing grime from many cheeks.

As the group rose, helping Buddy's stretcher back up the road to Chet's truck, the boy drifted in and out of sleep, or coma or consciousness or vision. He knew that he believed in the Prince of Peace, Wakan's Son. Not the fierce god of his white relatives but Jesus, born in a hogan, reared in the dirt of poverty, was his Lord. In the face of human cruelty and slaughter only the baby born in a barn, only the wrongly condemned, only the gentle one had the strength to overcome.

Lying in the truck bed under canvas again, Buddy saw the manger scene once more. Even in a vision he recognized that the Holy Family was really Herman Schmidt, Helen Parks and Helen's infant, Eric, dressed in Biblical costumes, presenting a living nativity scene. He had visited the "performance" three times last Christmas. It seemed appropriate that Herman, who was so kind and wise and strong, was Joseph, that Helen, so gentle, was Mary. Then the vision changed and Helen's face became the round, youthful face of Koito. Her blue robe became red and gold. Her soft blonde hair turned blue black, topped by a simple gold crown. Kuan-Yin, full of compassion, smiled at him. The figure of Herman-Joseph remained the same, but Helen, the Holy Mother, Mary the Virgin, changed places with Koito, Kuan-Yin, again and again. He remembered then that God is love and knew that Wakan, the great Jehovah, shone through everyone in whom love and compassion flowed. The vision, rushing in a confusion of color across the backs of his eyelids, faded into black, and sleep.

The truck which had been Buddy's home for several days rattled across the docks and rolled aboard the navy LST. He and the other injured marines felt an almost uncontrollable upsurge of joy. They felt as though they had passed some supreme test. If they did not know everything about life, they did know that they were survivors. They were the battling marines of the frozen Chosan, human beings who could cope with whatever obstacle life had to offer.

As his stretcher was picked up to be moved to the LST's crew quarters and medical attention, Buddy noticed that the pale winter sun seemed to magnify his reclining bulk as he cast a single shadow on the gray steel deck and bulkheads. Although he knew none of the smiling strangers who treated him gently as they moved across the ship, Buddy felt at one with them and knew that each suffering-stamped face belonged to a friend.

"We got to get you to Japan, kid," an old chief corpsman told him after examining his leg. "We'll get you to a hospital ship soon. You'll make it."

"I know I'm gonna make it," the youth answered. "Write 'Gordon, Charles' on that evacuation tag. The guys called me 'Buddy.' You can call me 'Buddy,' too, if you want, chief."

"Whatever's right, my boy!" the veteran responded with a wry grin.

"I always wanted to be called Hawk. It sounds so damned

dangerous, so Superman like. But they always smiled and just called me Buddy. They were right, I guess. I don't need that name anymore. I can hold my own."

"I expect you're right about that, Buddy. Now, hold still while I get this shot in your hip," the grandfatherly medic ordered, his mind already elsewhere, on the next patient.

"Sure," Buddy agreed, trying to hold still in the cold as he was rolled over on the narrow stretcher and his clothing was pulled away.

As the painkillers took effect, Buddy drifted back into the land of shadows visiting family and friends, the mountains and the sea, and waited to see what tomorrow would bring to a boy who cast a single shadow.